SMOKE AND MIRRORS

Books in the Ray Elkins Series:

Summer People

Color Tour

Deer Season

Shelf Ice

Medieval Murders

Cruelest Month

Death in a Summer Colony

Murder in the Merlot

Gales of November

The Center Cannot Hold

Destination Wedding

Smoke and Mirrors

SMOKE AND MIRRORS

AARON STANDER

Writers & Editors
INTERLOCHEN, MICHIGAN

For Beachwalker
who helps this all happen

1

After midnight, Sheriff Ray Elkins and Detective Sergeant Sue Lawrence were finally off duty and back home, sitting at their kitchen table with cheese, crackers, and fresh fruit between them.

"Not too bad for a July 4. We've had worse," said Sue. She cut a small wedge of Brie and balanced it delicately on a cracker. The department had responded to several calls over the previous twenty-four hours, including three nonserious fireworks injuries; a scattering of DUIs; one lost child—found and safely returned; and three domestics, all alcohol-related.

"The night's still young," said Ray as he fed Simone, their cairn terrier, a little bit of cheese.

"Hey," she responded, "no one maimed, no one died. And, thankfully, no drownings. All's quiet on the western shore. The summer people had a wonderful day. The local businesses, too. I'll put these things away. Let's go to bed."

Ray's phone started vibrating on the nearby counter. Sue's eyes locked on his as he picked it up and listened.

"Anyone close?" he asked. He nodded at the response from the dispatcher and said, "Okay, I'm rolling. Please alert Dr. Dyskin."

"What's happening?" asked Sue.

"Possible double homicide. The beach at Aral, just south of the creek. Pick up Dr. Dyskin on your way?"

They embraced for a long moment, and then Ray grabbed his shirt from the back of the kitchen chair and started buttoning it as he dashed out into the night. A sudden rush of adrenaline pumped through his frame as he sped across the narrow waist of the peninsula toward the crime scene, siren wailing, lightbar pulsing. The roads in Cedar County, bumper-to-bumper during much of the day on a holiday weekend, were deserted after midnight.

Ray slowed as he turned off the highway onto the narrow country road that snaked through rolling terrain as it descended toward the Lake Michigan shore. After a few hundred yards, the pavement became little more than a tattered ribbon of loosely connected potholes. Passing the few remaining cars pulled off to the side near the trailhead, he parked behind a patrol car nosed into the sand pathway leading to the beach. Flashlight in hand, he sprinted down the trail, turning south at the water's edge and moving toward a large bonfire. Slowing at the edge of a fast-moving creek, he gingerly waded across the slippery gravel, water seeping into his shoes. Once on the other side, he approached a tall woman in the crowd surrounding the fire, Barbara Sinclair, one of the younger patrol officers in the department.

"What have we got?" he asked.

Sinclair pulled him off to the side and moved in close. "Two bodies." She took a deep breath. "One of the kids," she motioned toward a couple standing close to the fire, "told me where to look. It didn't take long to find the victims. I checked. Both were dead. After, I made sure no one went up there."

"Anything more? The victims? Someone from this group?"

"No. These guys are college kids from downstate. I've checked that. Everyone's accounted for."

"So, two victims?" He looked directly at Sinclair, the bonfire's reflection flickering in her eyes.

"I scanned the scene with a flashlight. I only saw two bodies. They're nude, Ray. It looks like they were having sex. I could see wounds and blood but didn't look close."

"Who found them?"

"The little blonde wrapped in the blanket, Brittany." Sinclair gestured with her hand, "The girl with the big guy hovering over her. I just got bits and pieces. He did most of the talking. Brittany's hysterical and appears to be very intoxicated."

"Okay," Ray said, picking out Brittany in the crowd.

Sinclair continued, "She said she climbed over the top of the first dune looking for a place to pee. She must have gotten disoriented in the darkness. The bodies are a long way from the beach in the low shrubs near the base of that steep hill. She told me about tripping over something and discovering the bodies with the light from her phone. Alex, her guy, went up there and checked it out with a flashlight. He made the 9-1-1 call."

"Did anyone else venture up there?" Ray asked.

"I don't think so. I was in the area when I got the call. It took me maybe ten minutes to get here. Then, I took a few minutes to talk to Brittany and Alex."

He noticed Sinclair shiver. "Are you okay?"

"Yes, just wet. The dispatch call sounded like a shooting in progress. When I got here, I sprinted down the beach. I didn't see the stream until I tripped and fell in it." She shook her head, then said, "I've never seen anything like this. I guess I wasn't ready." Her words came slowly, quivering.

Ray nodded. "I understand." He made eye contact, letting her know that he had heard her. "We'll get you out of here as soon as we can. Backup is on the way. We need to get contact information for these kids. Do you know where they're staying?"

"They said something about a family cottage in the hills near here."

Ray looked at the kids, noting the coolers and the empty bottles and cans scattered on the sand. "I bet none of them should be driving. We'll arrange transportation back to their lodging."

2

~

Ray stood in the background, beyond the intense circle of light. Sergeant Sue Lawrence, the department's crime scene investigator, and Dr. Jon Dyskin, the county medical examiner—both clad in Tyvek suits—hovered near the victims. Sue listened intently and snapped pictures as her body cam recorded Dyskin's actions and comments as he moved around the corpses. Sometimes, he looked directly at the camera as he spoke.

"Victim one, female, Caucasian, body face down. Multiple entry wounds at or near the spine. Powder burns on the bare skin."

Ray moved away from the pathologist to take a question from one of his deputies, his eyes still fixed on the scene. He continued to watch as Dyskin, with Sue's assistance, rolled the small woman off the body of a much larger male.

Ray left the scene for a few minutes, walking with Sergeant Brett Carty to the top of the ridgeline overlooking the shore. They stood for several minutes and surveyed the rolling terrain—scattered patches of dune grass running up against stunted-looking bushes, mostly poplar and cottonwood at the foot of the steep, pine-covered slope. They discussed securing the area, a popular Lake Michigan beach, especially on a holiday weekend. Then Ray returned to the crime scene. Two black polyester body bags now encased the victims.

"What do you know?" asked Ray.

"First, the obvious," Dyskin answered. "Double homicide. You'll want a forensic autopsy."

"Have you ever seen anything like this?" Ray asked. "A couple killed while having sex?"

Dyskin was slow to answer. Finally, he looked up at Ray. "Once before, Wayne County, a long time ago. As I remember, the murders were rumored to be part of a feud between some recent immigrants from the Balkans—Albania or maybe Montenegro. The headlines screamed about honor killings. You know, mess with my sister, I kill you, maybe her, too." Dyskin stopped and focused on Ray. "You learn never to trust those headlines. They usually reflect the shared prejudices of the writer and the community."

Glancing back at the body bags, Dyskin continued, "The woman is young, middle teens, most likely. The male, late twenties or early thirties. Lots of tattoos, prison quality. Symbols of sorts with a few words. Could be Cyrillic script."

"How about time?"

"Based on rectal and ambient temperature, sometime late afternoon or early evening."

"Anyone we know?" asked Ray, looking at Sue.

"The male, definitely not. He has very distinctive features. It's a face you wouldn't forget. No to the female, too."

"The female is very thin," added Dyskin.

"And the wounds?" asked Ray.

"The female had gunshot wounds at the center of her back. One or more bullets traveled through her, killing the man. Also, a gunshot wound at the center of the man's forehead. Postmortem, maybe." He paused briefly, "Gratuitous?"

"The weapon?" asked Ray.

"A pistol, .40 or .45."

"The girl," said Dyskin, his voice full of sadness, "she reminds me of my granddaughter—so small and fragile. How did this kid end up here?"

3

~

Ray walked the grassy verge of the forest surrounding his house, a dwelling he had recently started sharing with Sue Lawrence. In the dappled morning light, he followed Simone, the terrier, as she inspected the world on her first outing of the day.

At the sound of the screen door slapping against the frame, he glanced back and watched as Sue approached, dressed in a crisp uniform, carrying two steaming mugs.

"You were good enough to start the coffee. So, I thought the least I could do was bring you a cup," she said, handing Ray one and then snuggling close, putting her arm around his back and briefly clasping his side.

Ray felt her still-damp hair brush against his cheek.

"Short night," she said. "Just enough time for a shower and change of clothes."

"Yeah."

She leaned away to look up at him. "You okay?"

Ray focused on the luminous shafts of sunlight pouring through the openings in the dense canopy high above the forest floor.

"Ephemeral," he said, pointing at them. "Here for a brief moment before the mist burns off."

Sue followed his gaze, then studied his face.

"No, I'm not okay," he said. "I'm never okay when I have to confront senseless violence. I don't understand how anyone can be angry or damaged enough to do that to fellow humans. I'm a stranger in a strange land." He sighed. "If I have a special place on this planet, it's that beach, that stretch of sand and water. From my earliest memories, that was my special place—the big lake, the rolling dunes, and the extended vista revealing the earth's curvature. Summer or winter, it is a place of wonder and beauty. These killings, what were they about? Why there?"

"Ray, you need sleep. You could catch a few hours—go in late."

"We're both tired." He sipped his coffee, then said, "The girl, did she look familiar to you?"

Sue knelt beside Simone, scratched the dog's ears with her free hand, and then looked at Ray. "I thought about it a lot."

"Reach any conclusions?"

"No. I'm glad I didn't recognize her. It's easier to keep my professional distance. That said—"

"What?" pressed Ray.

"She was at that age where kids grow and change so rapidly. If you don't see them for three or four years—"

"Yes."

"And then how do we identify people?" continued Sue. "It's more than physical appearance. It's the voice, personality, mannerisms, gestures, and facial expressions. So drain all that away, and what have you got?"

Ray nodded. "Yes, I know."

"I could see Dyskin was upset. I've never seen that before. There was a crack in his usual granite facade," she said.

"Yes. You two have bonded. Now you're right in there next to him. In the beginning, you loathed the man."

"Elkins, he used to reek of cigar smoke and too much aftershave. And he'd talk about bodies like cuts of meat."

It was true. In Ray's experience, people rarely changed, but Dyskin had.

"As he examined the girl," Sue said, "he used the word 'feral.' And then he showed me her hacked-off hair, clearly not the work of a hairdresser. Then he said, 'Bodies tell stories. This will not be a happy one.'"

"Why didn't I hear any of this?"

"Well, first, he almost whispered, like he didn't want to be overheard. He felt this one more personally, so his comments weren't meant for a larger audience. And then, Elkins, you always hang back when there's a body."

"I imagine you will need most of the day to work the crime scene," he said.

"Yes, at least a day."

"We'll need all hands on deck to secure the area and thoroughly search in the light of day. While you're there, I'll do a press release, talk to the TV news, and check missing person reports on the off chance that one or both of the victims pop up. Then we'll pull the team together to see where we are."

Sue stood and moved in close for a hug. "Elkins, it's been lovely spending a bit of the night with you," she said before heading for her car and back to the crime scene.

4

~

D r. Dyskin, his nylon running suit hanging on his narrow frame, stood at the head of the conference table, fidgeting with his iPad. Ray thought about the first few years after Dyskin had retired up north and become Cedar County's part-time medical examiner. He had always driven to an unexplained death in a battered Lincoln Town Car, his arrival preceded by the rattles and groans of the decaying vehicle. He would emerge from the sagging behemoth in a rumpled suit and a tie, stinking of tobacco, his manner gruff.

That was pre–heart attack Dr. Dyskin. After the coronary, Cassandra, his wife, had put the good doctor on a strict diet and forced him into an exercise regimen, driving him to the cardiac rehab gym six days a week. And during Dyskin's rehabilitation, Cassandra met with Ray. She stipulated that if her husband was going to continue as the medical examiner, a deputy must drive him to and from any incident requiring his presence.

But it was more than weight loss and a wardrobe change. Dyskin's once-granite exterior, reinforced by years of examining dead bodies at accident sites and murder scenes in Wayne County, had slowly crumbled away, revealing a kinder, gentler Dyskin. Ray wondered about the catalyst for the mellowing: the man's realization of his mortality reinforced by a life-threatening illness, the arrival of grandchildren he doted on, or perhaps just life in the woods away from the daily barrage of mutilated bodies.

Dyskin cleared his throat and gazed at his audience—Ray, Sue, Barbara Sinclair, and Brett Carty. "Early this morning, we were all at the murder scene. I started autopsies at about one p.m. with a video link to a forensic pathologist and her chief resident in Ann Arbor. I can give you some preliminary findings through the miracle of technology that should help connect the dots. The final report will include all the specifics in the appropriate medical terminology.

"Victim one, the female, was struck by several gunshots, as I indicated to Sue when we were at the scene. The exit wounds were consistent with those caused by a handgun, the finding confirmed at autopsy. All shots were fired from an intermediate range, a few inches from the skin. The track of the bullets suggests the shooter was on the left side of victim one, kneeling or bending close. The path of the bullets indicates the shooter was holding the weapon at an angle.

"The entry wounds were closely spaced and followed a similar path. I'm thinking maybe three or four bullets in this area. The first shot shattered the fourth thoracic vertebra, severing the spinal cord. The heart, liver, and lungs were also damaged. Death was instantaneous. The second and perhaps third or fourth bullets had a clear path through victim one into victim two. The male's heart sustained massive damage. His death, too, would have been instantaneous. The shot fired into the male's forehead was postmortem." He looked at Sue. "As I said at the scene, I'm curious as to why the shooter bothered."

Dyskin then provided the blood alcohol numbers and the stomach contents of both victims, adding, "Gas station food."

He concluded by saying, "Cocaine and its metabolites were found in the blood and urine of both victims. In addition, the nasal passages of the male showed long-term use of the drug. So, in sum, these two were under the influence of alcohol and cocaine."

"Dr. Dyskin, what can you tell us about the victims, especially the female?" asked Sue.

"The female weighed, let me see," Dyskin flipped through screens, "110 pounds or just under 50 kilograms and was five feet six inches or 168 centimeters in height. She was post-menarche. As you know, at the time of her death, it appeared that she was engaged in intercourse. There were traces of semen in her vagina. No injuries were found to suggest forced sex. At the time of death, the victim appears to have been relatively well nourished, but some markers suggest that hasn't always been the case. I think there were probably periods of long-term malnutrition during childhood. Best guess, the age of this victim was fifteen to eighteen years.

"The male was five feet eleven inches in height and 182 pounds. I speculate he was in his late twenties or early thirties. In his case, the long-term and heavy use of tobacco, alcohol, and drugs might make him look older than he was. Lack of health care and poor nutrition can also influence the aging process. And I think that is true in this case. As you know, comprehensive toxicology takes several weeks. Are there any questions?"

"The female, any signs of physical abuse?" asked Sue.

"If your question is whether this woman was knocked around or beaten up in the recent past, the answer is no. However, she did have several bruises that were faded and mostly healed. Whether these resulted from earlier abuse is impossible for me to say. She might have fallen off a bike or gotten into a dustup with a sibling, relative, or a friend a month or two ago."

"The caliber of the weapon?" asked Sue.

"Given what you uncovered at the scene, you may know more about this than I do," Dyskin told Sue. "These wounds were deadly because the bullets struck vital organs. I'd say .40 or .45. I wonder how the assailant got close enough to the victims to place these shots so precisely. I leave that to you, detectives."

"Anything else?" asked Ray.

"I don't think so but let me review my notes." Dyskin scrolled through the screens on his iPad. "Ah, I did leave something out. And this may be important. The limited powder stippling around the wounds suggests the weapon was fitted with a silencer."

"Photos?" asked Sue.

"Yes," said Dyskin. "Photos of faces, tattoos, and other distinguishing marks are appended to the preliminary report. And I assume Sue will help me get this file in the right place so you can all access it."

After Dyskin made his exit, Ray looked at his three colleagues. "We're lucky to have the autopsy available so quickly. Sue, how about the crime scene?"

"In addition to Barbara and Brett, I had help from our three summer interns, a couple of NPS rangers, and a DNR officer. I have extensive notes that I'll write up tonight. At this point, I have nothing related to this crime: no brass, no personal items like clothing, car keys, wallets, phones. Nothing. We started at the scene and moved out ten yards at a time. And Barbara used our drone to survey the whole area from above.

"We recovered a few bullets and bullet fragments at the crime scene," Sue continued. "The perpetrator was meticulous about not leaving anything at or near the scene. We searched the trails that run behind the beach to the scene. We worked the shoreline from the parking area, then over the dunes to the crime scene, and walked the near-shore water checking for a weapon. The NPS crew worked the sides of the road used for parking. We've got socks, flip-flops, shoes, clothing, bottles, cans, cigarette and cigar butts, etc. We found nothing we could tie to the victims, not a car, motorcycle, or bike they might have used to get there. I believe the perpetrator carefully removed everything belonging to the victims. They didn't want these people easily identified."

"Do you want to keep the area secure for another day?" Ray asked.

"No, I'm satisfied that the search was thorough. And thunderstorms and gale-force winds are forecast from this evening through tomorrow morning. I've already sent the bullets and lead fragments to the State Police lab. Not that they will yield anything unless we find the murder weapon."

"Same for you, Barbara?" asked Sue.

"Yes. I've got a huge amount of video. At this point, I've only seen the video in real-time. I'll be able to study the images over the next several days."

"Okay." Ray looked over at Brett. "The kids on the beach near the scene, is that all squared away?"

"Yes, we got statements, names, and contact information. The group didn't arrive until after nine. They planned to watch the sunset and return to their lodging."

"Where were they before?' asked Sue.

"They were at Art's—raved about the burgers and complained about the wait. But I think the important point is, based on Dyskin's estimated time of death, the crime took place before they arrived. And given the number of fireworks set off yesterday, a few extra explosives sounds would have gone unnoticed."

"Thank you for that, Brett," said Ray. "And I'd like you to take Barbara off road patrol and assign her to this team for as long as needed. Are both of you okay with that?"

They both nodded.

"Good," Ray said. Then, moving to a whiteboard, he started to write.

"First, Barbara, working from autopsy photos, would you use the facial composite software to make lifelike digital images of the two victims that we can circulate? You know, eyes open, looking alive, but drawing quality."

"Yes, Sheriff."

"And can you do that before you leave this evening?"

"That won't be a problem. I'll message you the images as soon as I'm done."

"And how much time will you need to analyze the drone video?"

"I don't know, Sheriff. This is my first time working with this type of video. I was taught how to fly the drone. How to analyze the video wasn't part of the curriculum. I'll start at the murder scene and move out across the area."

"Keep us in the loop," said Ray. "Sue will facilitate it if you think we should go outside for technical assistance.

"Next, Brett, keep the road closed until tomorrow morning. Then, I want a patrol officer and the interns in place when the road is reopened. As people enter the area, I want them stopped and questioned. Were they in the area on the Fourth, did they see the individuals in the digitized images? And if they did, is there anything they can remember, such as clothing, vehicle, or anything else? We're pulling at straws. Brett, please write up the questionnaire before leaving this evening and send me a copy. Tomorrow morning, walk the interns through the interview process early. They should seek help from citizens in a friendly manner without being officious. Have them observe you working with the public, then monitor them before setting them loose.

"Third, security cameras. This is your next project tomorrow morning, Brett. This is a follow-up on Dr. Dyskin's comment about gas station food. Only a few stations in the county sell food, beer, and wine. You know where they are. Focus on the stations close to the crime scene first. Take Barbara with you to handle technology issues like securing the security tapes. If lucky, our John Doe will be captured on video using a credit card. And if he got gas, we might be able to ID the vehicle and get the plate numbers."

Ray looked around the room. "We're all tired. Thank you for your hard work. Get some rest. We'll start fresh early tomorrow."

5

~

Barbara Sinclair maneuvered the Dodge Charger patrol car into the shade of a large maple at the far end of the Village Market parking lot. She sat for several minutes, squinting as she looked out through the windshield, thinking about the events of the last twenty-four hours. She closed her eyes briefly, momentarily overtaken by how exhausted and sad she felt.

She worked to pull herself back into the moment. Pushing the door open and ducking her head to avoid hitting the top of the door frame, she emerged from the car and rose to her full height. She stood between the vehicle and the door for a long moment, her arms resting on the roof, and gently rolled her head from side to side, working through the process her physician mother referred to in lay terms as *unkinking*.

She watched a woman walk toward the store's entrance with a young teen, *mother and daughter*, she thought. The mother marched forward, a woman on a mission. The girl followed, arms and legs sweeping in graceful turns, a lithe figure gliding across the blacktop. The woman paused at the door, smiled briefly, then motioned the girl forward.

Barbara thought about her childhood. She considered—not for the first time—that her mother had probably wanted a girl, a ballerina, her passion as a child. And her father, a teacher and coach, had probably longed for a son, a basketball player.

Her parents ended up with a bit of both. Barbara was a ballerina first, starting as one of the little girls in a community production of *The Nutcracker*. She continued to dance into junior high, towering over all the girls in her grade. She had suddenly leaped from the body of a delicate child to that of a gangly adolescent.

By then, a basketball had replaced the satin pointe shoes, and her coach father had replaced her stage mother. Not that her mother had ever voiced disapproval, but Barbara sensed some disappointment on her part.

Barbara was taller than her peers and most of the girls on the opposing teams. By her sophomore year in high school, her exceptional athleticism caught the attention of college recruiters. And then the future continued to open before her. Her father moved from personal coach to cheerleader in the stands throughout her high school and college career. In the end, there was even talk of the Olympics and a pro career.

Barbara looked beyond the police cruiser's hood at the bay glistening in the distance. "And then everything changed," she said, looking around, knowing anyone observing her would think she was on the phone. "A mangled knee, a fractured back."

The hoop hopes had suddenly vanished, but Barbara had a degree in criminal justice to fall back on. Even before she had earned her BA, her mother told her it was time to start considering a graduate or professional school, a law degree, medicine, or becoming a teacher. "Let me work a few years, and then we'll talk," Barbara said after joining the sheriff's department as a patrol officer. A response that she repeated until her mother gave up on the topic.

Barbara rubbed the knuckles of her right hand against her lower back and slowly twisted, releasing the tension. Then, reaching into the car, she grabbed a small shoulder pack from the passenger seat and closed and locked the vehicle before heading toward the store entrance, collecting a cart along the way.

The pre-dinner shopping rush had subsided, allowing her to move leisurely through the market. She stopped first to look at the produce and fruit. Catching the eye of a teenage stock boy in the area, one she'd seen there before, she asked, "Do you have any more of that lovely lettuce blend? The bin is empty."

"Let me check in the back," he said, taking the empty plastic tub. When he returned with a small amount of lettuce in the bin,

Barbara had already bagged some baby spinach and filled a plastic sack with new potatoes.

"Here's the last of it," the young man said. "We'll have more tomorrow as if that helps." He returned the tub to its place. "It's a little bit sandy. You have to give it a good rinse, or chewing will be a grind," he added. He was smiling, amused by his own joke.

"It's enough for supper. That's all I need. Thank you. What's your name again?"

"Jay, Jay Farnsworth. Hey, I told the coach about you. He said to tell you he'd love for you to come by this fall when we start practice."

"Yeah, I'll do that. I'm in here every couple of days. We'll talk. And thanks for finding some salad. By the way, how about the girls' basketball team?"

"Oh, yeah, that would be good, too," said Jay, blushing slightly.

Barbara moved on, selecting a loaf of fresh sourdough, some eggs from a local farm, a bottle of white wine, and the few other items on her mental list. She was thinking about egg salad sandwiches while waiting in the check-out line.

"And what is my attractive friend having for supper?" came a slightly familiar voice.

Barbara stood tall and looked down her nose as Scott Nelson— who had been a suspect in a murder case the sheriff's department had solved a year before—stood looking through the contents of her cart.

She cleared her throat. "Sir, would you please move away," she said.

Scott remained unabashed. He said, "Well, I was going to offer to make you dinner, but there's not much to work with here. It looks like you're going easy on the calories."

"I'm not looking for dinner company, thank you." She rolled the cart forward, turning her attention to the cashier, a girl of high school age. A few minutes later, Barbara returned to the warm afternoon sunshine, carrying two paper grocery bags, one in each arm.

"I hope I wasn't inappropriate," Scott Nelson said, momentarily blocking her way.

Barbara adroitly stepped around him, a basketball move, controlled and graceful. Grocery bags were held close, and her elbows were extended and menacing. She continued in the direction of her car.

Scott tried to stay with her. "I'm apologizing. Our initial meeting was at an inopportune time."

"Yeah," agreed Barbara, letting her disdain show as her eyes swept over him.

"But that's water under the bridge." Scott continued marching at her side. "And with that in the past, it would be nice to get to know you. Friendship, nothing more implied. Could we have dinner sometime?" he asked, moving into her personal space.

"I'm sorry, sir," she answered, balancing the bags as she unlocked the doors. After placing the groceries in the back seat, she turned in his direction, looked at him steadily, and enunciated each word slowly. "I am otherwise engaged. I am not looking for a dinner companion or someone to date. Please move away from my vehicle."

"Would you at least consider—"

She slid into the driver's seat and firmly closed the door, cutting Scott off mid-sentence.

Later, as she emptied the paper sacks onto the kitchen counter, she discovered a business card in one of them:

Scott Nelson
Executive Business Strategist
Heirloom Foods North

She folded the bags and slipped them into a recycling bin before tossing the business card into the garbage.

6

~

Sitting on a gentle slope above the big lake, Barbara Sinclair opened her pack and passed a carefully wrapped sandwich to Brett Carty.

"I hope you like egg salad," she said. "It's what I was making for dinner. You're lucky I boiled the whole dozen. And I brought some Perrier and some beer."

"Perfect," he said, pointing to a beer. "I wasn't expecting a picnic."

Brett had arrived at her door just as she was preparing dinner. She invited him in. Initially, he stayed near the doorway. Barbara could sense that he was ill at ease as he struggled to explain the reason for his visit.

"As head of the road patrol, I need to do more than just pass out assignments and make sure everyone's paperwork is up to date. I now see I need to take care of people, too." He paused briefly, then continued, "I'll admit I had to build up my courage to even stop by your place tonight, but I thought you might need someone to talk to."

Their conversation led to a dinner invitation, with Brett suggesting a picnic site overlooking the Manitou Passage.

As Barbara unwrapped her sandwich, she said, "Incredible view. Thank you for bringing me here."

He nodded as he bit into the thick slices of bread. After chewing awhile, he responded, "The view is always spectacular here. It's where I come to decompress."

They focused for a few moments on the food. Then Brett asked, "How are you doing?"

Barbara turned in his direction. "If you're asking about my emotional state, I'm still shaking. I'm still processing that whole… dreadful scene."

"Yeah, I understand. Like you, I got hired right out of college. I started in September. I was working nights. Everything was routine, almost boring. But then it happened, not a murder, a traffic accident, a sixteen-year-old girl at the wheel with three friends. Off the road into a tree. Speed and inexperience. The driver survived with serious injuries. The front passenger didn't. No seat belt. I found her outside the vehicle. The two girls in the back had fractures and lacerations— again, no seatbelts. I stood in fog and rain, doing what I could, waiting for the fire crew and EMTs. It was the helplessness. I wanted to scream at the kids. I wanted to fix things, but everything was so final."

Barbara nodded, flashes of memory racing by, moments she had pushed back into a subconscious part of her memory. She responded slowly, "Yes, I was running toward the scene to stop the violence, but the murders had already happened. The helplessness. That's it, exactly."

"This double homicide, it's so much worse than anything we've had during my career here." He inhaled deeply, "Sue's talked to you?"

Barbara nodded. "Yes, she's connected me with the department's psychotherapist, Wendy Morrison. Morrison is trying to work me into her schedule tomorrow or the next day."

"Dr. Morrison has helped many of our people over the last several years."

"Have you seen her?"

"Yes, briefly. I may not have been the best patient. Maybe I wasn't ready yet."

Barbara let his comment hang for a bit. Finally, she asked, "Why is that?"

"I don't know. I'm not good at talking about what's going on in me, my feelings. That's one of the problems my ex-girlfriend harped on. We moved up here together after college and even talked about marriage, but it all eventually went bust."

"What happened?"

"I don't know for sure. She's a nurse and works at the hospital. I think she fell in love with someone else, a PA. I didn't see it coming. She said that the fact that I didn't recognize we had problems was the problem."

Lost in her thoughts, Barbara was only half-listening. "Yeah, I'm sorry," she responded, noticing he had gone quiet.

She scanned the horizon, then looked at Brett. "I'm still shaking. I've started wondering if I'm cut out for this job."

She scooped up some sand and let it run through her fingers. "What keeps you here, Brett? I knew there would be bad days. That's life. I've been knocked down before. But… how do you cope? Why do you stay in this job?"

Brett considered the question. "I was the first kid from a large extended family to attend college. My goal was to get a job at the end of school. Most criminal justice majors got jobs. That's what I knew. I didn't know any cops; none of my relatives were cops. I had no role models. But within days of being on the job here, I knew I had done something worthwhile for this community. On one of my first marine patrol shifts, I rescued two people out there," he pointed out at the water, "in a swamped canoe. They were hypothermic. I probably saved their lives. Same thing for road patrol—I've been able to help in many different ways: people lost, sick, an older adult who needs a hand changing a tire. Like it says on our cars, *Serve and Protect*. That means something to me.

"My dad, he's gone now; he worked at the Buick in Flint, drove in from our farm in the Thumb. He hated the factory. He didn't much like farming, either. A sad character. I think about his life and know I'm lucky to have meaningful work." Brett seemed to catch himself. "Sorry about my rambling."

"Don't be sorry," she countered. "We've never really talked, even though I've worked with you for over a year. You're very professional, competent, and friendly." She hesitated before moving cautiously forward. "That said, I sense you're uncomfortable around me. I was surprised when you stopped by today."

"It surprised me, also," Brett said. "But I was thinking about you and what you've just gone through and that I'd made no attempt to reach out. I held back because I didn't want to give you the wrong impression."

"Wrong impression?"

"Yeah, you know. Senior male administrator being too… ah… well, you know what I'm trying to say. The whole male, female thing. The male coming from a position of power…"

Barbara explained that she understood what he was trying to say and that she had never felt that he had been inappropriate with her, adding she would have called him on it if he had.

Then she asked gently, "And you are comfortable around black people, especially black women?"

Brett nodded. "It's something I've struggled with. I hadn't met anyone much different from me until my first year in college. That was an adjustment. I came to school from a part of rural Michigan that was white and Christian. It took me a year or two to figure out we were more alike than different. I credit my soccer teammates for helping me understand this. But you must have faced prejudices and have some of your own?"

"Brett, my life doesn't look like the stereotype many white people have. I didn't grow up in the 'hood. I grew up in an affluent suburb. That doesn't mean I haven't faced racism. The school system was quite diverse. I seldom felt racism there. But I occasionally heard the N-word when my basketball team played at other school districts. Not from the other team but from the stands." Barbara made a popping sound with her lips before continuing. "I've been called the N-word far too many times, and I've had clerks follow me in upscale clothing stores. I understand prejudice. One of the nice things about living up here is I don't have to think about it as much. I don't understand why. Maybe the prejudices are less intense. Possibly people react to my uniform rather than my skin color."

Brett nodded. They sat in silence for a while. Then Brett pointed out to the islands. "The Manitous, have you been out there?"

"I went over on a Park Service boat with Sue last summer," Barbara said as she folded the wrapper for her sandwich and tucked it back into her bag. "I loved it. I've been a city person all my life. I'm learning about wild, empty spaces. At first, they were frightening, and now I'm learning to love them." She brushed the crumbs from her lap. "Brett, this has been lovely, but tomorrow's another day." She let her comment hang, and then she stood.

"Sure, sure, I'll run you home."

"Before we leave, I want to say I'm glad you reached out. I needed someone to talk with this evening. Thanks for being a friend."

Back at her apartment, standing in the shower, Barbara found herself going over the details of the evening. She wondered what exactly it was about Sergeant Brett Carty that she found so appealing.

Once in bed with the lights out, despite feeling tired, Barbara struggled to fall asleep. She tried several breathing exercises and finally drifted off. Later, wide awake again, her sleepwear soaked with sweat, she crawled out of bed, still shaken by the nightmare replaying the events of July 4, starting from the moment she leaped from her patrol car and started running toward the bonfire on the beach.

7

~

Midmorning the following day, Ray stood outside the open door of Maria Tillson's office and rapped gently on the doorframe. Maria, a veteran social worker in the Child and Family Services Department, looked up and smiled warmly when she saw him there. She walked around her desk to greet him. Even in flats, her height exceeded his. Her handshake was firm. As she clasped his hand, she touched his elbow with her other hand briefly.

"It's been a while, Ray," she said. She looked him over. "You're looking well."

He nodded in response and said, "As I mentioned on the phone, we need help with identification."

"This is related to the story on the news last night, the double homicide?" she asked. "I couldn't help but notice the lack of details."

"You know the steps to this dance," said Ray. "Identification comes first. We have two victims, just naked bodies, nothing else. One of the victims is a young woman, a teenager. No hits on missing person databases matched her description."

"What can you give me?" asked Tillson.

"The basic descriptors: race, height, weight, eye color, and a small tattoo of Dumbo, the Disney cartoon character, on her left shoulder. There were also multiple piercings: ears, nose, lip, navel." He opened a nine-by-eleven manila envelope and extracted a single sheet of paper. He passed it to her waiting hand.

"How about a photo, Ray?" she said after scanning the sheet.

He pulled a photo from the envelope and slid it in her direction.

A long silence followed. Ray studied Tillson's face as she examined Barbara Sinclair's digital rendering of the autopsy photo.

"Tammy Ogden," she whispered. She took a long breath. "With many of these kids, you spend so much time hoping for the best. Tammy was one of those kids. This is beyond my worst fears." Tillson's voice was filled with sadness.

"What can you tell me?" Ray asked.

"Oh, Ray, I'm surprised our interests didn't intersect on this kid before. Like her mother before her, Tammy was a habitual truant. But, you know, it's not the kid. It's mostly the parent. In this case, as soon as I contacted Annette, Tammy's mother, they would disappear out of state, or so the story went. Annette's father, Joe Ogden, would tell me about Annette and Tammy moving in with some relatives in Kentucky. But Joe was a habitual liar; I knew it was just a story. On the few occasions I could corner Joe, he always seemed drunk or stoned. You know what I'm talking about. The person is right before you, and their lips are moving, but no one is home.

"Anyway, Annette and Tammy would pop up on our radar a year or two later, but as soon as we tried to get Tammy back in school, they'd vanish again. They lived with Annette's parents when she and her mom were in this area."

"Tammy's grandparents?"

She nodded. "Annette Ogden was one of my first cases up here, so I also knew her parents. We had limited success keeping her in school for a few years, but when she turned sixteen, she dropped out with her parents' permission. The next time I saw Annette, she was at Walmart carrying a baby with some soldier boy not much older than her lurking nearby. I assume he was the father. I don't know if they were ever married. Then, not too many years later, I'm doing version 2.0 with Tammy, the next generation of the Ogden family."

"Might you have an address and contact info?"

Tillson sat down again behind her desk and pulled the keyboard close. After tapping away for a minute, she said, "I just have a PO box, nothing more."

"But you've been to the house?"

"An ancient trailer in a debris field filled with dead vehicles and decades of trash."

"How's your calendar?" Ray asked.

"Full—but I'll get free if you need a guide."

Ray keyed the address Tillson gave him into his GPS. The first few miles were on a state highway, a ribbon of carefully maintained roadway. The route to their destination led them through one of the county's most rural and impoverished areas. As they grew closer, the roads became narrower, the paving sometimes little more than patches of washboard with nonexistent shoulders.

Driveways—some covered in gravel, most just two-tracks—led to modest dwellings, house trailers dating from the 1950s—a few even older—and decrepit frame houses. Peering out of her window, Tillson observed, "It's a landscape of poverty and lost hope. Trips out here always take me down. It's impossible to keep a professional distance. You reach out and do your best, but breaking through generational poverty seldom happens."

"I understand."

"Ray, the first time I called on the Ogden family, I arrived with a road patrol officer."

"Who?"

"Ben Reilly, nice man. Is he still around?"

"Retired," said Ray. "Looking after a cherry orchard and grandkids now."

"Annette, Tammy's mom," said Tillson, "was in second or third grade then. The principal of her school had requested a welfare check. In addition to spotty attendance, the little girl was consistently unbathed and appeared to be poorly nourished. Polite terms, Elkins. The first thing I noticed about Tammy when I met her at the school was how small she was for her age. And Tammy reeked. Her clothes were soiled, and you just knew she was hungry. So, I told the principal, Ms. Smyth, I would do a home visit. Smyth was emphatic about my not going to Tammy's home alone. She called the sheriff's department and arranged for an escort. It was my first year on the job. I was starting to understand the meaning of *up north*. You know what I'm saying."

Ray nodded. He studied the GPS map. "It looks like we have a turn soon?" he said, slowing.

"Yes, just past this cluster of homes right where the county road does a hard left turn and meanders south, you make a dogleg to the right onto a two-track. The trail runs down along the river. Have you been here before?"

"Never," he replied, slowing to a crawl as he maneuvered through deep potholes. He stopped and looked at the valley below. Long-abandoned cars and trucks were scattered in the woods surrounding a decrepit hovel. Bits of plastic, the remains of thin grocery bags, clung to the limbs of nearby brush and small trees. The contents of piles of abandoned garbage bags, degraded by the elements or torn by scavengers, spilled into the abutting thicket.

"Looks like a long-abandoned deer camp," said Ray.

"Funny, I had the same impression years ago. But people were living there then and still are now. When I encounter this kind of neglect and chaos, I..." Her words trailed off as Ray stopped behind a battered black Chevy pickup.

They stood outside for a long moment before approaching the door, listening to the howls of more than one dog seeping from the interior of the dwelling.

"If Annette's here, we need to get her outside. You don't want to know what the interior is like," said Maria.

Ray reached up and rapped on the door, then moved back and waited for a response.

The animals went silent, and the door opened a crack, just wide enough for the short snout of a large dog to push into the void.

"What do you want?"

"Annette, it's Maria Tillson. It's about Tammy. I need to talk with you."

"She's not here."

"We need to talk to you. Please come out."

The door opened a little wider, and two dogs—Ray guessed

both were pit bull mixes—squeezed out and dropped to the ground, circling them suspiciously. Then, a frail woman slowly emerged from the shadowy interior, holding the doorframe with her left hand. Ray noted the deep wrinkles in her face and the ragged appearance of her long black hair. A shapeless cardigan sweater covered her faded blouse and hung over washed-out jeans. She shuffled down the rickety metal steps in misshapen slippers, clutching the handrail. Ray smelled tobacco, woodsmoke, and the sour scent of neglect.

"Why's he here?" Annette asked, looking at Ray as she addressed the question to Maria Tillson.

"It's about Tammy," Maria repeated.

Annette stared at Ray. Finally, she whispered, "It's bad news."

"We need your help," answered Tillson.

"She's dead, isn't she?" Annette said. Not waiting for an answer, she sank to her knees, buried her face in her hands, and began to sob. The dogs moved in close, one on each side, their flanks touching her.

8

~

Sue made a salad while Ray grilled whitefish fillets and asparagus over charcoal. After clearing away the dishes, they lingered over coffee.

Even before they were a couple, Ray and Sue had had an informal pact not to talk about work away from the job. Unfortunately, the agreement hadn't worked in the past and didn't this time either.

"You're unusually quiet this evening," said Sue. "I've been doing all the talking. Are you okay?" Ray didn't respond right away, so she added, "Rough day, huh?"

"Let's walk Simone," he finally said.

A few minutes later, Ray unclipped Simone's leash on a nearly deserted stretch of Lake Michigan beach, knowing the cairn terrier would lead the way but always stay only a few yards ahead.

"How bad was it?" Sue asked, shoes off, walking in the sand at the water's edge, the setting sun reflecting off the lake's mirrorlike surface.

Ray described the scene in detail, explaining that Annette quickly guessed why they were there and collapsed and how Tillson took control of the situation, kneeling at Annette's side, getting her back on her feet, into the car, and through the identification process. "I was grateful that Maria Tillson was with me. She and Annette Ogden, Tammy's mother, have a long history. And Maria has a rapport with Annette. Throughout our time together, through the identification and afterward, Maria carried the ball. She sensed what questions I would probably be asking."

"So, what did you learn?"

"First, Tammy hadn't been coming home for several nights.

Instead, she'd stop by for a short daily visit, bringing food. She told her mother she was working crazy hours at the West Bay Tap, and it was easier to crash with friends."

"Did her mother know the friends?"

"No, she didn't seem to. This was Tammy's other world. Annette had never met any of these people."

Sue stopped and picked up a stone from the shallow water. "A Petoskey," she said, holding the rock up for Ray's inspection.

"Nice one," he responded.

"Then what happened?" pressed Sue.

Ray stopped walking and turned toward the setting sun. Then he looked back at Sue. "After identifying the body, other than an initial gasp when the sheet was pulled back, she went silent. There was no effect. No tears, nothing. She seemed catatonic, didn't say a word as we drove her back to her trailer. Fortunately, Maria had reached out to one of Annette's relatives, a cousin who lives in Petoskey. The woman, Mirth Skelwith, was waiting for us when we took Annette back to her trailer. Skelwith was going to take Annette home with her.

"Later, as I dropped Maria off at her office, she assured me she'd make sure all the social services Annette might require would be put in place. We probably should question Annette again, but I'm unsure how much we'll get from her."

"Why wouldn't we get much from her? She's the victim's mother," said Sue.

"I had the impression that Annette isn't all there. She didn't question why her daughter wasn't coming home at night. Her daughter needed to bring her food daily. Annette couldn't take care of herself. Tammy was the caregiver."

Unhappy with their progress, Simone came prancing back, barking and circling them.

Sue scooped the small dog into her arms. "What are you working out in your brain right now?"

"Poverty, extreme poverty," Ray said. "But it's so much more. Maria said Tammy was Annette's anchor, her lone contact with the outside world. Now Tammy is gone. Annette has a history of depression and an addiction to opiates. And if that isn't enough, she has an autoimmune disease, rheumatoid arthritis. She's unemployable. I'm trying to make sense of all of this; that's where I'm struggling."

Sue nodded her understanding. "Should we go back? You look like you're crashing."

"Probably so. I'm weary."

9

~

Hours later, well after midnight, Ray was awakened by the dreaded ringtone.

"Ray, central dispatch," mumbled Sue, nudging him several times. Finally, he grabbed the phone off the nightstand.

"What's happened?" Sue asked a minute later, having only heard his side of the conversation.

"Five 9-1-1 calls in three minutes. Automatic gunfire and a forest fire," he answered as he crawled out of bed.

"Someone responding?"

"Sector three patrol and fire and EMT."

"You want me to drive?" Sue asked, sitting up in bed.

"Sure," he responded as he switched on the light and dressed.

Sue was already in her SUV—engine running, wipers slapping at the heavy rain—when Ray climbed in, carrying his shoes and socks. She traversed the empty roads. Switching on the light bar, she turned south onto the main highway. Ray looked at the map showing the route to their destination on a computer screen.

"Know the area?" Sue asked, catching his gaze.

"Yes, that's Annette Ogden's address," he said as he called dispatch on his cell to find out what was happening. "Fire and EMTs requested," he told Sue after completing the call. "The structure is fully engaged, and the surrounding brush and trees are burning."

"Annette? And her cousin?" Sue asked.

"Her cousin was going to take Annette to her home in Petoskey.

That was the last I heard," he said. Sue nodded grimly and turned on the siren.

As they approached the two-track, Ray could see flames in the distance reaching toward the sky, illuminating the low-hanging overcast.

Sue switched off the siren. "What's the access road like?" she asked.

"Let's keep it open. Park on the shoulder out here. We'll hike in."

They donned rain jackets. With flashlights in hand, they carefully picked their way along the rutted sand trail toward the pulsating strobes and the roar of the diesel engines. The first hundred yards were uphill on a modest slope, something Ray hadn't noticed when he drove in twice the day before. Reaching the top of the ridgeline, they paused briefly on a plateau, the whole scene opening below them in a small hollow in the landscape. Flames poured out of the windows and doors of the ancient trailer. The rear of the structure was partially collapsed. Some derelict cars and trucks closest to the trailer were also on fire, with fire-filled interiors and tires ablaze. The nearby brush and trees had become part of an expanding circle of destruction.

An EMT truck was pulled off the trail directly in front of them—rear doors were open. Noah Zanner, a recently hired patrol officer, stood at the back of the vehicle. The two EMTs inside the truck attended to a patient. One of Annette's dogs stood below the doors, alert to the activity above.

Ray and Sue approached the truck. "What's happening?" Ray shouted over the sound of the idling diesel.

Zanner bent close to Ray's ear. "The firefighters carried her up here and said she was out of the trailer and clear of the fire when they arrived. Her eyes are open, Sheriff, but she's otherwise unresponsive. The dog won't leave her." Zanner covered his mouth and started coughing uncontrollably. He straightened and turned away.

"Follow her to the hospital," said Ray. "We need to provide protection."

"The dog?" asked Zanner.

"Take it with you. Talk to dispatch. Let them coordinate with animal control for a pickup."

They moved closer to the fire as the EMT truck departed. Ray and Sue could see the firefighters moving around the pumper truck, a tanker, and a pickup truck, getting equipment in place, and beginning to direct powerful streams of water at the hottest parts of the inferno. Tongues of fire at the center reached into the sky. Pine trees exploded in flames as the perimeter of the conflagration continued to spread outward.

Later, the rain now falling in sheets, they could see people with shovels working at the fringes of the burned areas, searching for and extinguishing the last glowing embers before the firefighters began collecting and stowing their equipment.

Ray headed toward Tom Butler, the township fire chief, standing near the remains of the trailer.

"Not much left," shouted Butler, gesturing with his hand. "Never is with these."

Ray nodded. "You were the first one on the scene?"

"Yeah, me in front, the pumper. The tanker followed us in."

"Did you see anyone around when you arrived, in vehicles or on foot?"

"Just the woman, the resident I guess," Butler answered.

"In my headlights, she looked like a pile of rags directly in front of me as we rolled in. Good thing that dog was with her. The mutt stood in the middle of the trail, blocking our way. The dog refused to move. That's why I stopped."

"Did you see a second dog?" asked Ray.

"No, just the one. Our EMT was following us. They parked off the road so additional tankers could get through. Job one was evacuating her. Do you know how many people were living here?"

"As far as I know, just the woman and two dogs currently, and she wasn't supposed to be here last night," Ray answered.

"Hope the place was empty. It was too far gone by the time we got here to check the inside," said Butler.

"Tom, any idea of the cause of the fire?"

"Hard to say." He gestured with his hand. "There's not much left."

"Could gunfire have started it?" asked Ray.

"Possible. Dispatch alerted us about that. We were hypervigilant on the way in. To answer your question, core bullets produce a lot of heat when they strike something solid. I'd be suspicious of the electrical if someone sprayed the trailer. Say the fuse box got hit or some of the wiring. Ray, it doesn't take much in these old trailers. Once they get started, they burn hotter than hell. But you know that already."

Butler searched under his coat, pulled out a bandana, and wiped his glasses, one lens at a time. "We were lucky with this rain. It could have been a lot worse. These woods are just ripe for a big one. Lots of fuel in here. And this has been the driest spring in years. It's going to be a bad fire season."

Ray nodded. "I'll leave you to it."

Rejoining Sue, they started up the trail, stopping at a high point and turning to view the scene again. Bits of twisted steel were all that remained of the trailer. The collection of junked vehicles nearby was now blackened, burned-out shells. The air reeked of burning rubber, plastic, garbage, and wood. Annette Ogden had lost her only child—her daughter—and now everything else but one dog and the clothes on her back.

The two fire trucks crawled back up the sand trail past them, the drivers carefully maneuvering the ponderous vehicles between the trees lining the narrow, twisting trail. A large pickup adapted for firefighting remained below. The chief and another firefighter moved around the perimeter, extinguishing the remaining flare-ups.

Ray and Sue followed the trucks on foot to the paved county road. Then Sue moved her vehicle down the trail closer to the scene, parking at the side in a narrow clearing. They started toward the scene, pausing to survey the area again carefully.

"Are you in the shooter's head?" asked Sue, noting that Ray had slowed to a reflective pace.

"Yes. First, they'd need a clear view of the trailer. And given how thickly wooded the area is, the shooter wouldn't have had it until—" Ray walked on, pausing just over the ridge line. "About here," he said. "So the brass should be…"

"In this area at the right," said Sue, moving off the trail. As he watched, she carefully searched the thick mat of decaying leaves on the forest floor. Then, after a brief hunt, she held up a brass shell casing with a gloved hand.

"Are there more?"

"Yes, lots," Sue answered. "My work is cut out for me. I'll have the interns come out and help me work the area. It will be a learning experience for them. One more thing, Ray."

"Yes?"

"You started this conversation with 'first.' What was your second point?"

Ray took in the scene of destruction in the small valley below. Finally, he said, "Was the shooter aiming, or was it just spray-and-pray? At three a.m., it was dark here, heavily overcast, and with a dense forest canopy above. Was there a light source?"

"Maybe in the trailer or a yard light?"

"That's possible. Either way, someone had to know the lay of the land. I'm assuming the violence had something to do with Tammy. I don't think you could find this location in the dark if you weren't familiar with the area. And if there was no light from the trailer or yard, they might have used their headlights, a flashlight, or a laser sight on the weapon." Ray paused, then said, "Okay, I'll leave you to it."

"What are you going to do?" asked Sue.

"I'll canvass the neighborhood, starting with the people who called 9-1-1. If we're lucky, someone noticed something during the night or perhaps yesterday, like if the shooter had come by to check out the area."

"Elkins, people will be just getting up. They'll just be starting their coffee."

"Yeah, coffee would be good."

Before leaving, Ray stopped and looked at the remains of the trailer in the center of the fire-blackened perimeter. Even in the dull light of the gray, rainy morning, he was struck by the contrast between the scene of catastrophic destruction and the lush green foliage of early summer just beyond the reach of the flames.

At the center of the blackened area, all that remained of the mobile home was the subframe on which the structure rested, now just pieces of steel twisted by the intense heat on the forest floor.

The mist hanging over the small valley was redolent with the vile scent of burnt rubber and plastic and the ashen remains of decades of abandoned or discarded belongings and rubbish. He quickly captured the image with his phone to remind him later of his emotions. *How had this happened? Why was Annette still at the trailer? Why hadn't he followed up to make sure her cousin took her away as planned?*

As Sue talked with dispatch to organize the crime scene team, Ray walked off to meet the neighbors, heading toward an old frame house with interior lights glowing through the windows.

10

Later, as the team gathered near the end of the workday, the photo of the fire scene Ray had snapped in the morning filled the giant screen at the front of the conference room, setting the tone for the meeting. At one end of the table, Ray waited for the others while reading through the case notes, paying particular attention to the new material that had been added during the day.

"Did you bring snacks for everyone?" asked Brett Carty with a chuckle, noting the large plastic bottle of antacids stationed next to Ray's coffee mug as he dropped into a chair.

"Always happy to share," he responded.

Sue, the last one to enter the room, carried a coffee flask in one hand and her laptop cradled in her other arm.

"Brett, Annette Ogden, do you have an update?" asked Ray.

"She's being held for observation—smoke inhalation and psychiatric issues. Per your instructions, an officer is assigned to provide protection while she's hospitalized."

"Good, thank you." He looked at Barbara. "Barbara, I just read your notes. Please share."

"Brett and I made the rounds of gas stations with convenience stores near the scene and collected their archived video."

"Any problems getting their cooperation?" asked Sue.

"No. All the clerks were eager to help."

"We got lucky early on," Sinclair continued. "At the second place we stopped, I described the individuals about whom we were seeking information. I showed the two clerks the digital images of the two. Both women said the man looked familiar, and one offered that he had paid for gas and some snacks with a crisp hundred-dollar bill. The older of the two, the manager, gave us access to their security system footage." Sinclair's fingers moved across the keyboard. First, the image she had created of John Doe filled the screen.

"They told us C-notes get a lot of attention. They're the favorite of counterfeiters. They also recalled the man's companion, whom they called a 'girl.' They wondered if they were father and daughter, given their age difference. But they also said the pair didn't look like family. And they both mentioned that the guy's English was limited.

"So we got to the needle without going through the whole haystack," Sinclair said. "Here's the video of our John Doe. Please note the time and date stamp. Sunday, July 4, starting at 1:17 p.m. John Doe approaches the counter and tells the clerk the pump number, setting the C-note and some food and beverage items on the counter. Then Tammy enters the picture, adding chips to the other items. She leaves the frame at that point."

"Run that by again," said Ray. "Is there any chance she's carrying a phone in her hand or a pocket?"

Sinclair walked the video frame by frame. "Looks like one in her back pocket, Sheriff. Anyone else?"

"I agree," said Sue. "But the man, I don't see one. Anyone?"

"Are we good to go on that?" Sinclair asked.

"Yes," said Ray, when no one replied.

"Notice that the transaction takes a lot of time. First, the younger clerk takes the bill to the older clerk. The manager, Linda, scrutinizes the bill and nods to the younger clerk. Finally, the first clerk totals the items, makes change, and gives it to the man."

Sinclair stopped the video, leaving a profile of the live John Doe on one side of the split screen with the software-assisted image she had created, also in profile, on the other side.

Ray commented on the remarkable likeness of the two images. He was startled by the images of these two people a few hours before they were murdered. Finally, he said, "I can't imagine that C-note is still hanging out in their cash register."

"My first thought, too. But Linda said she deposits most of

the cash at the branch bank just down the road at the end of her shift. She works till eight. Then, with only one employee there, they lock the doors and go credit card only at the pumps until closing at eleven."

"How about the vehicle they were driving?"

"Good video of the vehicle and license plate, too." The car appeared on the screen, first with a view from the front and then from the rear with a clear view of the Michigan license plate. "It's a current model Audi Q8. The manufacturer calls the color Florett Silver Metallic."

"And the plate info?" asked Sue.

"Well, here's where the information gets interesting," explained Barbara. "The plate is registered to a Ford Escape belonging to a woman in Royal Oak. I got the owner on the phone and identified myself as a police officer. I asked if she still owned the Escape. She answered in the affirmative and said the car was waiting for parts at the Ford dealership on Woodward. Then she wanted to know what happened to the drunk who rear-ended her. Was he in jail? I explained that this was a question about the license plate, not the vehicle." She shook her head. "I didn't do it well. I'm afraid I left her confused."

"And then?" prompted Ray.

"I called the Ford dealer and got the body shop manager on the line. When he went outside to check the vehicle, I could hear Woodward Ave. in the background. I almost got homesick. Then, there were some quasi-religious oaths, followed by expletive-filled expressions of disbelief. Finally, he told me the plate was missing. He said it might have fallen off at the accident scene or been lost during transit.

"I thanked him for the help and did a missing vehicle check on an Audi matching that description," continued Sinclair, "and guess what?"

"A stolen vehicle," Sue said.

"Bingo, a rental from Metro, went missing while parked at the Dearborn Inn."

"Another piece of the puzzle," Ray said. "Now we know our John Doe came from or through Detroit a few days ago. Good work, Barbara. Anything else?"

"Yes, one more item. Perhaps this is more for me than you guys. I prepared a map. Let me bring it up."

The screen briefly went black, and then a topographical rendering of the beach area and countryside appeared.

"I'm still trying to get the lay of the land. I started with an image from Google Earth. I've marked the areas of interest in this case. You'll notice the red *X* is the crime scene. I've also traced the paved road and two-tracks leading to this beach area in red. Finally, you'll notice that the gas station convenience store is at the far left end of the map, only eight miles from the beach.

"South of the crime scene, there are all these little roads, lots of two-tracks, leading to cottages and the public boat launches and picnic areas on these two small inland lakes. My question is, should we be checking these areas, too? Might the Audi be stashed somewhere in the area?"

"Good thought," said Brett. "I rolled through that area yesterday. I think a high-end vehicle would have caught my attention. But to be sure, I will ask the sector patrol officers on all shifts to drive through there and look for the Audi or anything suspicious."

"Thank you all," said Ray. "Please try to get some rest tonight."

In the quiet of his study that evening, with a print of the fire scene he had captured that morning lying on his desk just beyond his journal, Ray thought about the lives of the two people who had inhabited that space. As he guided his pen across the paper, a trail of brown ink flowed into letters, words, sentences, and paragraphs. His pace was irregular, with stops and starts, long hesitations, and occasional quick dashes to catch a thought before it slipped away.

Ray's pen hovered over the page. He felt exhaustion running through his frame. Picking up the pen cap, he mated it to the barrel and slid the pen into the desk drawer. He switched off the lamp and lingered at the desk in the dark. His eyes burned, and his throat was sore from the smoke he had inhaled in the early morning. Closing his eyes, he thought about the footage of Tammy Ogden from the convenience store video—her delicate features, animated face, and shy smile. Then, the image of the cold, lifeless body illuminated by white beams of the crime scene lights flashed across his consciousness.

After reading through his entry, he closed his eyes briefly. Childhood memories came rushing back, filled with the sunshine, sand, and warm breezes of that beach. His mother's laughter, her arms pulling him close and wrapping him in a towel after he ran to her from the cold water, shivering. He could hear the sound of wind and waves.

He flashed forward, now a young man on that beach with his first real love, the daughter of some summer people. Like most summer romances, the relationship ended with tearful goodbyes and promises to write.

Ray knew this terrain: the dunes, the stream, the beach, and the water out to the second bar. And even beyond that, to the Manitous and the gentle slope of the horizon. This was his special place on the planet. And it had been defiled in the most gruesome way.

11

〰

Ray stood in the shower, letting the water cascade down on him, still lost in a trance. Finally, he worked through his usual routine of shampoo and soap.

Sue was still awake, propped up on pillows reading, as he approached the bed. Simone had cuddled in next to her.

"Thought you'd be out cold by now," he said.

"Should be," she responded. "I had to shampoo my hair twice to eliminate the grime and smell. Then, I tried to soak the day away in a long, hot bath. That usually guarantees instant oblivion when I hit the sheets. Not tonight. So, I did some yoga. Simone helped me with the down dogs, head to head. Then, she was ready for playtime. We had a few games of fetch and tug of war. Now she has finally conked, and I'm trying to read myself to sleep."

Ray pulled back the blanket and settled in, stretching his arms above his chest before pulling up the covers. Simone tunneled over, her head popping out near his face.

"She's missed you, Ray. How was the writing? Any new insights?"

"I wish," he answered. "Just thinking about everything that's happened. I put Annette's dogs back in the trailer before we took her to identify Tammy's body. I stepped inside…"

"And?"

"The interior was as bad as the exterior. I could see a small trail through the debris to the other rooms. And the place reeked from the wood stove, rotting food, and unwashed bodies. But sadly, we've been in these places too many times."

The old and the poor—often a combination of the two—seemed to need to cling to things, even junk mail and fast food containers.

"I hope I don't become a hoarder in my dotage," Sue said. "That poor kid was growing up in that environment. Can you imagine if that's your norm?"

"Yes, I was thinking about that. And then I was thinking about my life and the lives of some kids I grew up with."

"From what you've said, your mother was a smart woman who turned you on to reading before you could walk. Didn't you tell me she was the valedictorian of her high school class?"

Ray looked over toward Sue. "That's true. There were seventeen in her class, five boys and twelve girls. Did I tell you she was pregnant with me at the time?"

"What? You omitted that part of the story."

"Fortunately, she wasn't showing. She said the superintendent expelled girls from school when they were pregnant. She didn't tell me this until much later in her life. But that's not the half of it."

Sue sat up and turned in Ray's direction. "What's the other half of your late-night bombshell?"

"My dad, he was just in ninth grade. She said he was the cutest boy in the school. She said the winters were so long, and my father was the cutest and nicest guy around. He had to get his parents' consent to get married. He was long dead by the time she told me this."

"So, how did they live, teens and a baby?"

"My father dropped out and went to work for his uncle Jake, the eponymous owner of Jake's Masonry Service. Dad liked to tell me how hard he worked when he was just a kid, ten-hour days carrying a hod filled with bricks or mortar and lugging cement blocks. He did that for ten years. Then Jake keeled over on the job one day, a heart attack. Dad's story was that as soon as Uncle Jake was in the ground, he went to town and got a job painting at the state mental hospital. He never wanted to touch bricks and mortar again."

"Where did they live?" asked Sue.

"At first, with Mom's grandparents on their small farm."

"How about her parents or his?"

"I never got the story. The grandparents had the room and desperately needed Mom's help. She ran the house, cooking, cleaning, and looking after the bills. It was a trade-off. She and Dad inherited the farm when her grandparents died and spent the rest of their lives there."

"What's gotten you thinking about all this?"

"I was born in up north backwoods poor like Tammy. But I was dealt a better hand than she was. Despite all the hardships, my mother was a cheerful, happy, energetic person. She made me a reader and pushed me to do well in school. Our old house was a remnant of the lumbering era, but she kept it neat and clean. Much of what we ate came from her garden and the chickens she raised. And in winter, we lived on her beautifully canned fruits and vegetables."

"What about your dad?" Sue asked. "You hardly ever talk about him."

"He was a drunk. His alcohol was an enormous drain on the family finances, but he wasn't violent or destructive. And much of the time, he was a pretty good dad. He taught me basic carpentry and mechanics. These skills helped me get a job with Nora and Hugh, the summer people I worked for as a teenager. I was their full-time handyman and gofer. Eventually, they made sure I had the funds to get through college. They changed my life."

"Maybe Tammy's life was starting to change, too." She turned off the light on her side of the bed.

12

Chuck Gunderson lay wide awake, stirred from a deep slumber by a too-familiar dream of war, filled with the sounds and smells of battle. Alexis, his wife of over sixty years, lay curled up on the other side of the bed. Tonight's dream—a slight variation of the same recurring dream—began before their wedding, shortly after he was discharged from a military hospital in Okinawa and returned home. Chuck had no memory of how he got to Okinawa, only waking up in a strange place filled with hospital smells and sounds, surrounded by nurses, doctors, and orderlies. A few months later, physically healed, he landed at Detroit Metro. Expecting his family to greet him, he only found his girlfriend, Alexis. They arrived at the old farmhouse near Lake Michigan four hours later, where he anticipated a big family gathering. Instead, they had a quiet meal with his parents and Alexis, enjoying his mother's signature meatloaf, mashed potatoes, and green beans from the garden.

And over the next few days, his siblings and a few of his high school friends still living in the area dropped by to welcome him home. There was warmth and friendship in these gatherings. But he quickly realized that he had returned from an unpopular war to a nation that didn't welcome the returning veterans. There were no ticker tape parades, no joyful victory celebrations. The atrocities of a few still smoldered in the public memory. The blood, sweat, and tears, the sacrifices of so many, were forgotten. And the politicians who had sent the sons of yet another generation off to fight a needless war had moved on to other issues.

Chuck felt that his family and friends expected him to take up exactly where he left off before he was drafted. His physical injuries would heal, and he'd return to his old life. But no one other than Alexis seemed to understand the psychic wounds that would remain with him forever.

That first night home, he climbed the creaking staircase to his bedroom, which he had once shared with his brothers. It was the old, the familiar. But he also knew that the innocence of childhood had been stripped away in the jungles of Vietnam. And now he had a new companion; the dream—the thumping blades of the chopper, the sensation of falling out of the sky—had already taken up residence.

The years unspooled. He and Alexis married. With his father's death, he took over the farm. And then there were children and all the events that filled people's lives over the decades, rearing a family and making a living. But the dream remained a constant.

Chuck looked at the clock glowing on the dresser—5:37. The dream started as it always began. He was in the right-hand seat going through the pre-flight checklist, his copilot, Doug, confirming his actions. Doug's voice faded out as the scream of the turbine started to build. "Front row seat," Doug yelled, his private joke repeated before every takeoff. "Front row seat to our death. How fucking lucky is that?"

The air filled with the stench of burning jet fuel. The speed of the turbine increased. Their clothes were already soaked with sweat in the heat and humidity; Chuck could feel rivulets running down his chest. The slapping sounds of the rotors grew louder, the wash from the blades scattering dust and debris as the ship broke free from the ground and slowly turned and followed the line of choppers toward enemy territory. Chuck glanced back at the young Marines huddled behind him. He never knew how to read their faces—fear, terror, resignation, boredom. He didn't want to think about the hell into which these boys would soon be dropping.

In the dream, they reached the landing zone without any incoming fire, the squadron flying low and descending into a narrow opening in the jungle. Endless radio chatter filled his headphones: "Friendlies on the left, VC on the right." He watched Eager Ed in the lead ship move into the clearing and hover just long enough for the Marines to jump to the ground. Chuck could see men scampering away as the chopper rose and turned.

Chuck moved forward, struggling to hold the machine level as his human cargo dropped to the jungle floor. Then he twisted the throttle control, pulling his machine away from the LZ, following on the heels of another ship.

Chuck's dream always had one of two possible endings. The most common was waking up in the hospital. The second ending, the darker and more frightening, started with an explosion and the sensation of falling, the chopper on fire, breaking apart as it hit the ground—the dream ending with his body pinned in the burning wreckage. At the end of either version, he was always wide awake.

Guided by a pale blue nightlight, he pulled himself from the sheets and blankets, carefully stepped around the two aging farm dogs that slept at the foot of the bed, and crept into the bathroom.

Alexis kept a stack of ironed and folded PJs in a cupboard. Dropping his sweat-soaked garments to the floor, Chuck toweled off and pulled on some dry pajamas.

Back in bed, still wide awake, he tried to focus on the breathing exercises the psychologist at the VA had taught him. His concentration wandered after just a dozen or so slow inhalations. The explosions and machinery of war had permanently damaged his hearing. Tinnitus, the buzzing in his head, now dominated his attention.

Anger, the last act in the nightly drama, ran through his system. His muscles were tensing. Pain ran through his frame.

Chuck went back to the breathing exercises. "Follow the breath, follow the breath." Loosening his jaw, the pain across his temples and forehead gradually lessened. He slowly moved his head from side to side, old muscles aching and worn vertebra grinding. He could hear the therapist's voice as he worked down his arms to his fingers, upper legs to toes, his breathing slowing, sleep seeping in as the war slipped away.

Minutes maybe, but perhaps only seconds later, he was awake

again. An explosion rattled the old farmhouse. He pulled himself from the bed again and looked out the front window. He could see the flames reflecting against the walls of the gravel pit across the road. A second, third, and fourth explosion soon followed, each burst illuminating the billowing black smoke as it unfurled skyward. He stood momentarily, rubbed his eyes to ensure he was awake, then walked down the steep staircase to the kitchen and dialed 9-1-1.

He waited until the first sheriff's car rolled past, followed by a fire truck a few minutes later. Then he returned to his bed.

Ray turned off the rural county road, parking on the gravel drive near a weather-beaten farmhouse.

"Mr. Gunderson?" Ray called to the man, stooped from age and wear, arranging vegetables at a roadside stand.

"Yes, can I help you?"

"I heard you had some excitement during the night."

"Oh, Sheriff, yes, more commotion than I like in the wee hours. Didn't expect to see you so early."

"The car involved. It's one we've been looking for. You want to tell me about it?"

"Not much to tell. Just a couple of loud bangs at night, enough to wake me up. Then I went to get a drink of water and saw something burning in the gravel pit across the way. So I called it in, and there was a little commotion, fire trucks, and probably one of your guys. And Alexis, my wife, she slept through it."

"Did you see anything beforehand? Suspicious vehicles?"

"No, Sheriff, as I said, I was sleeping. The first explosion woke me. I thought about getting dressed and walking over. I would have done that years ago." Gunderson pulled off his faded baseball cap and rubbed the grayish stubble on his mostly bald head. "Then I thought whatever was happening could happen without me."

"Thank you for calling it in, sir."

"Call me Chuck. 'Sir' frightens me—flashbacks of the military, Nam." Pointing to his stand, he continued. "Things are just starting to get ripe. Everything was picked this morning. This is all I do now, the stand, the garden. My neighbor farms my fields. I leased the gravel pit to Tony Nelson, a small-time excavator. I don't see him around much, but I called him this morning. I thought he should know what happened. The wife answered, says he's in the UP on a job. So I went over and had a look after breakfast," Gunderson said.

"And?"

"Well, I guess you know this already. It was a newish car, I think, totally destroyed. I looked inside. Nothing much left, seat springs and stuff. Guess someone was trying to get rid of something."

"Has anything like this happened around here before?"

"Never. I mean, occasionally, kids with twenty-twos shooting bottles and cans. There's something about a gravel pit. If I hear them, I run them off. But nothing like this."

"And you haven't noticed anything suspicious in recent days?"

"No, traffic's mostly local and cottagers in the summer. Haven't seen anything unusual."

"Well, thanks for the help," said Ray.

"Vegetables, Sheriff? Fresh. Good prices."

Pointing, Ray said, "My detective has just arrived. I need to get over there. I'll try to stop back. Thanks again. And if you think of anything else, let me know." Ray handed Gunderson his card and drove across the road down into the gravel pit, parking near Sue's truck. As he approached the remains of the passenger car, she was walking the perimeter, taking pictures.

"Isn't much left," she said. "The incident report from the fire company stated that the vehicle was fully engaged when they arrived. They checked the interior for occupants. There were none. Then they pulled back and waited at a safe distance until the fire burned itself out. Finally, they cooled the wreckage with water and did an environmental damage assessment."

"So, what have we got?" asked Ray.

"A roasted Audi. Looks like our missing vehicle. I'll confirm that with the VIN."

"So what's the plan?"

"Flatbed to DPW garage. Then I'll see what I can find with the appropriate tools and good lighting."

"How long?"

"Elkins, you're so impatient. The flatbed will be here soon. I should have something for you later today."

13

〜

Amanda Slosson, a commanding presence—tall, strikingly beautiful, with long blond hair—stood behind the bar of the West Bay Tap, a trendy brewpub and eatery built in a rehabbed warehouse in the historic harbor area of the village. The north side of the building stood at the water's edge. Slosson's gaze locked onto Sheriff Elkins as soon as he came through the main entrance. Catching his eye, she gestured over the late breakfast crowd toward an exit door at the far left side of the building.

Ray had known Amanda since high school. She was two years ahead of him. They rode the same bus, and he—then a very shy sophomore—always felt lucky that the coolest senior girl always had time for him. She sometimes helped him with homework on the bus, and sometimes they just talked. After she graduated and went off to college, he lost track of her. They reconnected years later when Ray returned to Cedar County. Amanda, by then divorced with two daughters, was running the family business.

A few moments later, she approached him, pushing the door open with her hip and passing him a mug of coffee. "Still take it black, I imagine?"

"Yes," said Ray.

He followed her to a picnic table under the trees. "I'd like us to be out of eyeshot as much as possible," she said. "The kids who work here, well everyone, is wondering…"

"Tammy Ogden."

"Oh, no. Oh, Ray," Slosson said, her eyes welling with tears. "When Tammy didn't show up for work or call in, I knew something was wrong. The buzz started after last night's first report on the eleven o'clock news, quickly spreading on social media. Imaginations ran wild. I began getting texts and emails from the kids. Oh, Ray, this will be so hard. And you know what it's like. Most of them have never lost a peer. Dying is for old people—ancient relatives, grandparents. But not people like Tammy. Oh, Ray, she stole our hearts."

Slosson pulled a tissue from her pocket and dabbed at her eyes and nose. "The seasonal kids—servers and bussers, mostly the children of locals or the kids of summer people—had never met anyone like her before. When she first came to us, Tammy was so sad. And she was hungry like none of the other kids had ever seen. And she needed clothes, kindness, and friendship. Over the last few months, we all watched her blossom. We were all thrilled by it."

"Maria Tillson told me Tammy worked here," explained Ray. "She thought you might have seen something that would help our investigation. At this point, we know almost nothing about Tammy. You said she was seen leaving with a man?"

Amanda brushed a strand of long blond hair away from her face. "Yeah, there was this creepy guy in here on and off the last week. Thirty-something, maybe older. He had a lot of bad miles on him if you know what I mean. He took a real liking to Tammy—big tips, chatting her up—dirty old-man stuff. He had thick black hair, lots of it, combed back and oily-looking. He had a sort of swarthy complexion—maybe Mediterranean or Eastern European? I don't mean to sound xenophobic. That's not me. Lots of the people we see aren't from here. But there was something bad about this guy."

"What else do you remember about him?" Ray asked. "Other physical characteristics? How did he dress? Did he have any visible tattoos? What was he driving?"

"He was about my height, pushing six feet, trim and wiry. His clothes were different, tighter than American men wear, dark colors, mostly black. But good muscle definition, like a bodybuilder. He was hairy, too, real hairy. And the guy liked showing off his body."

"How do you know?" asked Ray.

"He caught me looking at him. I knew what he was thinking.

A woman knows. But that's not what I was thinking. I didn't want Tammy getting tangled up with a sleazeball. And older guys are only after one thing. Oh, and he did have tats on both arms."

"Can you describe the tattoos?"

"I didn't get that close."

"Anything else?" Ray asked.

"He didn't have much English. Lots of pointing at the menu."

"How did he pay?"

"If you're hoping for a credit card, no luck. He had a large roll of cash, and he enjoyed flashing it. Big denomination bills."

"Did this man have a name?"

"Not that I heard. I asked Tammy, and she didn't seem to know, or perhaps she wasn't telling me."

"Other than Tammy, did this man meet with anyone else?"

"He came in alone and left alone. Other than the hostess and servers, I don't think he talked with anyone."

"Anyone snap a photo of the man?"

Amanda shrugged. "I don't know, but I'll ask around. Not likely. The kids are forbidden to carry a phone. I drill it into them: 'Leave your phone in your car.'"

"Did you see what he was driving?" asked Ray.

"Sort of. Trying not to be obvious, I followed him out one night. The car was something low." Amanda made a motion with her hands, fingers open, rolling outward. "Curvaceous, sensual, you know what I'm trying to say. Probably black or dark blue and expensive."

"Make?"

"European, I think, or high-end Japanese. They all kind of look alike to me. And no, I didn't see a plate if that's what you're about to ask."

"Transportation, how did Tammy get to work?"

"An old van, a Dodge or Plymouth. A real beater."

"Did she leave the vehicle here after her last shift?"

"I'm not sure, but it's gone now."

"Was there anyone Tammy didn't get along with?"

Amanda took a moment to answer. "Yes. Dakota Dirks, one of the dishwashers. That kid's got a hair trigger. He got in a dust-up with Tammy just before she went missing.

I wasn't here. Olivia handled it."

"Dirks, is he around?"

"No, he hasn't shown up the last few days. That's his usual MO. He gets in trouble here and disappears for a week or so. Then he comes back all apologetic. He's a good dishwasher. They're in short supply. We always take him back."

"We need to talk with him. Contact info?"

"I'll email what I have."

"Any cameras inside or in the parking lot?"

"No, sorry. I've been thinking about that, but it seems Big Brotherish."

Amanda averted her eyes and chewed on her lower lip. "Tammy was a sweet kid, Ray. I failed her. I didn't protect her. I didn't want to be a mother hen. That's what my girls always accuse me of being." She sighed.

"You have always been an incredibly caring person, Amanda. There is no way you could have anticipated this."

Amanda remained silent, pondering Ray's words. Finally, she said, "My daughter, Olivia, remember her?"

"I remember the girls, but it's been a while."

"Olivia, she's my baby, twenty-two, graduate school in psychology. This is probably the last summer I can hold onto her. She looks after the summer staff: servers, bussers, and dish crew. She's close to these kids. Olivia's the one you should talk with."

"Is she here?" asked Ray.

"No. She's just working dinner today. She's at the cottage, reading, and probably trying to improve her tan. I'll give her a call. I know she'd be happy to help."

"I'd appreciate that," said Ray, passing her a card. "If there's anything that I should know, please call. And as things develop, we may need your help again. So either Sergeant Lawrence or I will contact you."

"Can you tell me anything about what happened to Tammy?" Amanda asked, her eyes pleading with him.

"Not at the moment," Ray said, trying to unclench his teeth. He didn't ever want to have to tell her what had happened to Tammy Ogden.

14

〜

Olivia Slosson stood waiting near the circular drive at the family cottage as Ray parked his patrol car. She led him to a deck facing the lake. With only memories of Olivia as a child to go on, he expected a young woman who looked like her mother. By contrast, Olivia was petite, and her dark brown hair was cut close. She had a ballerina-like grace and delicacy, a striking difference from her mother's cheerful, rugged, take-charge physicality.

They settled at a table on the deck, shaded by a large umbrella from the afternoon sun. After Olivia had shed her oversized sunglasses, Ray could see that she had been crying.

"A difficult day," he said.

"I've been running possible scenarios since Tammy disappeared. Her getting harmed or killed is the one I didn't want to imagine." Olivia inhaled deeply and slowly exhaled, meeting Ray's gaze. "The man Tammy was found with, is he the guy my mother told you about?"

"Yes," Ray answered. "I assume you saw him, too?"

"I did, but I was late hearing about this hot romance. I'm sure my mother has told you what little we know about him?"

"I'd like to hear your impression."

She shrugged. "First, I keep everything moving from the kitchen to the front of the house, the servers and bussers, but I'm not often in the front. Their flirtation continued for days before anyone called it to my attention. Once I knew, I checked the guy out—European, maybe, and older. My first impression was that he was not anyone

I would feel safe with. I warned Tammy off. She didn't take me seriously."

"We know so little about her," said Ray. "You've worked with her for several months. What can you tell me?"

Olivia touched her face with both hands, an unconscious gesture of horror. "Mom hired her a few days before I returned from Ann Arbor. That was weeks before most of our summer staff started. She was shy and needed a lot of help and reassurance, and I was glad I had the time to spend with her before the season started. It's not that she didn't catch on quickly, but her basic knowledge of almost everything was limited."

"For instance?"

"How to set the table: flatware, dinner plate, salad plate, water glass, wine glass, napkin. I learned these things as a little girl helping my mother at home. But this lack of world knowledge was more extensive than that."

"So you taught her what she needed to do restaurant work?"

"Yes. And in the process, I realized the advantages I had growing up. Generational poverty is something I learned about in a sociology class, but I didn't fully comprehend the concept until I spent time with Tammy."

"Understood."

"It's like this, Sheriff: We started serving local asparagus before Memorial Day. Tammy didn't know what it was. She had never tasted it. The staff gets a meal with every shift. I'd eat with Tammy, ordering our meals to give her a taste of everything on our menu. I probed her about her usual diet. It was a short list: cold cereal, Pop-Tarts, frozen pizza, saltines, Kraft Dinner, and lunch meat sandwiches."

"Nothing that requires much preparation," said Ray.

"Exactly. She said the only fruits and vegetables she ate came in school lunches, which she disliked. But that's only half of it."

"I'm listening," said Ray.

"Hygiene, personal grooming, how to wash clothes, simple mending—the list is endless. First, we worked on the basic life skills most kids have learned by third or fourth grade. Then, we focused on job skills: arriving on time, dressing appropriately, and grooming. Again, she was an adept student. Her transformation was amazing. And she seemed to appreciate all of our help. She wanted to please us."

Olivia fell silent and looked vacantly across the water to the distant shore.

"How did she get along with her coworkers?"

"For the most part, well."

"But she didn't get along well with everyone?"

"Staffing a restaurant is always difficult, especially one like ours, which requires so many seasonal employees. Turnover is constant. Sometimes you put up with people because you have no alternative."

"Your mother told me about Dakota Dirks?"

Olivia's body tensed, and Ray could see she was struggling to hold back the tears. He waited.

"The guy's a freaking lowlife. I could go on and on. That said, Dakota can wash dishes and shows up for work—or at least he did. Other than that, he has no redeeming qualities. He lives near Tammy and made it clear they shared a *history*." She opened her eyes wide, making sure Ray comprehended that she was talking about sex. "If I had a replacement, he'd be gone in a heartbeat."

"How did you know they didn't get along?"

"Everyone knew," Olivia said. "Whenever they were working the same shift, Dakota would make inappropriate comments when Tammy came into the kitchen to pick up her orders. If I was there, I'd get on his case, and he'd shut up. But I wasn't always there. Then, one night, they really got into it."

"They argued?" Ray asked.

"More than an argument. It was about the guy, the foreigner. It was about sex. I came into the kitchen just as the last words were exchanged. Then it went postal. Dakota said, 'Whore just like your mom,' and Tammy went totally feral. She was slapping the shit out of him before three or four of us could get in and pull them apart. Dakota got the worst of it. I sent him home early. Since he was off the next day I gave him his check, then I walked him to his truck and watched him drive away. And that was also the last night Tammy was at work. I never saw her again. I'm not accusing Dakota of anything, but I have suspicions."

"Because?"

"After we pulled Tammy off him, his eye was swollen, and he was bleeding from multiple scratches, and he just seemed humiliated. He was almost crying, and then he started screaming that he'd get even with her 'big time.'"

"Have you ever seen him in possession of a gun of any type?"

"No, but one of the kids told me he bragged about having an AR-15."

"Aside from Tammy, has Dakota Dirks physically or verbally assaulted or threatened you, your mother, or other employees before this incident?"

"No. He knows better than that. He'd be out of here permanently. And I have no evidence that Dakota has a history of harming small animals," she hissed sarcastically. "That said, I know he was very possessive of Tammy. He always addressed her as 'my bitch.' Got that, Sheriff?"

"When did this fight between Tammy and Dakota happen?"

"It was Saturday, the third."

"Did Dakota come to work the next day?"

"No, Sunday is his normal day off."

"How about Monday?" asked Ray.

"He hasn't been back since then. One of the other dishwashers said Dakota mentioned heading to the U.P."

"Did he let you know…?"

"Oh, hell no. That's not how it happens with some of our workers. They just disappear. Some wander back, looking to get hired again. Most show up wanting their final check."

"Other than Dakota Dirks and the nameless foreigner, were there other employees or customers who might have had a romantic interest in Tammy, or vice versa?"

"Maybe," Olivia said, "but who knows what's going on in their heads? Some kids at this age are mostly hormones. I see the summer romances. I imagine there are one-night stands and encounters of convenience. Some of the kids are always looking, especially the guys. Others are at least subtle or perhaps shy. Let me think about who might have had a thing for Tammy. Give me your cell, and I'll message you if anyone comes to mind."

Sue stood watching Ray work at the keyboard, his handwritten notes from his interview with Olivia Slosson on the desk.

"Dakota Dirks, what do we have on him?" asked Sue.

Ray told her what he'd learned during his interview with Olivia Slosson.

"He sounds like a real smooth talker," said Sue. "Priors?"

"Two moving when he was a minor," Ray answered. "And one first offense OWI with high blood alcohol content two years ago. He's not attempted to get his license back."

"Once you lose your license, you've got nothing left to lose. Getting it back doesn't matter. Most of these guys follow the same script," Sue quipped.

"If the address on file is accurate, he lives less than six miles from Tammy's home. I called Maria Tillson to see if she could provide any background on Dirks."

"And?"

"The Dirks family has a long history with social services, too. It's not a happy story. An alcoholic, abusive, seldom-employed father and a poorly educated mother who tried to hold the family together by working at low-wage jobs. Eventually, Dakota's mother was too ill to work—bowel cancer. By the time she sought medical care, the cancer was inoperable. Then Dakota's old man, Billy K. Dirks— who insists on being addressed as BK—pulled one of his frequent disappearing acts. Dakota, then sixteen, dropped out of school to be his mother's caregiver and look after a younger brother and sister. His mother died a few months later."

"Tragic story," said Sue.

"Yes," said Ray. "According to Tillson, an aunt, the mother's sister, took in his siblings, but the aunt and Dakota didn't get on. So, he was left in the care of his mostly absent father. Tillson thinks Dakota was mostly without adult supervision from that point forward."

"Did he go back to school?" asked Sue.

"Tillson said she tried to get him back into school–vocational programs, online courses, and an alternative high school. No success. School had always been a disaster for the kid since first grade. He was diagnosed as learning disabled, and from that point on, there's a long history of truancy and suspensions."

Ray glanced through his handwritten notes. "He confronted Tammy on July 3, the last day she was at work. He hasn't been back since. We need to bring him in."

"Any idea what he might be driving?"

"No car listed in his name. Among the vehicles listed for that address is a fifteen-year-old Chevy pickup titled to Billy Kendall Dirks. I assume that's what Dakota is driving. It fits the description Olivia gave me.

Ray quickly copied the information from his screen to a sticky note and passed it to Sue. "Would you please get this out? BOLO. Dirks is wanted for questioning in a murder investigation. He should be considered armed and dangerous. Alert the interagency SWAT team. Get aerial maps of his address. You know all the steps to this dance."

Less than an hour later, Dakota Dirks was located. A 9-1-1 call from a motorist reported seeing a vehicle zigzagging down a county road, eventually going onto the shoulder and rolling several times before crashing into a tree. By the time they reached the accident scene—Sue at the wheel, Ray in the passenger seat—the east side of the road was lined with emergency vehicles. Walking along the shoulder, they could see members of the township volunteer fire department and their EMT team working to free the passenger of the overturned pickup truck in a steep gully far below the highway.

From their vantage point, they watched as emergency workers struggled to pry open the door of the mangled vehicle with mechanical jaws. Finally, with the door torn away, the EMTs carefully slid the injured man onto a backboard. Once he was secured to the board, the crew slowly carried him up the steep slope to the waiting ambulance.

"What can you tell us?" Ray asked the fire chief as the ambulance rolled away.

"Not much, Sheriff, other than that the victim was alive, breathing, vitals not bad, and had no noticeable injuries other than a small laceration on the forehead. Who knows what they'll find at the hospital."

"Conscious?" asked Ray.

"Not really," the man answered. "He seemed to be in an alcohol or drug stupor. Most likely both. At best, he'll probably be plenty sore and have a bad hangover."

15

〜

Dakota Dirks, dressed in an orange jail jumpsuit, arms and legs shackled, slumped in a chair in the interview room, arms on the table, his head resting on his arms. A steel table painted institutional gray separated Dirks from two empty chairs on the other side. The corrections officer, Darleen, an imposing woman of late middle age, stood guard near the door.

Ray nodded a greeting toward Darleen as he entered. Sue followed and looked up at the camera, verbally identifying the room's occupants and the date and time. Then she settled in one of the chairs, arranged her notes, and Mirandized Dirks.

"Do you understand what I've just read for you, Mr. Dirks?" she asked.

With his head cocked toward his left shoulder, Dirks just glared at her. Then, finally, he emitted a low guttural sound.

She repeated her question.

Lifting his head in her direction, Dirks slowly uttered a stream of profanities. In this way, during the opening minutes of the interview, he avoided answering any questions. He just rattled off the same obscenities, changing the order occasionally.

Over the years, Ray had learned to tune out angry words and focus on the nonverbal information a suspect communicated. Dirks' anger and disdain remained constant. He appeared to be highly agitated. Streaks of sweat had soaked through the front of the jumpsuit.

Dirks' hair was long and shabby, a ragged, oily mop that extended beyond the base of his neck. His face was pockmarked. Tattoos covered the visible part of his neck.

Sue repeated her question a third time, "For the video, did you understand what I read to you? I need a 'yes' or a 'no.'"

"Yeah," he eventually uttered without making eye contact.

"Do you want an attorney?"

Dirks slowly moved his head from side to side and exhaled audibly.

"I need a verbal response, Mr. Dirks."

"No," he said, slightly pulling himself up in his chair. "Why am I here?" Another blast of obscenities followed. Then he raised his cuffed hands and slammed his fists against the metal tabletop.

"You crashed your truck yesterday," Ray said. "Do you remember that? They had to cut you out of your vehicle before they could take you to the hospital."

Dirks muttered a single obscenity, intoned in a manner to suggest complete despair. "I should be in the hospital."

"You were transported to the hospital from the accident scene and held overnight for observation. Other than a small cut, you had no physical injuries. But your initial blood alcohol was at a level that could have killed you. The accident might have saved your life by getting you immediate medical attention."

Dirks shrugged.

Ray waited, wondering if Dirks comprehended what he had just said.

Then Ray continued, "We found beer cans and whiskey bottles in your truck, Dakota. It seems like you've been on a major bender."

Dirks didn't respond or even look at Ray.

Ray continued, "We also found two weapons, a .38 caliber pistol, and a military-style assault rifle. Both the rifle and pistol are ghost guns with no serial numbers. Would you tell us about them?"

"Not mine. I don't know how they got there," Dirks responded, clumsily using the cuff of his jumpsuit to mop away some of the sweat running into his eyes.

"What do you mean, not yours?" Ray asked.

"Found them."

"Where, Mr. Dirks? Where did you find them?"

"A hitchhiker left them in the car. The guy must have tossed his duffel bag behind the seat when he got in. Total stoner. Guess he forgot it."

"Can you give us the name of this hitchhiker?"

"Naw, he wasn't a talker."

"How about a description?" asked Ray.

"Just some Black guy. Shouldn't be hard for you to find him up here," Dirks said. "I didn't look too close. I was driving."

"Come on, Dakota, let's not play games. You said you didn't know the guns were in your truck. We checked the weapons for fingerprints and compared them with those on file from your last arrest. Can you explain how your prints, and only your prints, are all over the guns—and the ammo, too?" said Ray.

"Maybe I took them out and looked at them."

"You said you didn't know the guns were there."

"I found them a few days after I picked up the hitchhiker. I just figured that's how they got in my truck."

"So it's possible the guns didn't belong to the hitchhiker?"

"Must of. Don't know how else they got in there."

"Where and when did you pick up the hitchhiker?" Ray asked.

"Saturday night after work, late. I can't remember where. I was just driving."

"Where did you end up?"

"I don't remember. I slept in my truck somewhere. Maybe along the Manistee."

"Dakota," said Sue, "you haven't been at the West Bay Tap since Saturday. Can you tell us where you've been since you left work on Saturday night?"

"What does it matter?"

"We're just trying to get your story sorted out," said Sue. "There was a shooting at Annette Ogden's house. We found your prints on some of the brass recovered at the scene. When we get the ballistics back from the state police lab, I'm sure we will find the rifle in your truck was the one used in that incident."

"Not by me. Someone's trying to blame me. Probably you effers planted it."

Sue began again. "Dakota, you're racking up a long list of charges against you. By not cooperating, you're making things worse. We know you and Tammy Ogden argued and came to blows Saturday night in the kitchen at the West Bay Tap. We have a witness who said you threatened Tammy. Less than twenty-four hours later, Tammy was murdered. The next night, her home was sprayed with bullets from a semi-automatic rifle."

"I didn't know the bitch was dead!" Dirks yelled at Sue, slamming his fists down on the table time after time. "I didn't know. I didn't know," he chanted.

Finally, he started sobbing. Tears ran down his face. They waited several minutes for him to regain some composure. Sue pulled a few tissues from a box and pushed them toward his cuffed hands.

"The shooting at her house, what was that all about?" asked Ray as Dirks dabbed at his tears and blew his nose.

"I didn't think anyone was there. Her car wasn't there. I thought she and her mother were gone. I just wanted to show her."

"Show her what, Dakota?"

"Bitch. That I was good enough till—"

"Till what?"

Dirks looked straight into Ray's eyes as he rose abruptly from his chair, grabbing the table's edge and trying to flip it. His action came to a jarring halt as the table, bolted securely to the floor, held fast. Quickly, the corrections officer's hands were on his shoulders, pushing him back into the chair.

Gasping for air, he sputtered, "I didn't know she was dead. I didn't do it." He pulled his arms up to shield his face.

"Let's go back to Saturday night," Ray said. "After your fight with Tammy, what did you do? And take your time, Dakota. See if you can tell the truth."

A long silence followed. Dirks swiped at his nose.

Then he said, "Olivia ordered me to leave. She gave me my check and walked me to my truck. And she stood there and watched me drive away. Ask her."

"Then what did you do?"

"I went to the Beer Depot, cashed my check, and got some stuff."

"Then what?" asked Sue.

"Like I said, I just drove around. Manistee maybe. Then, I decided to go to the UP. I stopped outside Grayling to pee."

"When did you wake up?"

"Sometime during the day. Noon like?"

"Then what?"

"I don't remember. I was hung."

"So if we check the bridge cameras, will we see your truck crossing?" Sue asked.

Dirks thought about it. He mumbled a response.

"We can't hear you, Dakota," said Sue in a carefully modulated tone.

He looked in her direction. "I don't know. I musta hit a bar in Mac City. I woke up in a parking lot by the bridge. I drove home and slept it off."

"Then what?"

"Hair of the dog. Nothing left. Was on my way to get some beer. And then…"

A long silence followed. Dakota seemed to be struggling with something. Finally, he said, "I'm going to be sick."

"Want to do lunch?" asked Sue as they walked toward Ray's office.

"I'll take a pass for now," he said, looking at his watch.

"Elkins, you're looking a little green," she said, giving him a knowing smile.

"Look," he countered, "I've got a news conference in twenty minutes, and I want to pull my notes together."

"What do you think?" said Sue.

"Make sure he gets his shower and some time to sleep it off," said Ray. "That'll give you some time to request a search warrant for his phone. We're especially interested in the location data. We'll see if that supports his story. Also, request a search warrant for his house. I think his version of the truth is probably reasonably close to the reality of what happened."

"Yes," Sue agreed. "These murders weren't a solo operation. They required two or more people and careful planning. This isn't our man."

"Let's make sure there's no handgun at his home that could be the murder weapon. We need to get him ruled out as quickly as possible."

"Expecting a big turnout for the news conference?" asked Sue with a wry smile.

"Yes," he responded. "The usual suspects—local TV, regional print news, and maybe public radio." He reconsidered. "That's not quite true. TV News, someone new. A woman, young, a summer intern. It took a while for her to get a camera set up."

"Remember the old days, Ray, when they'd come with a cameraman?"

"Yeah, the old days. That was only a couple of years ago," he responded.

At the news conference, the print news reporter, Katy Boyd, asked, "Sheriff, you said earlier that the murders appear to have been targeted. What does that mean for the general public?"

"It means we believe someone was specifically targeting these victims for reasons we are still piecing together," Ray said. "That means the general public is in no danger, and it is safe to use the public land where the crimes were committed."

The public radio reporter, Abi Gear, asked, "Sheriff, what can you tell us about the victims?"

Ray described Tammy Ogden and John Doe and held up the digital sketches Barbara Sinclair had created from the autopsy photos and that Sue had distributed to the same news sources and others around the state the previous day. He reiterated the department's earlier requests for community help. He asked the reporters to remind their audience about the community tip line.

The TV intern said, "Holly Pride, TV News. Sheriff, do you have any leads on who might have committed such a horrific crime in such a public place?"

"We're following multiple leads," Ray said. "When we have something definitive, we will make that information available."

"What about the shooting and the fire at the residence of the mother of victim Tammy Ogden?" Holly Pride asked. "For viewers who are feeling nervous about having a murderer on the loose, can you tell us if this incident is related to Tammy Ogden's murder?"

"We don't believe there is any connection between those two incidents," Ray said. "We currently have someone in custody for the shooting at the Ogden residence. We also have the weapon that we believe was used in that incident. We're waiting for verification from the MSP lab. We don't believe the person in custody was responsible for the murder."

"Would you give us the name of the person under arrest?" asked Abi Gear.

"Not at this time. We're still collecting evidence."

When there appeared to be no more questions, Ray ended the news conference. As he collected his notes, the print reporter, Katy Boyd, approached him, and they chatted briefly as the others were leaving. Boyd noted that a double homicide on a July Fourth weekend, where there had been two mass shootings in other parts of the country, wouldn't attract much attention. As was her usual MO, she said she would continue to follow the story and put it on the wire. And then Boyd reminded Ray that on a typical three-day holiday weekend, more than a thousand people were injured by gunfire, and a third of them ended up dead.

When Ray caught up with Sue later, he repeated what Katy Boyd had said to him: "You only make CNN if it's a mass shooting or a dead celebrity."

16

~

Carrying a brown paper bag, Ray walked through the main entrance door of the Cedar County DPW garage, pausing briefly to allow his eyes to adjust from the brilliant midday July sunshine to the dusky interior of the old cement block building. After scanning the area, he headed for a corner at the back of the garage where the burned-out hulk of the Audi—circled by four bright banks of lights on tripods—rested on the remaining bits of the scorched and mostly melted-away aluminum wheels. Both doors, the hood, and the rear hatch, distorted and misshapen from the intense heat, were propped against a nearby wall. The air was thick with the smell of burnt rubber and plastic. Sue—clad in a Tyvek suit, booties, hood, and face mask—was peering into the rear opening of the car.

"Find anything?" he asked. Sue moved in his direction. With a gloved hand, she passed Ray an evidence bag.

"What am I looking at?" he asked.

Pulling down her mask, she answered, "A man's belt buckle. Interesting design. There was also some hardware, which looks like a suitcase's metallic parts."

"Anything else?"

"Seat frames, some blackened coins, a Yeti insulated coffee mug—the plastic top seems to have gone missing."

"The doors, hatch, and hood, you didn't take those off yourself?" said Ray.

"The guys," she pointed toward the repair area of the garage, "saw me struggling and offered to get the parts 'out of my road.' I think they wanted to practice using the Jaws of Life. So, what's for lunch?"

"Your usual medium-rare burger, fries, large Diet Coke." He looked down with disdain at the bag he held in his hand. "I always feel like I'm aiding and abetting."

"Let's go outside. I need some fresh air," said Sue. Out in the sunshine, she headed for an old oak tree shading a grassy slope near the back of the building. She pulled off her mask, cap, and rubber gloves. Last, she shed the Tyvek suit before settling in the shade.

"I was hoping for more than a belt buckle," said Ray as he emptied the paper sack.

Sue attacked the Coke first, then moved on to the burger. Eventually, she said, "There is a bit more. I reached out to my buddy at the Bureau this morning. I forwarded the autopsy photos of our John Doe late yesterday. He didn't have anything solid for me yet. But he had liaised with the DEA. He said he'd email more later today or tomorrow. He reminded me of the rapidly changing cast of characters in the drug trade and the constant probing for new ways to smuggle drugs into the country."

"Everyone wants a piece of the American market," said Ray.

17

Ray stopped at the information desk near the hospital's main entrance, provided ID, and asked for Annette Ogden's patient room. The woman at the desk, her gray hair pulled back into a tight bun, peered at his photo first, then up at Ray, who momentarily pulled down his mask so she could see his face.

"You've been cleared to visit this patient, Sheriff. Follow the blue line to the East Elevators. Go to the fourth floor. The nursing station is just to the left of the elevators. Please check in with the nursing station. I'll alert them that you are on your way. They'll escort you to the patient."

Ray went through the almost empty halls until he reached the 4 East nursing station. He looked across the work area—men and women in scrubs seated at desks, heads down, looking at screens, fingers moving across keyboards. Finally, a thirty-something man looked up and made eye contact. "Can I help you?" he asked, rising to his feet and approaching the counter.

"Yes," Ray answered, showing his picture ID. "I'm here to see Annette Ogden."

"This patient is heavily sedated. She's mostly sleeping," said the man, whose tag identified him as a nurse named Tony. "And currently, there are two visitors with her—a social worker and a relative."

"I need to talk with those people, too," said Ray.

"Please take the conversation to the visitor lounge area. Let me escort you."

Ray followed the nurse to the room at the end of the hall. He stood at the open door and peered into the dimly lit interior as Tony exchanged a few words with the women sitting near the side of the hospital bed, one of whom, as Ray had suspected, was Maria Tillson. The other was Mirth Skelwith, Annette's cousin from Petosky. Skelwith, a mask covering her face, wore a dark blue blouse, tan slacks, and sandals—Up North professional apparel.

Tony guided them to the lounge, a room with several groupings of chairs and sofas. The three of them settled into chairs arranged around a wide ottoman.

"How's Annette doing?" Ray asked Maria Tillson.

"A bit better. She has breathing problems from the smoke inhalation, and she has so many pre-existing conditions. Yesterday, the hospitalist wasn't sure she would survive; today, he's more optimistic."

"Were you able to talk with her?"

"Today, yes, a bit. Annette doesn't remember how she ended up in the hospital. She's completely disoriented."

Ray focused on Mirth Skelwith. "When we left you and Annette, it was my understanding that you were going to take her home with you. What happened?"

"Annette said she needed to pack a few things. Initially, I followed her in, thinking I could help. Then she became angry and started screaming at me. So I went outside and waited. After about half an hour or so, I reentered the trailer. She was sitting in there drinking wine, I think. I told her we needed to go. She started yelling at me again. The dogs were becoming very aggressive. I was frightened, so I just left. I should have called Maria. I'm sorry I didn't."

"How do you two know one another?" Ray asked.

"We met through a series of professional continuing education classes," said Skelwith.

"It was one of those six-degrees-of-separation moments," continued Tillson. "When Mirth found out where I worked, she asked if I had ever had any contact with a certain family who lived in an old trailer at the edge of a swamp. There was only one family in my caseload that fit that description."

Skelwith picked up the narrative. "There is a family story I heard growing up about cousin Matilda Jane, the daughter of my great-great-grandparents, how she had been institutionalized in a state asylum in Traverse City, how she died there. When I got interested in genealogy, MJ's history was one of my first searches. And it turns out she didn't die in the asylum. Instead, she ended up marrying a man who I think worked there. I found the marriage certificate and followed the line down to the current generations, Annette and Tammy."

"So you met them?" asked Ray.

"Yes, with Maria's help, I tried to reach out to them and attempted to build a relationship. It never worked out. Tammy was open to me. Annette was hostile. I kept trying over the years. Finally, I gave up. But I continued to wonder how they were doing. I've always been interested in the differences between the two branches of our family tree. We share the same gene pool, but the people on my side of the family have had good lives, whereas Annette's family has always lived in poverty. Why? That's what I puzzled about."

Ray had wondered about the same thing many times, seeing some families caught in the cycle of poverty generation after generation.

"What happens with Annette now?" asked Ray.

Tillson answered, "Well, she's now homeless and incapable of caring for herself. I'm in the process of exploring possibilities. And my friend here," she motioned toward Skelwith, "has offered to provide for Tammy's burial and help with finding a placement for Annette. One question for you, Ray. The man killed with Tammy. What do you know about him?"

"We're working on that. No answers yet."

"So you don't have a possible motive for either of these crimes."

"Correct," said Ray. "We don't know at this point in the investigation."

As he walked toward the elevators, Ray found the thought almost unbearable that these women had reached out to Annette over the years, and she had refused their help. And because of her pride or some other reason that Ray could not fathom, she had insisted on imprisoning her own child in abject poverty.

18

Ray added to his earlier notes on the large whiteboard as Sue and Brett Carty entered the room. Barbara Sinclair, the last to join them in the conference room, was uncharacteristically late. She set a large wicker basket laden with fruit on the table. The necks of two bottles of wine were visible above the fruit in the artfully arranged basket bearing the label of the new boutique gourmet food and wine store in the county, Heirloom Foods North. Everyone in the room noticed a degree of agitation in Barbara's usually composed demeanor.

"Apologies," she said. Then, pointing to the basket, she continued. "I stopped at my apartment on the way back to the office. This basket was on the porch."

"Do you have a secret admirer?" asked Brett.

Sue thought she heard a certain something in Brett's question. It was more than collegial banter. She looked from Brett to Barbara.

Barbara passed a card to Sue. After absorbing the contents, she read the message out loud:

> *Hey, Barbara, here are some goodies to help you celebrate summer. I'm glad to see this address stayed in the department. Of course, if someone on the county board reads the employee nepotism policy, Sue may need her old pad back.*
>
> *I'd enjoy spending time with you and would love to show you some fantastic places that aren't on the usual road patrol routes.*
>
> *Your friend, Scott.*

"He knows where I live." She looked at Sue. "So what the hell's going on? And what do I do with this?" She gestured toward the basket.

"Scott Nelson, he's playing head games. Yes, he knew where I lived for several years. The duplex is right along the main drag. He must have noticed the change in vehicles and made some assumptions about the identity of the new resident." Sue locked eyes with Barbara. "Scott can be charming, but he's a liar, manipulator, and narcissist. Some other appropriate nouns describe him, but I'll hold back on the expletives."

"Yes, to liar, manipulator, and narcissist. I'm not sure about the charming part. I met this guy my first week on the job. I thought he was a creep then. That hasn't changed. What about the nepotism thing?"

Ray grabbed her question. "Scott is wrong. If you were my daughter, and I hired you, that would be nepotism. Or if a county official became involved with one of their employees and gave them preferential treatment or promoted them, that would be nepotism. There's nothing in our relationship," he gestured toward Sue, "that violates the nepotism policy. He's just blowing hot air."

"What's he trying to do?" said Barbara.

"As far as we know, he's still under investigation by the feds. So maybe he'd like someone inside our department who could provide a heads-up on anything that might involve him," said Sue. "And like I told you early on, Scott Nelson goes out of his way to chat up any pretty woman he encounters. He thinks he's an Adonis."

"What do you hear from your friend at the Bureau about that investigation?" asked Ray.

"Matt has been unusually quiet. Last time I probed him about Scott and Yuan Zheng Hong, aka Mike, his Chinese immigrant friend, all I got was that things are moving slowly, and the State Department hasn't been getting much assistance from the Chinese government," said Sue. "I keep wondering if Scott got away with murder."

"So what do I do with that?" Barbara pointed at the basket of goodies. "I don't want any part of his gift. How do I make sure he gets that message?"

"I will have a patrol officer who covers the Heirloom Foods North sector return this," said Sue. "And I'll ask them to insist on getting Nelson's signature on the department *Returned Property* form. I'll make this happen as soon as we're done here."

Ray considered the basket. Then he said, "I'll run it out to Scott at Heirloom Foods North. I want Scott to know we're still around."

"Maybe you'll get to meet Victoria Wainwright. Don't call her Vicky!" said Sue.

Ray gave her a long look. Then finally, he said, "What do you mean?"

"Remind me to tell you later," she answered. "Privileged information from my yoga group."

"Okay. Back on task," Ray said. "First, regarding the fire at the Ogdens' trailer." He told Brett and Barbara about Dakota Dirks' confession of shooting up the trailer and his relationship with Tammy. "He's our perpetrator in that shooting, but neither Sue nor I think he's a suspect in the murders."

Sue nodded.

"I saw Annette Ogden at the hospital. She's in no condition to answer any questions about who she thinks might harm her daughter. That said, I doubt if she'll know anything helpful. The social worker who has had past contact with Annette and Tammy, Maria Tillson, says that Annette is more or less nonfunctional.

"That's all I've got for now. Sue, would you share what you learned when you liaised with the Bureau guy about our John Doe?"

She keyed a few more strokes on her laptop, then said, "Here are the essential points from the material he just emailed me: First, the FBI and DEA had no matches in their file to the autopsy photos of our John Doe. They will reach out to their colleagues in Europe. In response to the tattoo on John Doe's arm, the double-headed eagle is a *Shqiptar*. This common prison tattoo identifies the person as being of Albanian descent.

"My contact speculated that Doe could have entered Canada

illegally on a ship and then entered the US, also illegally, through Windsor. His passport would have probably been Greek, fake, and with a fictitious name." She looked around the room. "Any questions so far?" she asked.

"Okay, some historical background: After the breakup of the Soviet Union, an organized crime gang dubbed the Albanian Mafia, but including an array of criminals of other nationalities, started moving into Western Europe. They are now the primary source of cocaine in Europe, especially in the UK, Spain, and Italy. They are also involved in prostitution, human trafficking, and money laundering. The gang has been in Canada's major cities for over a decade. And now they may be trying to get a piece of the American market.

"In the US, their primary objective seems to be the cocaine market. Of course, that would upset the established players and, as you know, these people don't play nice."

"Where does our John Doe fit in?" Brett Carty asked. "If he is part of this gang, what was he doing here?"

"That's what I've been wondering," Sue said. "Was Tammy Ogden just collateral damage? Was Doe trying to take over an existing dealer's patch? Was he the victim of a turf war? There are lots of possibilities."

"Didn't Dyskin say that Tammy and John Doe both had cocaine in their systems?" Barbara asked.

"Yes," answered Sue. "So, did he bring it up here with him, or did they buy it from a local source? Cocaine is not necessarily uncommon in these parts, but meth, heroin, fentanyl, and Grandma's oxycontin are more popular because they're cheaper. Coke is a bit upmarket for much of the local customer base. That said, I've heard it's the drug of choice among our affluent users, both residents and tourists." Sue closed her laptop. "That's all I've got for now. Any other questions?"

Barbara and Brett shook their heads.

Barbara said, "Someone mentioned earlier that John Doe had to be staying somewhere around here: a motel, an Airbnb, a tent, his car."

"Brett, I'd like you and Barbara to take a few hours tomorrow morning and find out if Doe was a registered guest anywhere in the area," said Ray. "Start with the motels near the crime scene—there are only a few of them, and they're small-time operations. See if anyone remembers anything."

The sun dropped toward the horizon as Ray and Sue followed the path on the dunes above the beach. Simone was in the lead, her enthusiasm restrained by the leash wrapped around Sue's wrist and hand. Ray followed—a large pack on his back, a hiking stick in his right hand. Finally, the threesome settled on a gentle slope at the leading edge of the dune on a blowout created by the wind.

Ray pulled a beach blanket from the pack and tossed it to Sue. As she unfurled it in the strong breeze coming off the lake, he moved to the opposite side. Together, they quickly anchored the blanket to the sand with hiking boots and the pack. Then they peeled down to swimsuits, headed to the shore, and waded into the water, stepping gingerly across the band of stones near the beach.

Hip-deep in the rolling surf, Sue turned and splashed water in Ray's direction. He stumbled as he tried to retreat from the cold spray, falling backward and sinking under the surface. When he regained his footing, Sue was swimming in an athletic crawl toward the sun. She stopped on the second sandbar and waited for Ray to join her. Simone stayed on the beach, avoiding the surf, her excited barking lost in the wind.

"What was that all about?" Ray asked.

"You looked like you were going to stop at your knees. I wanted you to follow me out."

"Why?"

"Because I like you," she answered in a peal of laughter. She stood on her toes, arms spread, then briefly dropped below the surface, re-emerging and shaking the water from her hair.

"It's gone, I think," she said.

"What?"

"The smell of smoke finally washed away in this lovely soft

water. I've put that part of the dreadful scene behind me. Now I can eat, then sleep. Maybe I'll even get lucky," she giggled. "Race you to the beach."

Ray watched her swim toward shore for a few moments, then followed, switching from a crawl to a backstroke, staring at the sky. The crest of a wave occasionally washed across his face. When he reached the shore, Sue was toweling off as Simone circled her, barking. Sue pulled on a hoodie and settled onto the blanket.

Ray, wrapping himself in a large towel, moved to her side. "Vicky? Victoria? The woman at Heirloom Foods North, what were you going tell me? Your yoga gossip."

"Well, first, she's the woman who bought up everything this past winter—the tech millionaire or billionaire who moved to her family's summer home sometime during the pandemic. She's been dominating our post-yoga gossip for months. I'm sure I told you about it."

"I don't remember." Ray was usually in bed when Sue returned from yoga.

"You probably had your nose in a book and weren't quite listening."

"Run it by me again."

"Okay, Trudy has been doing Victoria Wainwright's hair for months. Trudy's first tidbit of advice on how to get on with this woman is never to call her Vicky. She'll bite your head off."

"Okay," said Ray, gazing out at the big lake. "That's it?"

"Tip of the 'berg. While home prices, especially waterfront property, have skyrocketed during the pandemic, many small businesses have crashed. So Victoria, who appears to have endless funds, has bought a select group of businesses in the northern corner of the county. She started by buying Heirloom Foods North and its extensive orchards. Next, she acquired assets and equipment from a chocolatier and a cheesemaker. Next, she moved those businesses to her farm and hired the original owners to work for her. Then, she bought the long-defunct Piping Plover Winery. Finally, she's having a spectacular post-and-beam pavilion built to house all these businesses. And, as you know, Scott Nelson—who managed to game the system and stay out of prison, at least so far—is her marketing guy."

Ray chuckled and tossed a small pebble in her direction. "There's something in the tone of your voice. What are you trying to tell me?"

"Well, it's been rumored—after a few glasses of wine—that 'boy toy' is listed as one of his duties in the Executive Business Strategist description."

"So there's a pattern here?" said Ray.

"Yeah, you got it. Old enough to be Scott's mother, Alice Ingersoll bent over backward to protect him when things went south. And his new employer, Victoria Wainwright, a handsome woman in her late fifties, is allegedly similarly taken with Scott. But, of course, there may be little or no truth there."

Ray thought of the gift basket meant for Barbara sitting on his office desk. Perversely, he looked forward to returning it to Scott the next day and getting a sense of what the man was up to now.

19

~~~
</center>

Barbara Sinclair was driving north and thinking about breakfast—a steaming cappuccino and a buttery chocolate-filled croissant—when the call came: "Sector officer or any available unit. Shooting accident. One victim. Immediate medical attention is required. EMS dispatched."

After making a U-turn, she responded to dispatch and headed toward the scene, the siren blaring and the light bar flashing. She glanced at her computer screen for the map showing the route to the incident. The roads narrowed as Barbara drove away from Lake Michigan into the county's interior, rolling terrain covered with orchards and vineyards.

On the final turn, her body pulsating with adrenaline, she left the paved surface of the state highway for a narrow lane of fresh gravel. As she accelerated, the tires of the rear drive vehicle broke free, throwing the patrol car into a violent fishtail. She fought to bring the vehicle under control, sliding first into a shallow ditch, then rebounding off a bank back onto the road, finally stopping at an angle in the middle of the road. Her body shaking, Barbara sat for a moment. A horn blast from approaching traffic stirred her back into action. Pulling into the right-hand lane, Barbara carefully accelerated toward her final destination, marked by an address on a mailbox at the end of a sandy two-track that led back to an old farmhouse at the edge of a wooded hillside.

Bolting from her car, she focused on an agitated young teen—skinny, barefoot, in cutoff jeans and a T-shirt—yelling and motioning for her to follow him. Barbara was quickly on his heels as
~~~

he sprinted up a trail into the woods. Finally, he stopped, standing over a sobbing woman clutching a small boy in her arms.

Kneeling at the woman's side, Barbara palpated the boy's neck, eventually finding a shallow pulse. Then she saw the wound, blood oozing into the front of the boy's light-colored T-shirt.

"My poor baby," sobbed the mother. "It was an accident, an accident."

Looking into the mother's eyes, Barbara said, "Let me take him. There's an ambulance coming."

Barbara gently lifted the young boy into her arms, securing him close to her, and started down the trail, moving quickly while carefully watching her footing to prevent a fall. Two EMTs ran to meet her as she emerged from the woods outside the house. They guided her to their waiting unit, the rear door standing open, the cot on the ground ready for the victim. Lifting the limp body from her embrace, they positioned the child on the gurney and lifted it into the brightly lit interior of the truck.

Barbara stood back and watched the flurry of activity—the EMTs assessing the child's condition, a second firetruck and two more patrol cars arriving, and the child's mother being assisted into the ambulance just before the doors were closed. Seconds later, the vehicle disappeared down the drive onto the gravel road. The howl of the siren slowly faded. She stood, dazed, listening to the wind moving through the trees.

Barbara jumped slightly as a hand touched her shoulder from the back. It was Brett Carty. "Sorry," she said. "I didn't know you were there."

"Just arrived. Are you okay?"

"Did I do the right thing?" she asked, reaching out to him, grateful when he wrapped his arms around her. "The wounded kid was way up in the woods. I didn't wait for the EMTs. I carried him down."

"You got him to care faster. Seconds often count," answered Brett, holding her gently.

"I got a pulse; then I could see he was breathing. I didn't want him to die in my arms," she said as she brushed away some tears. She looked down as she pulled back, noticing her shirt was covered with the child's blood.

"I got some blood on you," she said. "Sorry."

"No problem. I want you to take the rest of the day off. I can arrange a meeting with a crisis counselor."

Barbara rolled into her next question as if she hadn't heard Brett. "What happens now?"

"We hope for the best." His gaze moved over her face. "You were the first one at the scene, right?"

"Yes."

"Tell me what happened."

Barbara described the teen waiting for her, following him up into the woods, and eventually finding the mother cradling the wounded child.

"Did you see a weapon?"

Barbara was slow to answer. She looked up toward the sky, then back at Brett. "It was on the ground. Probably a twenty-two."

"Is it still there?"

"I think so. They followed me down. I just wanted to get the kid help."

"Would you show me where it is? I'll take an evidence bag."

Brett followed Barbara up the path into the thick woods. The trunks of ash trees, victims of a deadly exotic beetle, littered the forest floor between the standing timber of oak and maple. Barbara stopped several times at forks in the narrow sand trail, starting up one leg, retracing her steps, and taking the other. Finally, she stood in a small clearing and pointed.

Brett retrieved the small bolt-action rifle with a gloved hand and slid it into an evidence bag.

"Did the mother tell you anything?"

"I was moving fast, Brett. As soon as I had a pulse, I wanted to get him to the EMTs. If she said anything, it didn't register."

"Understood."

"Do you know something I don't?" Barbara asked.

"Dispatch kept her on the line till you arrived."

"And?"

Brett shrugged. "A kid with a gun, most likely a tragic accident. The older brother was taken to the hospital in a squad car. Someone, probably Sue, will be waiting at the hospital and will stay with him. Then, the process will be tied to what happens with the victim. But at some point, the brother will be questioned with a parent present. Then, there's an elaborate process to get to the truth while protecting the juvenile's rights. How old do you think the shooter was?"

"Hard to say. Best guess, twelve? Fourteen? Accident or not, these kids are forever changed."

"Yes," he answered. "Let's get you out of here. Okay to drive?"

Barbara nodded.

"I'll follow you home just to make sure," said Brett. "If you change your mind, pull over, and I'll drive you. We'll take care of your car."

"I'd like a bath and fresh clothes," she responded.

As they returned to their vehicles, Brett noticed her cruiser's scraped-up right front fender. A conversation about the damage could wait a day or two.

20

〜

It was mid-afternoon when Barbara Sinclair encountered Sue Lawrence as she entered the Cedar County Sheriff's Department building from the parking area.

"How are you doing?" asked Sue.

"Okay, sort of. I think. I am going to talk to the crisis counselor late this afternoon. Can't hurt."

"I'm glad you're doing that," said Sue. "It helped me get through a tough time a year ago. I was on the edge of PTSD." She looked at Barbara with curiosity. "When I suggested you see our psychologist the day after you found the two murder victims, you turned me down. So what's the difference?"

Barbara looked down. She shifted her weight from foot to foot. Finally, she said, "Two things come to mind. First, the bodies. That night, standing on the back side of the dune—" Her words came slowly. "I had never been close to death before. The violence. The finality. My senses, sight and smell were overpowered. Their skin was so cool when I felt for a pulse. Their lives were over. All I could do was protect the scene. So when you suggested I should see a counselor, I thought, how would that change anything? I wasn't there yet. You know what I'm saying?"

Sue nodded.

"But this little boy had a pulse. He was breathing. There was a chance he could be saved. I heard the sirens. I could get him down the hill to the EMTs. As soon as they lifted him from my arms, I noticed this blood on my shirt… it was so real. His life had been in my hands."

"I understand," said Sue. "You made a difference. They got him to the hospital in time."

"How is he?" asked Barbara.

"His name is Noah, and he's not out of the woods yet. He was in surgery for hours. He might be transferred to Grand Rapids or Ann Arbor for more diagnostic work and possibly another surgery."

"Did you get the full story?"

"I think so. After Noah was out of the OR and things were starting to look hopeful, I interviewed Lucas, the older brother, with his father present. And later, I talked with the mother, Amanda. Their stories were all consistent. The shooting appears to have been an accident. It should not have happened. The parents did almost everything right. But they were outfoxed by a teenager's fascination with guns.

"His mother said Lucas is often off to the woods at first light. While making breakfast, she sent Noah to find his brother and bring him home. As it turns out, Lucas and Noah had been building a fort up on that hill. Noah decided to sneak up on his brother and frighten him.

"The boys had heard rumors that a cougar had been sighted in the area—we get those yearly. According to Amanda, the boys had been obsessed with the idea of a cougar running wild and had been playing at being big game hunters. Noah snuck up on his brother but then made some noise in the brush, and that caused Lucas to panic. He shot toward the noise, which he thought was the cougar stalking him. He quickly realized he'd hit his brother and had the good sense to get his mother immediately. You were quickly on the scene."

"So the gun, where did that come from?" Barbara asked.

"It belongs to the boys' father, Randy. He told me that while the boys were still toddlers, he decided to get rid of the rifle. But he didn't. He pulled the bolt out and stashed it in one of the drawers of his workbench in the garage. He hid the rest of the gun up in the basement ceiling, in the floor joists."

"But they found the pieces," Barbara said.

"Yeah, you got it. Lucas said he found the gun first. He and his brother had been using it to play war since early spring. He said he found the bolt a few days ago while looking for a wrench to fix his bike."

"And the cartridge?"

"He had one bullet, just one. He got it from a kid down the road, Bobby Carpenter. I talked to Bobby and his parents late yesterday afternoon. Bobby confirmed that he traded a bullet to Lucas for a Swiss army knife with a broken blade. His parents were very cooperative and appeared to be enormously upset. Bobby's father, Dan, showed me the locked gun safe where the weapons and ammo were stored. When he confronted Bobby about where he got the bullet, the kid said he couldn't remember. And then he said he'd had it in his room for a couple of years. And then he said maybe he found it. So who knows."

"What happens now?" Barbara asked.

"We'll turn everything over to the prosecutor. After that, any further action is at her discretion. That said, both sets of parents acted responsibly, for the most part. But that wasn't enough given teenage boys' inability to comprehend possible consequences."

Barbara nodded. "A whole lot of passion in your words."

"Boys, teens, nice kids, for the most part, get into so much trouble doing stupid things." She sighed. "Shifting gears, did you find where our John Doe might have stayed?"

"Still working on that," said Barbara. "Tomorrow, hopefully."

21

Ray turned off the state highway at a new impressive-looking sign—two fieldstone pillars supporting a heavy wooden beam with carved letters welcoming visitors to Heirloom Foods North. He quickly realized how extensively everything had changed since his last visit to the farm, probably two or more years before. A blacktop ribbon of asphalt had replaced the sand and gravel drive that snaked back to the sales area. The original parking area near the sales structure, a century-old barn, had been extended and paved. And the barn itself had been expanded, tripling or quadrupling the size of the original building.

Ray, carrying the basket Scott Nelson had gifted Barbara Sinclair, stood for a long moment, taking in the many changes made to the structure. New post-and-beam framing connected the original structure with the new addition, creating a large, brightly lit display area. In place of bushel baskets of heritage apples that once covered the crowded dirt floor of the old barn, wide aisles provided easy access to the whole interior. Large signage identified the various sections of the sales floor: vegetables, fruit, wine and spirits, coffee, chocolate, and baked goods.

"May I help you?" asked a woman peering at Ray through gold-framed trifocals. Her pleated gray skirt and tailored blazer with an embossed company logo suggested the upscale nature of the business.

"I'm looking for Scott Nelson."

"I don't believe Mr. Nelson is in today," she responded, looking into his eyes and then over to the basket he was carrying.

"I'm here on official business." Ray fished his ID from an interior pocket of his sports coat.

"Perhaps you'd like to talk with the owner, Ms. Wainwright."

"Yes, that would be perfect."

"Let me see if she's available. I'll be back in a few moments."

Ray was inspecting a display of dried fruit, some local and others from exotic sources when a different woman approached him.

"Hello, I'm Angie Monti, one of the managers here. Ms. Wainwright will see you. Follow me, please."

"What do you manage?" he asked as they moved through the market.

She slowed and turned toward him. With a sweeping gesture from left to right, she said, "This area, local retail. Everything you see here is the brick-and-mortar end of the business. We're also developing an online store." There was a touch of tease in the way she moved and talked.

"Are you new to northern Michigan?" Ray asked.

"No, I grew up on the peninsula but have spent most of my adult life on the East Coast. I was happy to have the opportunity to move back here."

"When did the business open?" he asked, walking at her side.

"Just last week, more than a month past the planned date. Everything's been delayed—shipping, getting craftsmen on-site, and the residue of shortages still blamed on the pandemic."

Ray stopped and gazed at Angie. "I have a sense I know you, but I can't quite place you."

"I was wondering if you would recognize me. I didn't want to embarrass you. And why should you remember me? I'm Tod Voss's sister, the kid sister, the eight- or nine-year-old girl in awe of the incredibly mature high school boys like my brother and you. How's that for an oxymoron? Mature high school boys."

Ray extended a hand. "I remember you," he said, "the wiry little girl with the high-pitched voice who usually hung at the crowd's edge when I was at your house."

"Yeah, 100 percent tomboy, desperately wanting to hang out with you cool guys."

"Tell me about Tod. He hasn't made it to any of the reunions. I've lost track of him. Last I heard, he was in the military."

"That's right. It worked for him. Along the way, he got an education and became a fighter pilot, his big dream growing up."

"Where is he now?"

"Back in Michigan, Detroit area. After retiring, he flew commercial for a few years, then moved on to executive work. Says those little jets are much more fun than 737s."

"Please say hello for me." Ray. "Tod was in a special group of friends. After graduation, we wandered off in different directions." Ray pointed to her name tag. "Monti, your married name?"

Angie exhaled and nodded. "It's some baggage I should have unloaded long ago. I kept my married name for my kids when I divorced. I wanted their mom to have the same last name."

Angie pointed to the basket Ray was carrying. "Returning some defective product?"

Ray considered his answer. "This was dropped off at the home of one of my officers. We have a stringent department policy on accepting gifts."

Angie brightened and started to chuckle. "I assume the recipient was female and probably young and attractive?"

Ray nodded.

Angie flashed a joyful smile. "Our resident Adonis. You might want to walk softly with this problem. He may be Madame Wainwright's boy toy du jour," she added mockingly.

Ray gave her a long look. There was a flash of memory, a spindly girl with an insolent lip.

"It's not that she's overly possessive. But one should expect a certain level of loyalty to the person providing you with an executive benefits package."

Angie's final remarks were delivered almost gleefully as she opened a door marked private and then led Ray down a hallway at the back of the building. He could smell fresh paint and new lumber.

She guided him to a final door, knocked quietly, and conducted him into a brightly lit office space.

Ray was surprised by the stark interior. A long, sleek, elegantly designed executive desk stood at the center of the room. Only a keyboard and monitor shared the large expanse of the rosewood desktop. The room was void of other furniture, save two perfectly spaced mid-century modern chairs facing the front of the desk. No artwork adorned the walls. The plain interior contrasted with the chaos of the natural world visible beyond the titanium-tinted floor-to-ceiling windows lining the back wall.

At the desk, a woman worked at the keyboard. When Ray and Angie entered the room, her eyes initially remained focused on the large computer screen. Finally, she looked in Ray's direction, peering over the top of her glasses. Then she stood.

"Sheriff, please have a seat," she said, her eyes refusing to notice the gift basket in Ray's hand. She had a trim athletic frame, like a gymnast, runner, or dancer. Her salt-and-pepper hair was meticulously cut and styled. Later that evening, when he described the hairdo, Sue suggested that Wainwright's hair sounded like the current version of a pageboy.

"How can I help you?" Wainwright asked.

Ray placed the basket on the left corner of the desk and settled into a chair.

"One of your employees, Scott Nelson, left this basket on the doorstep of one of the department's patrol officers. Our officers are not allowed to accept gifts. I had hoped to return it to Mr. Nelson personally, but since he is not here today, I wonder if you would take possession of this item."

Ray removed the Returned Property form from his jacket, opened it, and set it on the desk in front of her. "And I'd appreciate it if you would sign the bottom indicating you received this package."

Wainwright eyed the basket from afar and then finally stood and moved closer to get a better view of its contents. She wore a gray suit and a white blouse with ruffles at the neck, the one suggestion of femininity in her outfit. Her eyes were pale blue, and light pink lipstick provided a bit of color to her face.

"We've just added basket assortments to our product line. Scott suggested this concept. As you can see, we're just ramping up the operation, and these baskets have been surprisingly successful in the store and online. We call this product *The Taste of the Peninsula*—three sizes at different price points." She rearranged the contents of the basket. "This is the gold standard." She looked at Ray with a hint of a smile. "The officer is female?"

"Yes."

"I don't understand, Sheriff, why giving someone a basket of goodies is inappropriate. Scott appears to be extremely generous with his friends. I think this is his normal MO. It's not as if he's slipping a cop a roll of twenties at a traffic stop."

Ray was annoyed by her tone. "Our policy is unambiguous regarding gifts," he responded.

Wainwright stared into his eyes for a long moment, then she stepped back from the basket and dropped back into her chair. She picked up the form, scanned it, signed and dated the sheet, and pushed it toward him. Her manner was imperious.

"What exactly is Mr. Nelson's position here?" Ray asked, curious as to how Scott had reinvented himself.

"Scott has many skills. The man is adept at operation pieces, like getting the online store up and running. He's helped find and train people and initiate them into our culture. I'm thinking about how we can—in our modest way—imitate the efficiency of Amazon and the quality of Zingerman's."

Wainwright's eyes narrowed a bit as she looked at Ray. "Sheriff, I want our brick-and-mortar operation to be a destination. But I don't wish to be a seasonal business. I want to provide my people with year-round employment—good wages, health insurance, and retirement benefits. And that's what a thriving internet business will provide." As she warmed to her subject, her tone became less officious until it bordered on unctuous.

Then she changed tack once again. Her superior attitude seemed to evaporate. "Sheriff, believe it or not, I'm happy to meet you. Your reputation in this community precedes you. And I hear that besides being an esteemed civil servant, you are known as one of the region's most discriminating gourmets."

Ray wondered how to respond to the sudden change in the direction of the conversation. "I don't know about the gourmet part. I like to cook," he said. "I traveled extensively in Europe as a young adult in the service. I sampled a large range of beautifully prepared food during that time."

She nodded approvingly. "Our long-delayed grand opening is scheduled for next week. The main event will be an invitation-only dinner featuring locally produced food and wine. Four of the region's premier chefs will be preparing the food. It's just your kind of event, Sheriff. I considered comping you two tickets, but now that you've explained your department gift policy…"

To Ray's surprise, she suddenly smiled. Within a few milliseconds, her amused expression faded. She appeared to be momentarily lost in thought.

"I've meant to call you for several weeks," she said. "But I've been hoping the problem would disappear."

"What's the problem?" Ray asked, wondering if she was playing him. The woman's rapidly changing demeanor threatened to give him whiplash.

She pulled a folder from a drawer and pushed it across the desk toward him. "I've been getting these messages and letters almost since we began the new construction, but I didn't take them seriously. Then the vandalism started."

22

~

Ray opened the folder and paged through the documents—letters, handwritten notes, copies of emails, and electronic messages. A separate page at the back of each item contained Victoria Wainwright's careful annotations, including the date, time, and other relevant information. A few of the earliest pieces were formal, with a pseudo-legalistic tone. That veneer disappeared quickly, replaced by notes filled with obscenities and illogical ramblings gathered from the internet's darkest corners.

After reading through the folder, he was at a loss for words. Ray looked up at Wainwright and thought he saw a hint of panic in her carefully controlled demeanor. Finally, he asked, "Why didn't you contact us immediately?"

"I'm a big girl, Sheriff. I've run into hostility before. As an HR executive with a law degree, I hired and fired. I'm used to fighting my own battles."

Yet Ray noticed she was gripping the edge of the desk, less cool than she claimed.

"The messages mention a carpentry crew. What can you tell me about them?" asked Ray.

"We're talking about a dozen men who arrived just after the lockdown ended. They were here from early summer through the winter, much longer than I originally anticipated." She paused for a moment. "Sheriff, the events of the last two years seem lost in a fog. I don't have a sense of chronology like I used to."

"It's been a strange time," Ray agreed. "I think we're all struggling with that."

"So you understand my situation, let me give you some

background. My parents passed several years ago. My brother, Ted, and I inherited the family cottage on Sandpiper Point. Ted likes sailboats and warm climes, so he was delighted to trade his share of the property for cash.

"The house stood unused, even unvisited, for several years. I knew the place needed work, but I put it on the back burner. Then, finally, I had time to fly up here and look the site over. I had set up a meeting with a local builder. We did a walk-through, and the man pointed out the urgent repairs needed and suggested other improvements to bring the place up to date. It didn't take him too long to get me an estimate and timeline. Getting started and completing the work is a different story.

"As you probably know, the little gravel road from the highway out to Sandpiper Cove runs along the side of this farm. So, during the week or ten days I was here, I couldn't help but notice a weathered for sale sign at the front of the property. So, one day, I drove in and looked around. The buildings had fallen into disrepair; the orchards and fields were long neglected.

"Sheriff, I loved this farm as a kid. It was magical, especially when the apples started ripening in the late summer. The farmer and his wife, Ted and Maddy, were always welcoming. They let me feed the chickens and play with the barn cats. And the two made time for me, which most adults didn't. They taught me about old-time heritage fruits and vegetables. Some were ugly, but the flavors were unique compared to the hybrid stuff I'd grown up with from grocery stores.

"So, on a whim, I called about the property. Compared to West Coast prices, it was a bargain. I bought the property, not knowing what I'd do with it. And then my life changed overnight. I had been part of the management team of a tech company from its infancy. A larger competitor bought us out. They were bringing in their leadership team. Suddenly, I was without a job. Fortunately, the terms of the sale provide upper management with a golden parachute."

Ray nodded, saying nothing, knowing the woman was still on a roll. Her enthusiasm and sense of mission struck him.

"I'd spent thirty years in that industry. I was ready to do something else. So I started thinking about my impulse buy—this farm—and what I could do with it. And voila! Heirloom Foods North was born."

She paused briefly, then continued. "I wanted to save the barn and extend it into the primary sales area. But, after bringing in a structural engineer, I learned it was barely salvageable. That's when I decided to focus on creating a master plan for the farm, including rehabilitating the original buildings." She made a sweeping motion with her right hand, a characteristic gesture delivered randomly throughout her narrative.

"Once I had the architect's renderings, I started looking for contractors. I couldn't find anyone local who wanted the job, so I decided to be my own contractor. The first thing I needed was a roughing crew. No luck finding a crew, either. As I'm sure you know, there's a shortage of skilled tradespeople here. Finally, a contractor friend of my brother's in Arizona found a crew for me, a foreman and a group of young men, mostly in their twenties. The whole team was of Mexican descent. Some were born in Mexico, and some were born here—citizens by birth, just like you and me. My brother's friend said he'd carefully vetted the crew. ICE wouldn't be a problem. He FedExed me complete documentation before the team arrived.

"They were great workers and skilled carpenters. They'd been here for six weeks when I got the first obscene letter. It was in an unsealed envelope without an address, mixed in with the rest of my mail one morning. The writer accused me of bringing a group of Mexican drug dealers and rapists into the community. Not long after receiving that letter, ICE staged an early morning raid. First, they got my crew out of bed. When I got on the scene, the agents in their black bulletproof vests had all my workers surrounded outside. There were black vans parked nearby, ready to haul the men away.

"Confronting the lead agent, I waved my thick file of documents providing the legal status of each of the workers in front of him and demanded to see a search warrant. When he couldn't produce one, I ordered them off my property. Finally, after much huffing and puffing, the agent signaled a retreat." Giving Ray a sidelong glance, she asked, "Did you know about this?"

"Immigration and Customs Enforcement seldom inform local law enforcement agencies when working in a jurisdiction." Ray asked, "Was that your only contact with ICE?"

"Yes, but that's not the end of my troubles," Wainwright said, rising to her feet. Let me show you some recent vandalism. And I was going to call you about this."

23

That evening, fighting exhaustion, Ray made it through dinner: cheese omelets, his go-to entree at such times—two ingredients, two minutes of cooking time, and one pan to clean up. Fortunately, it was one of Sue's favorite meals. Simone, the terrier, appreciated the few bits of egg topping her usual meal.

Over dessert, he told Sue about his encounter with Victoria Wainwright, the vandalism to her orchard, and the cutting down of heritage apple trees.

Then Ray collapsed on the couch, book in hand. Soon, the book was resting on his nose, and sometime later, Sue herded him toward the bedroom. But his dreams, nightmarish in nature, did little to knit up the raveled sleeve of care. Jagged flashes from the recent violence kept his psyche from sliding into deep repose.

Near morning, distant, dull flickers of light started at the verges of the bedroom, seeping around the drapes and through the skylight. As the storm moved across the big lake from the southwest, the flashes of lightning intensified, and the rumble of thunder grew louder and more sustained.

Simone moved from her usual station on the pillows near the headboard. Her initial utterances were low, rumbling growls. But as the storm moved closer, her agitation grew. Growls became sharp barks. "What's happening?" Ray asked sleepily.

"Something's bothering her," said Sue. "Maybe the storm. Maybe a skunk or porcupine is wandering around the yard. She senses things we don't."

"You want to take care of it?" he asked.

"Could be dangerous. Better you. You're the sheriff," she said before rolling to her side of the bed and pulling a pillow over her head.

Whatever prescient awareness of marauding wildlife Simone had displayed sitting on the edge of the bed had vanished by the time they were out in the cool night air. Simone pulled Ray across the driveway. Slowing, she focused on the delicate light-green moths she flushed from the myrtle as they walked around the edge of the property in the gentle glow from the porch light. She snapped at the tiny Lepidopterans, pursuing a few with her nose or paw, watching others with total fascination. Ray stood by wearily.

Eventually, tired of that pursuit and her bodily functions attended to, Simone pulled him back toward the house as large drops of rain began to splat on the paving around them.

"Prowlers?" asked Sue sleepily as Ray and Simone settled back into bed.

"We put them to flight," he responded. "All's quiet?"

"Dispatch called twice," said Sue. "Missing boater. Brett's handling it. He's already talked with the wife and started organizing the search."

Ray listened to the rain beating on the roof. The house reverberated with each roll of thunder. His day was beginning before first light.

The first glimmers of dawn—none of that rosy-fingered stuff, just a lighter gray line on almost black—were visible to his right as he sped along the main highway on the eastern coast of Cedar County. Turning left, he raced across the narrow waist of the peninsula, finally seeing the glow of the marina lights against the still-dark western horizon. He asked the dispatcher for a marine weather update as he rolled through the village to the shore.

"Gale-force winds from the SSW diminishing by daybreak. Near-shore wave height dropping to 3 feet to 5 feet by 9:00 a.m. Small craft advisories ending at 11 a.m."

As he walked toward the docks, he saw that every slip in the marina was filled, the norm for the summer months. Boats seeking refuge from the storm filled every available space along the docks and seawalls, secured to any available mooring post.

Ray found Brett Carty working through the prelaunch checklist on the department's rigid-hull inflatable patrol boat.

"What do we know?" asked Ray, moving close to be understood.

"Not much. Male, solo, small sailboat."

Ray gave him a questioning look, signaling that he wanted more than Brett's usual laconic answer.

"Wife was on the last evening flight into TC with the couple's two small children," Carty continued. "You know, the one from Detroit that arrives around eleven. The husband didn't show up as expected or answer his cell. She caught a ride with a friend who was on the same flight. In their last conversation earlier in the day, the husband said he was going for a quick sail but would be at the airport to pick her up.

"Once home, the wife checked the beach. The boat was gone. Then she looked at the security system video. Her husband left at 2:00 p.m. but didn't return. By then, she's in a panic and calls 9-1-1."

"Did she have any idea of a possible destination?" asked Ray.

"Yeah, Platte Point, Empire, Leland, South or North Manitou." Brett smiled without humor. "Only a few hundred square miles of water and coastline."

"Assets?"

"Coast Guard will start an aerial search pattern after daybreak. The NPS will do a nearshore search with two patrol boats and rangers onshore. Township fire departments have been alerted to help with shore searches."

"What's the plan?"

Brett pointed to a location map on the screen mounted on the dash between them. "Here's the initial Coast Guard flight plan. They will start twenty miles south of the initial launch site and do a slow pass up the shoreline for twenty or more miles. Wind direction, speed, launch time, and boat type have been factored in. The logic is that, given the high winds and seas, the sailboat will probably be found on or near the shore. Same for the missing mariner. A rescue swimmer will be deployed if they see someone in the water. If the boat or wreckage is found, we'll get the coordinates, and they will stand by till we're on the scene. If nothing is found, they will start their preprogrammed search patterns."

"Names?"

"Family name, Atwood. Claire and Bob. Know them?

Ray shook his head. "Anyone with the wife?"

"Yeah, Becca Johns, the community relations summer intern. Some family, too. Mid-lake water temperature is sixty-three, warmer near shore but not much with this storm bringing in the colder water."

Ray nodded.

"Now, do you want the bad news?" Brett asked. Without waiting for an answer, he passed his phone to Ray, who looked at the image from a marine weather app.

"It looks like a big blow," said Ray as he handed the phone back.

Brett dropped the phone into his chest pocket and pulled the zipper to close it. Then, he brought the two big outboards roaring to life as he completed the last few items on the checklist.

24

Brett nodded toward the moorings, and Ray climbed on the dock, freeing the bow line and then the stern line before jumping back on the boat. He settled in the chair at Brett's left, attaching and tightening the harness system until he felt his PFD tight against the seat back. Brett passed him a headset.

Brett reversed out of the slip and slowly turned the boat toward the path to open water. The rain had stopped, but spray from waves topping the seawall splashed against the windscreen.

Ray peered at the largest screen on the dash and noted that the wind speed was dropping, as predicted. But he knew the energy absorbed from the gale-force winds by the big lake over many hours and the long fetch starting somewhere south of Chicago would dissipate slowly. He held on as Brett maneuvered the boat into open water, steering diagonally into rolling surf and then turning northeast, toward the missing boater's launch point. Ray watched as Brett punched the throttles forward. The boat ricocheted wildly off the first waves as it began to accelerate, then settled into a rhythmic bounce as the specially designed hull cut through the steep waves, its outer ring of inflated collars providing a stable platform and shock mitigation.

As he scanned the array of screens and the LCD dashboard, Ray thought, *"A giant video game on steroids."* He noted his much younger colleague's relative comfort in absorbing and reacting to digital information. On the largest screen, the images from the onboard radar were superimposed on a marine map, the Lake Michigan shoreline glowing at the bottom and an outline of the Manitou Islands at the top.

Ray looked left toward the Manitous as they motored north following the shoreline a quarter of a mile from the beach. The island's upper topography was clearly outlined against the sky. The steep waves obscured the lower half, giving the illusion that they were floating above the water.

This piece of water stretching from Platte Point to Pyramid Point, thirty or so miles, a tiny fraction of the lake's shoreline, felt like part of Ray's DNA. Stories from his mother and old photographs preceded his earliest memories of this place, bathing as a toddler au natural in warm pools at the edge of the big water. Later, his boyhood memories, exploring the miles of beach on foot at the edge of the dunes or peering down the steep sandy slopes at the big waves, later poling or oaring anything that would float on one of the shallow, small inland lakes. And finally, memories from his teens and adult years, exploring the edges of the big lake in a canoe, later a kayak, moving over the decades from canvas-covered wood frames to fiberglass, then carbon fiber.

The common denominator was the direct connection between the water and the paddler—body, blade, boat, a relationship unchanged over millennia.

Skimming across the lake, information flowing into the cockpit via screens and headsets, voices in his ears from the various responding agencies, and a computer guiding and stabilizing the boat, Ray felt disconnected from his preferred place in a kayak, where he experienced the storm firsthand, battling each wave from crest to trough, fighting to keep from capsizing.

A female voice in his headset brought his attention back to the present moment: a sighting from a helicopter, a blip on a screen. Brett changed direction and accelerated. Ray had become a mere observer.

Then he saw the target—jagged pieces of a white and red plywood hull, tangled ropes, ripped nylon sails, and a snapped wooden mast that would appear momentarily and then disappear in the surf zone near the beach.

Brett sped toward the shore, cutting the power and raising

the two large outboards at the last moment, the bow coming to a grinding halt against the shore.

Ray tossed his headset aside and followed Brett into the surf. They waded toward the wreckage, first searching for a body, then dragging the shapeless debris—jagged pieces of thin marine plywood tangled with rigging and nylon sailcloth—up onto the shore, attempting to separate the entangled parts and find the Michigan watercraft registration numbers.

Ray followed the conversation as Brett read the numbers to the waiting dispatcher. He nodded in Ray's direction. "It's the boat."

Brett looked skyward at the hovering chopper, his hands cupping his headphones close as he struggled to hear over the screaming jet engine and the percussive pounding from the rotating blades. Finally, he nodded his comprehension to an unseen speaker and started moving south along the beach, motioning to Ray to follow as he broke into a sprint.

The chopper led the way, hovering over an area of rolling sandy terrain just beyond the high-water edge of the beach. A swimmer had already been deployed and hunched over an unmoving body on the beach. The torso was partially covered with a large piece of weathered plastic sheeting, flotsam the man must have wrapped himself in for warmth. At one end of the sheeting, a head. At the other end, two legs from the knees down, a worn deck shoe on one foot, the other bare.

Ray watched as the rescue swimmer carefully palpated the man's neck, searching for a pulse. Finally, the woman looked across at Ray and nodded, her lips forming "yes."

Peeling back the plastic, they helped her wrap the injured man in a thermal blanket and carefully position him in the rescue basket. They watched as the victim and the swimmer winched up to the chopper. Then, the rescue craft slowly rotated and moved away, the noise from the jet engines fading. Finally, just the blinking lights remained. The sound of wind and waves had replaced the roar of the helicopter. They lingered for a bit, thankful for what they had achieved.

They slowly walked back toward the scattered remains of the sailboat.

"Didn't know we went so far," Brett said.

"Adrenaline," said Ray, "We're on the downside now."

"Surprised the guy was still breathing," Brett said, almost as an aside, his attention now directed at his phone.

"Yes," agreed Ray, trudging through the sand at his young colleague's side. More than ever before, Ray felt the generational divide between them.

25

~

Early the following day, Ray stood looking over the remains of the sailboat spread out on the concrete drive behind the county garage.

"This boat was cut in half," Ray said to Sue. "Look at it. Propeller slashes everywhere: top, bottom, fore, aft. It looks like it went through a blender. Could that happen in one accidental pass? It makes no sense. Didn't the power boat see him? Were they on autopilot? Was he invisible in the tall waves? Any reports of a boating accident?"

"The first thing I asked," Sue said. "Dispatch checked and said no reports of boating accidents to the Coast Guard or any regional police agencies in the last twenty-four hours." Sue circled the pieces of the boat, making a photographic record of the damage to the thin plywood hull.

"Anything we can learn from this to help us figure out who did it?"

Sue snapped a few more photos, then said, "Reconstructing marine accidents is not on my CV. However, I'll contact the feds and see if they have any suggestions."

"Okay, let's do a press release about this incident. Give the approximate location and ask the community for information on this accident." Ray looked over the torn pieces of thin plywood. "I don't know if any materials here are substantial enough to damage a prop, but we should contact prop repairers and boat shops. That said… given that this kind of damage is common…" His voice trailed off. "The victim?"

"Yes, Robert Atwood was hypothermic and in shock

when admitted. The ER doc said the guy was lucky to be alive. Unfortunately, Atwood also has a hip fracture. There's bruising and damage to the femur," said Sue.

"Yeah, having a large boat crash into… I'm surprised he wasn't pulled into the prop wash. So what do we know about Atwood?"

"Barbara Sinclair is working on it. On the first pass, she said his background check looked unremarkable. He's thirty-four years of age, married with two children, and a high school teacher in suburban Cincinnati. He coaches swimming, too."

"Did the doctor know when we can talk to him?" Ray asked.

"Not today. He's heavily sedated and on lots of pain meds. They'd like to schedule hip replacement surgery when he's medically stable. Hopefully tomorrow."

"The people on the powerboat, why didn't they come to his aid?" Ray thought about it and then provided some possible answers to his question. "Something to hide? Operating under the influence? Did you talk with his wife?"

"Briefly this morning, just as she was heading to the hospital."

"I imagine she's still there," said Ray. "Let's start with her."

"Okay. I've got her cell. I'll check that she's still there and see where we can find her. I'll quickly get a press release out before we leave."

As Sue drove toward the hospital, Ray asked, "What else is happening?"

"The usual for a normal July. Or I should say the pre-COVID normal, lots of people and not enough patrol officers to cover all the calls immediately. That said, nothing major. A couple of medical emergencies, a DUI, and one domestic."

"How about Victoria Wainwright, the damage to her orchard? Did you have time to see her?"

"Briefly. She showed me what you saw yesterday. The damaged trees were located at the back of the property, with no easy access to a nearby road. So, the vandal had to hike there or use the tractor paths behind the barn.

"And since we know most vandals aren't into heavy lifting…"

"You think they rode a motorbike or ATV/UTV?" Ray said. "That would give them access without going near the main buildings."

"Right, Elkins. And they probably used a battery-powered chain saw. You can hear the gas version's scream a mile away. The electric ones are almost silent."

"Anything else?"

"Just some speculation on my part."

"Let's hear it," said Ray.

"The trunks on the first few trees were cut through. After that, the rest were just girdled. Cutting them down is dramatic, but girdling is more efficient when you have limited battery power."

"Did you have time to look at Wainwright's collection of threatening letters and messages?"

"Briefly. I was also trying to keep tabs on you and Carty so I would be available if you needed anything."

"What did you think?"

"Oh, Ray, it was a litany of angry phrases from the far edge of the blogosphere: open borders, rapists and drug dealers, radical left-wing Marxists, socialists, etc. And assorted obscenities. It's all tedious reading. How seriously do we take this?"

Ray had been wondering the same thing. "In the current political climate, we must pay attention to this. And using the USPS to send threatening mail is a federal offense."

"I'll contact the Bureau," said Sue.

"Okay," said Ray. "Alert the patrol officers in the north sector of this situation. Ask them to be extra vigilant. We don't want anything else happening on our patch."

At the medical center, they followed the signage to the ICU Family Lounge, a rectangular space on the second floor decorated in earth tones, wall units of faux paneling, indirect lighting from above, and epoxy-covered floors. The chairs and couches—covered with scrubbable materials—lined the walls. The magazine racks now hung empty in the post-COVID smartphone world.

Two women—one thirtyish, the other appearing to be in her sixties—were huddled together, talking quietly in the far corner of the room. "Mrs. Atwood?" Sue asked, approaching the younger woman, who nodded and came to her feet. Sue handled the introductions. The second woman was a family friend whose cottage was next to the Atwoods'.

Ray, notepad in hand, said, "It appears that your husband's boat was struck by another vessel."

Claire nodded, "Yes. One of the doctors said his injuries…" Her voice faded as she struggled with the vision of the incident.

Ray waited as she dabbed at her eyes with a tissue. When she looked up at him again, he said, "Mrs. Atwood—"

"Claire, please," she directed.

"Claire, we don't know what happened. We won't know until we can talk to your husband. Has he told you anything?"

"He's mostly sleeping when I'm with him," she answered.

"We have recovered his boat. It was severely damaged, apparently by a powerboat. We don't know if your husband was still on board or in the water when this happened. Perhaps the sailboat was turtled when the collision occurred. We need more information."

"Yes, the motorboat, wouldn't they…?"

"No one has come forward to report this incident as yet. So all we know is that your husband was injured, and his boat was destroyed."

"Tell us about the sailboat," asked Sue.

"He built it in our garage," Claire explained. "You know, from a kit, stitch and glue. Our cars spent most of the winter outside. Before building his boat, he used a Sunfish for years—my dad's boat from the seventies. Bob loved it. He's athletic, a collegiate swimmer, but no sailor. We call him Captain Turtle. He's always capsizing. The girls and I gave him a hoodie for Christmas with that written across the front." She smiled for a brief moment.

"I was happy about the new boat—a place to sit without always being wet. Bob said it would be more stable, and I wanted to believe him."

"So this was the first season for this boat?" asked Ray.

"Yes. We brought it up here to the cottage in June. He first trailered it to some small inland lakes to get comfortable before using it on the big lake. On Michigan, he mostly sailed near shore for a few weeks. If he capsized, I wanted him close enough that I could rescue him with our Jet Ski."

"And did he flip?" asked Sue.

"Yes, but he managed to right it every time." She exhaled an audible sigh, her eyes anxious. "I was worried about being gone this weekend. I wouldn't be around to be a naysayer. He's got this thing about the Manitous. No summer is complete until he'd solo sail out there. He always did that once or twice a summer with the Sunfish."

"Hours before you reported your husband missing, a PFD with *Capt. T.* stenciled on the front was picked up by an NPS boat close to South Manitou. So now we can connect the dots," said Ray.

"Oh, God. He's such a risk-taker. He always carried that PFD, but I don't think he always wore it. He must have lost it in a capsize."

Ray could see the wheels spinning.

"So he made it out to the islands," she said. "He was having trouble tacking in high winds with the new boat. Where did he finally end up?"

Ray looked over at Sue.

"About ten miles north of your cottage," Sue answered. "By afternoon yesterday, we had strong winds from the south-southwest. As a result, small craft advisories were posted."

"So you think he was probably having trouble tacking back to our cottage."

"Just speculation on our part. We need to talk with your husband," said Sue.

As they stood, preparing to take their leave, Claire said, "This getting hit by another boat...?"

"We just don't know what happened," said Ray. "If we learn anything more, we'll contact you."

26

~

Ray and Sue stood at the counter of the ICU nursing station behind which all eyes were focused on screens, fingers moving across keyboards. He cleared his throat impatiently. Then, finally, a woman looked in his direction.

After he flashed his identification, she stood and came around the counter to speak to him. She was masked and dressed in purple scrubs and a cap. She identified herself as Dr. Stephens. Ray focused on her gray eyes above her mask.

"I was wondering when I might be able to have a conversation with Bob Atwood."

Stephens's answer was slow in coming. "The patient is being prepared for surgery… but I'll permit it if you're brief, just a few questions. And one person only. If I signal you that it's over, it's over. And you'll have to mask up." She reached back over the counter and handed him a mask.

"I'll be there," said Sue, pointing to the ICU Family Lounge.

"The patient is determined to tell his story. When he's awake, he's been obsessing about what happened. Remember, just a few questions." She gestured toward the open ICU patient room door and followed him in. Bob Atwood lay with his eyes closed.

"Sheriff Elkins is here, Mr. Atwood," Dr. Stephens said, placing her arm gently on his shoulder. Bob Atwood's eyelids fluttered and opened with seeming difficulty. "Please tell him what you think he needs to know. I've told him he can only spend a few minutes with you."

Ray pulled a chair up near the head of the bed. "How are you doing?" he asked the man.

"Okay," the man's voice came out hoarse. "My wife says you were the people who found me."

"Yes, part of a team." Ray searched Bob Atwood's eyes. "The doctor says you have something to tell me?"

Atwood winced. His next question came slowly. "Where did you find me?"

"Approximately ten miles north of your cottage."

Atwood nodded. "Dead reckoning," he mumbled. "Almost dead… reckoning?" he added with a weak smile.

"You're going to tell me…" Ray prompted.

"About the boat. It ran right over me. The waves were so big that they probably didn't see me, at least at first. But I think they ran over me again."

"What kind of boat, Robert, do you remember?"

"A powerboat, a fast one. I was turtled, off to one side, trying to recover. I heard the motors screaming. I dove deep. I got hit hard. The world went silent, just the pinging sounds. The boat went over. I knew I had to stay away from the props."

"How many times did the boat run over you?"

"Maybe two or three. I don't know. They never slowed down. I swam away, surfaced, waited, waited. The motor and prop sounds disappeared. I held onto the mast and spar. Some flotation there. Two arms, one good leg, lots of pain. Fucking cold water. I knew I had to get to shore. Floated, backstroke. I don't remember much more."

"You were rolled in a piece of construction plastic when we found you."

"Don't remember that. I was so cold. I knew I needed to get warm."

Ray looked up at Dr. Stephens. "Can I ask a few more questions?"

She gave him an approving nod.

"Can you tell me more about the boat that hit you?"

"No. The waves were huge. I couldn't see much."

"Inboard, outboard?"

"Don't know."

"Can you tell me about your route, just briefly?"

"I set out later in the morning. North-northwest wind. Crossed to North Manitou, then over to South. Piece of cake, that first crossing. I beached and walked around, ate a sandwich. I relaunched; the wind had swung around. I capsized, lost my PFD and phone, righted the boat and started again. All I could do was tack, tack, tack. Wasn't getting far. I decided to just run for shore. Didn't matter where I landed. I'd find a phone or catch a ride."

"Is that enough, Sheriff?" Stephens asked.

"Yes, for now."

Dr. Stephens accompanied Ray out of the room. In the hallway near the exit, she asked, "Did you get what you needed?"

"I have a sense of what happened," Ray said, "but without any information about the other boat… or the intentions of those aboard the boat…Was this an accident or something more?"

"Yes," she agreed. "Guy's lucky to be alive."

"How long will you keep him?"

"Hard to say. Atwood has been treated for hypothermia and shock. The surgeons will make the call when it's prudent to go forward with the hip arthroplasty."

27

Before entering the old North Bay Marina building, Ray retrieved the largest piece of Robert Atwood's sailboat from the back of his car, a torn fragment of plywood a little more than four feet long. He stood at the service counter for several minutes, listening to voices echoing in the labyrinthian interior. Then, finally, after repeatedly hitting the dented brass bell on the counter, he heard a voice he recognized shouting, "Hold on, I'm coming!"

A slim, wiry man entered the customer area. "Oh, Ray, it's you. Why didn't you shout?" he asked.

"Zack," said Ray, extending a hand.

Zack looked at his hand and tried to wipe the grime off by using his coveralls. Finally, he just offered his elbow over the counter. Then he turned and yelled, "Hey Harry! Elkins is here." Turning back to Ray, he looked at the plywood and asked, "What's this?"

"Part of a boat," said Ray. "I need your help."

"Hey, Ray," came an excited voice as a taller, stockier version of Zack appeared. "What's going on?"

"Ray says this is a piece of a boat." Zack slammed an open hand down on the plywood.

"Where's the rest of it?" asked Harry.

"This is the biggest piece, and I have a question—"

"Oh, Ray, we can't get that to float. There's not enough there. You need a bottom, top, sides, and a back, all sealed together." Harry looked at his brother. "Tell Ray how many miracles we've done since the boating season started."

"Too many. People bring in the bits and think we can make their boat float or their engine run," said Zack.

"Yeah, exactly. Maybe it's 'cause we're close to water? But they get confused, the fish and bread story, you know, miracles."

"What?" said Zack, addressing his brother. Then, turning to Ray, he continued, "My brother, he gets allegorical sometimes." He shrugged and looked at the ceiling. "Anyway, I agree with Harry, Ray, no miracle will make that a boat again."

Ray waited. When no more dialogue was forthcoming, he said, "If you guys are done with your Click and Clack moment, I've got a serious question."

"Shoot," said Zack.

"There was an incident yesterday on the big lake. A powerboat collided with a small sailboat. I know you watch the weather; small craft advisories were up. The sailboat was capsized at the time of the collision."

"And this piece is from the bottom of the sailboat?" said Zack.

"My best guess," Ray answered.

Zack picked up the torn fragment of plywood and inspected it closely. Harry moved in as well for a closer look.

"Light construction, Okoume 4mm, one layer of fiberglass, homebuilt." He looked at Ray, "And this happened close to shore, not in the deep."

"Correct."

"So, how can we help you?"

"Can you give me a possible scenario? For example, what type of boat might have been involved? Most importantly, would they have been aware of the collision?"

"Scenarios, that's our specialty," said Harry. "Usually, our customers tell us an implausible story and beg for help to make it almost believable. You know, what should I tell my woman or the insurance company? And their version always starts with 'the shoal wasn't on the chart,' or 'I must have hit some flotsam.'"

"In truth, Ray, all we can do is walk you through possibilities," added Zack.

"Fair enough," said Ray. "You identified the type of construction—homebuilt, from a kit assembled last winter. At the time of the collision, the sailboat was turtled. The wave height was five to seven feet or more."

"Starting with that," said Zack, "other than freighters, there wasn't much out yesterday, not in those waves. So, the powerboat had to be designed for rough water. We're talking about a tiny niche in the recreational boating market. I'm guessing it's something with outboards. And if I'm right on that, there's a good chance the guy at the helm didn't see the sailboat before the collision. Did the sailboat have any flotation—foam, sealed bulkheads?"

"I don't think so. There wasn't much left," said Ray.

"Okay, so the only thing showing would be the bottom of the hull, about ten feet by maybe four feet."

"That's about right."

"In steep waves, the sailboat would have been almost invisible. The powerboat pilot might have felt the collision, but in big pounding seas, maybe not."

"And these cuts in the plywood?"

"The prop or props," said Zack.

"Would the motorboat have been damaged?" asked Ray.

"Unlikely. The plywood is cut through. I won't say a hot knife in butter but damn close. And the powerboat hull probably crushed the sailboat before this bit was swept through the prop wash. Lots of horsepower turning big-assed stainless props; think about the thin wooden boat getting hit by a giant inversion blender on steroids. My guess is the sailboat weighed less than two hundred pounds."

"A lot less," answered Ray. "Brett and I had no trouble dragging it up on the beach."

"Okay," said Harry. "So just a guesstimate: Let's say you got two big outboards, that's half a ton for starters. And those engines are probably hanging on a boat designed to handle rough water—we're talking a ton or two more. And that mass comes smacking down at speed on this fragile plywood hull. It's all she wrote before the fragments went through the prop wash."

"The sailboat guy was in the water at the time of the collision. He thinks the powerboat came about and passed through the wreckage a second time," said Ray.

"Was he wearing a PFD? Was he trying to make himself visible?" asked Zack.

"He had lost his PFD in an earlier capsize. He says he dove to stay away from the props."

"I can see someone doing a second pass. Can't you, Harry?"

"Yeah, the guy at the controls might have felt something and come around to take a look. And from what you're describing, it wouldn't have looked much like a wreck, Ray. And in big water, there wouldn't be much to see."

"So you haven't had anyone needing a prop repair or anything of that nature?" asked Ray.

"Elkins, prop repair is our bread and butter," Harry said. "Prop repair keeps the lights on and food on the table. We give thanks for all the bass boat yahoos running around unfamiliar inland lakes, hitting deadheads, and shearing blades off. But that's not like this. I'm guessing a monster outboard, V6 or V8, two or four of them hanging on the back of a big rough-water boat. The boating mags refer to them as offshore boats designed for suboptimal conditions. I love that phrase, 'suboptimal conditions.' Translated, that means you are dumb enough to get caught in some wicked shit and rich enough to have a boat that will save your sorry ass. We don't sell anything like that. You might see one at a large marina. Not around here. Maybe Petoskey, Harbor Springs. Or maybe the boat's tucked away in one of those old boathouses on Lake Charlevoix. This is saltwater stuff. And you need big bucks for those boats."

"Elkins," said Zack, "these aren't family cruisers. These are showoff boats—'My balls are bigger than your balls' boats. Expensive to buy and a ton of money to fuel."

"Yeah, Ray," said Harry. "Think drug runners in the Gulf of Mexico and around Florida. You don't see the ocean versions on the Great Lakes—at least, I haven't. Here, we occasionally see scaled-down versions with design features similar to ocean boats. Remember the last one?" He looked over at Zack.

"On, yeah, the first COVID summer. The short guy with the bowling ball head."

"That's the one, the guy from around Chicago. He hit something and tore off the lower unit of one of his two Merc 250s. First, he insisted that the motor must have been defective and demanded that the company replace it. Then, when that didn't fly, he asked us to fix it. When we couldn't get parts—remember how screwed up everything was during the early stages of the pandemic?—he threatened to sue all of us. Sue us for what? We hadn't touched the damn thing. The boat sat out there for months," Harry gestured toward the weed-covered storage lot behind the marina. "He finally had the boat trucked back home."

"The boats we're talking about are like your new patrol boat, Ray. But sleeker and less military-looking. They're made with higher-end materials and better cosmetics. If one comes in for service or repair of any suspicious damage, we'll rattle your cage," said Zack.

"Thanks, guys."

"Ray, I hope you are planning on our class reunion this fall," said Harry.

"It's on my calendar."

"Be nice to catch up, like the old days," said Zack. "You know, sitting up on the dunes, having a few brewskis, watching the sun drop into the lake."

"Yeah," Ray agreed.

28

Ray stood looking at the whiteboard, then turned to Sue, sitting on the opposite side of the conference table, laptop open, folders and papers carefully arranged.

As they waited for Barbara Sinclair and Brett Carty to join them, Ray asked, "Our John Doe, anything new?"

"Yes, but not anything that moves us forward. There is nothing new on the DNA or fingerprints. In terms of our guy being identified or a match on any FRT in Europe, nothing."

"FRT?" asked Ray.

"My friend at the Bureau has been on my case for 'old speak.' I kept saying *facial recognition software*. So it's now called *facial recognition technology*, commonly referred to as FRT."

"Just what we need, another acronym. I'll add it to my new vocabulary-to-learn list."

"Elkins, this is so interesting, but it never crossed my mind. I mean, this FRT stuff has been in use in England and Europe for several decades. Over that time, hardware and software continued to evolve. And here's the part you don't want to hear..."

"But you're going to tell me there's a problem," Ray said. He waited impatiently while she looked through her folder.

"Yes," she said, holding up what appeared to be a handwritten note. "And it may not apply to our John Doe, but during the first wave of COVID in Europe, when all the countries required masks, much of the facial recognition system stopped working. I mean, not all systems or software packages, but the masks disabled most. It didn't take long to adjust the algorithms and get the programs running again, maybe six or eight months. But in that time, millions of people moved across European borders."

"So what does that mean for us?" asked Ray.

"The FRT data allows police agencies to track criminals across national borders. And as your mother probably said, you're known by the company you keep. The facial data helps establish new connections. If we had the facial ID for the man," Sue continued, "we'd know when and where he was first spotted in Europe. Europol and the police agencies of the EU countries now use the FRT data to build connections between faces, much like DNA is used to search families when looking for a suspect. Gangs, criminal groups, and criminal families are connected using FRT."

Ray gave her a long look.

"Okay, Elkins, you want me to cut to the chase?"

"Exactly."

"If there were FRT data, the FBI would probably have a good idea why our John Doe was in this country."

"But there isn't?"

"Not at this time, Elkins. I know. And next, you'll ask, 'What if John Doe wasn't the killer's primary target?'" said Sue.

"We've looked at the possibility that Tammy was the target. Dakota Dirks is the only person we've come up with so far who had a motive, warped as it was, to harm her. And you've established, based on Dakota's cellphone locations, that his story holds together. He has a solid alibi."

"I'm still wondering if we've mined the Tammy Ogden vein enough—school friends, people with whom she worked at the restaurant, or maybe a customer who was attracted to her? Should we talk to Amanda and Olivia Slosson again? Maybe Maria Tillson, also. They've had a few days to mull this over. Perhaps now they have something new to offer."

Ray began to answer, but his response was lost when Brett and Barbara entered. Barbara's joyful laughter filled the room as she settled at the conference table. Barbara looked slightly abashed as she peered over at her more senior colleagues.

"What a lovely sound," said Ray. "Thank you for reminding us of laughter. Coloratura?"

"In my dreams, in my teens, voice and dance. The voice is mostly mezzo ranges now. My mother can still hit those upper notes. She went to Ann Arbor at eighteen, thinking her next stop would be the Met, but by her junior year, she decided she needed a career with a more secure future." Looking over at Sue, she asked, "How does he know this stuff?"

"His late wife was a classical musician."

"The cause of the laughter?" asked Ray, looking at Barbara.

"As we came down the hall, Brett was complimenting me on my sea legs during our rough water outing this morning. I was laughing at him," she paused and gestured toward Brett. "He watched me max dose Dramamine and then strap on anti-nausea wristbands before we even got near the water. And then the big lake was as flat as a pancake."

"What did you learn?" asked Ray, noting Brett's doting expression as he looked at Barbara.

"You said you'd take North Bay Marina," answered Brett, "so we stopped at the other marinas in the area selling fuel and offering repair services."

"Anything?"

"No. We heard the same story at every stop. The almost daily predictions of gale-force winds over the last week kept most recreational boaters tied up. And no one has seen any exotic rough-water boats. And you know, these guys, mostly teenage boys, are all boat geeks. How about Harry and Zack?"

"Ditto," Ray responded. "So we have a mystery ship. But it would have been nice to get closure on the incident." He turned a mental page. "Sue has brought me up to date on what little we know about our John Doe. It's all in the case file for your perusal."

Sue added, "There's an explanation of how he might have traveled across Europe during the early months of the pandemic without being noticed by their elaborate facial recognition systems.

And that leaves us nowhere. He had to be staying somewhere in the area."

"We've covered all the hotels, motels, Airbnbs, and campsites. He might have been living out of his car. We see this happening a lot in the summer," said Brett.

"Yes," Ray said, "but mostly teens and college kids, who find many places to crash along the National Shoreline during good weather. But this guy…"

"This guy," said Sue, picking up Ray's phrase, "could have been familiar with living rough. No one so far has described him as particularly refined. And Tammy wasn't expecting to be whisked off to the Ritz, but he had a fancy car and a big roll of cash. That would have been exotic enough in her world. And it's safe to assume he was the one who introduced her to cocaine."

"So why was this guy here? We need a motive." Sue looked around the table. "My contact at the Bureau said there's no intelligence suggesting an eastern European crime group trying to expand operations across the border from Canada. Our interagency narcotics team is mostly focused on trying to stop the flow of fentanyl into the area. And that's all coming from Mexico and points south."

Ray nodded his agreement. When no one else had anything to add, he said, "Moving on, I looked over the reports from the sector patrols, Brett. Can you add anything more about the vandalism at Victoria Wainwright's business?"

"No. Nothing new has been reported since the incident in the orchard, but the property is vulnerable to this type of vandalism. It's in the middle of nowhere. Did you talk to her about security cameras?"

"I did, briefly," said Ray. "She rejected the idea emphatically. She said security cameras intrude on the kind of world she's trying to preserve."

"We all know that's a widely held opinion, and not just by recent refugees from Silicon Valley," said Sue.

"Barbara," said Ray, "Brett and I have been discussing permanently taking you off road patrol and making you our technology officer. This is not just a desk job. You would still often be in the field helping with investigations, as you do now."

Barbara considered the offer soberly, and Ray wondered if he should have waited to ask her about the issue in private. Finally, she responded, "Deputy Geek. It does have a certain ring to it. I would like that."

"And," added Ray, "Brett's been our point person on home and business security questions. As part of your new assignment, I'd like you to take that over, too. Brett will share what he's been doing in the past and help you with training goals. Maybe the two of you can work with Wainwright on possibly installing security cameras. I'll give her a call as a way of introduction."

After the meeting, Ray waited as Sue collected her folders and computer. Then he asked, "Is there something going on between them?"

Sue looked as though she was struggling not to laugh. "Ray, something was going on from the outset when he was her training officer. It was just a spark initially. Lots of differences separating them. First, mutual respect, then friendship. And, lately, Brett's been following her around like a puppy dog."

"How did I miss that?"

"Elkins—" She considered how to explain it to him but then thought better of it. "What's for dinner?"

29

The pre-dawn mist was still clinging to the countryside as Ray carefully navigated the twisting gravel road, trying to avoid the deep chuckholes. His destination was a long-abandoned industrial site, a cannery, tucked away in an interior part of the county.

Finally, the flashing lights from a patrol car and a fire truck guided him to his final destination, a decaying cement block building surrounded by broken pavement and derelict vehicles. The patrol car was parked off to the side on a small plateau above the site.

"What do we have?" Ray asked, coming to the side of Stan Gill, one of the department's veteran patrol officers—ex-military and special forces. He had positioned himself on a rise above the firefighters.

"First, a 9-1-1 report of the fire," answered Gill.

Gill gave Ray a quick nod, then returned his focus to the scene below. "I had just finished a domestic when I got the call from dispatch. It still took some time to get here."

"Did you notice anything on the way in?" Ray asked.

"Other than a few deer for the last few miles, the place appeared deserted. When I finally got here, just one wreck was burning, that old panel truck off to the side. The fire hadn't spread to the other vehicles and junk." He pointed. "I did a quick drive around. Didn't see anyone. Then I parked here. I could smell gasoline as soon as I got out of the car. It had to be arson. There wasn't much left when the fire crew arrived. Just the tires, and they were mostly gone. The guys have been shoving sand on the flames. It's better than foam or water on rubber. Looks like they're almost done."

"I'm going down to speak with the firefighters before they leave. Then let's check this building."

Gill nodded. At first, he stayed at his post. Then he joined Ray, and the two men worked their way around the perimeter of the old building. It began to rain. In the dull morning light, they carefully moved around the exterior, tall weeds partially obscuring long-abandoned machinery and derelict fifty-five-gallon steel drums.

Ray ran the beam of his flashlight over the cement-block walls and steel-framed windows, most broken or missing glass.

"What do you know about this place?" Ray asked.

"Elkins, even when I was working days, I seldom got back here. I think we had a couple of reports of vandalism. People were trashing the area, dumping old appliances and junk. Back in the day, a steel cable blocked the drive at the road. I don't know what happened to that. But the place was long deserted when I came along."

They stopped at an overhead door and a nearby service door on the side of the building facing the road. Both were secured. They circled to the far side, illuminating another entrance. The rusting steel door, slightly ajar and opening to the outside, was riddled with bullet holes. Gill moved to the right of the door about ten feet. He knelt briefly, then stood, showing Ray a handful of shiny brass shell casings. He motioned with his head toward the door. "I guess I was wrong," he said. "Someone was playing with an assault rifle."

As Ray unholstered his Glock, Gill cut in front of him, hooking the door with the toe of his boot and kicking it open. The explosion was instantaneous, the brilliant flash and a torrent of searing air tossing Gill away from the opening and knocking Ray to the ground.

The world came back slowly. First, Ray knew he was being dragged away from the tongue of flames pouring out of the building. Later, he was in a vehicle, and someone was talking at his side. He opened his eyes, blinking, trying to eliminate the stinging sensation.

"How are you doing?" came the voice at his side. He tried to focus on the source. Finally, he nodded, just giving a one-word reply.

"Okay," he mumbled, his throat sore. Still fading in and out, people talked around him, over him, and a mask-covered face peered down at him—the beeping sound of a monitor droned on and on.

Then, a voice again. "He's awake."

"How's…?" Ray muttered, just a fragment, but enough to elicit an answer,

"Your friend's here, too. In the next room," came a female voice, calm and attentive. "I'm Doctor Chou. How are you feeling?"

"Head?"

"Yes. I've just put a dressing on the back of your skull. It looks like you hit something pretty hard. Anything else?"

"Blurry."

"Double vision, maybe?"

"Yeah, I think that's it."

"Okay. You're going for a CT. Then we'll talk again."

"Gill?" questioned Ray.

"A bit battered. Hair singed. His dislocated shoulder has already been reduced. He's awake and asking for breakfast. One tough guy, Sheriff. Nurse Madison here will put in a line before you go to radiology. I'll talk to you after."

"Which arm?" another female voice, a bit higher, almost musical.

His nonchalant manner suggested he didn't care. He felt the prick on the inside of his left elbow, then a few gentle taps to the area. "You're set to go, Sheriff. They'll take good care of you."

Eyes closed, head spinning, Ray felt the gurney being rolled through the hospital's hallways. He opened his eyes briefly in the dimmer light of the elevator and then pushed through to consciousness as three people in scrubs helped him off the gurney and onto the patient table extending from the scanner. "I'm putting earplugs in," came a male voice. "It gets noisy in there. You have to hold very still. This will take about 30 minutes. If it gets to be too much, squeeze this ball."

Ray felt something being inserted in his right hand just before the earplugs were firmly inserted.

He felt the hands of two nurses, one on each side, carefully cradling and cushioning his head. Then they lowered a cage-like structure over his face, locking his head to the table before he was slowly pulled into a narrow pipe-like tube. He closed his eyes, trying to blank out feelings of claustrophobia, focusing on his breathing.

Then the pounding began, low pitched, metallic, regular, but not rhythmic. Machine clanging and bashing. Starting and stopping, changing pitch and duration. Demonic.

Eventually, the pounding paused. His body emerged from the machine. A face moved close to his, shouting to be heard, "Adding contrast. Ten more minutes."

Finally, it was over. He was out. The cage was pulled away from his face. He adjusted to the light. Two sets of hands, one at each side, brought him to a sitting position and helped him onto a gurney. Then, in a hospital room, he gave up struggling to be awake.

Hours later, before he opened his eyes, he was aware of a familiar scent of soap and shampoo, then the touch, gentle.

"Ray?" Sue was hovering over him. She stroked his cheek. "You okay?"

"Now, yes."

30

Ray remained quiet for several minutes, slowly pushing away the fog. Finally, he said, "What can you tell me?"

"Why don't you rest. It's not important. Everything is being taken care of."

"I… just…" he sputtered.

"You just need to know. Right?"

"Yes," he answered in a raspy voice.

"Do you remember getting to the scene?" she asked, pulling a chair to the side of the hospital bed.

Ray nodded.

"How about being with Stan?"

Another nod.

"How about the explosion?"

"No."

"Well, you've got most of what we know. Stan remembers kicking open a door and the explosion. He said it was like a flashback to Iraq."

"Cause?"

"The MSP fire investigation team is probably at the scene by now. They will have an explosive expert with them. We should have some preliminary information by the end of the day."

"Your old boyfriend, is he leading the team?"

"No, silly. I heard he's moved on to cybercrime."

"Who called you?"

"Fortunately for you guys, the fire crew was still around," she explained. "They heard the explosion, found you, and requested the EMTs. Dispatch called me. I initiated the calls to get the investigation rolling." Sue reached for and held onto his hand, trying not to break down.

"The property, who owns it?"

"Cedar County."

"You've got to be—"

"No. A tax foreclosure sometime after the cannery closed. Then law enforcement removed some squatters—auto repair or a chop shop. I can tell you when the county evicted them, but there's no record of how long they occupied the property. We've both heard stories about the lack of enforcement of building codes back in the day. After the foreclosure, the building and surrounding area was designated a toxic waste site. It's been sitting in the queue for years, waiting to be cleared and cleaned up so it could be sold."

"Did you bring some clothes?"

"Elkins, you're not going anywhere. Concussion protocol. Forty-eight hours. You're going to be held overnight for observation. Then, at least a day of rest at home. Simone is looking for some quality time with you."

"But…"

"Twenty-four hours here closely monitored, then bed rest for several days with limited physical or mental activity. And then a checkup before you return to work. And I've saved the worst bit for last. I'm going to be doing the cooking."

Sue stood and kissed him gently and held him for a long time. Finally pulling away, she said, "Gotta run. I'll be back this evening sometime."

"Simone?"

"I'll see if I can smuggle her in."

31

Detective Sergeant Sue Lawrence started the meeting by introducing the Michigan State Police's new arson investigator, Sergeant Emily Larson, to Barbara Sinclair and Brett Carty. Larson had briefed Sue earlier at the scene, and Sue had asked her to share her findings with the team. She explained to Larson that while she was the only department member with the official 'detective' title, they were all part of the department's ad hoc team of detectives.

Sue provided a brief medical update on first the sheriff and then Stan Gill. She warned Carty and Sinclair not to answer any of the sheriff's appeals, including direct orders, to liberate him from the hospital. The two officers tried without success to suppress their laughter.

"He is spending the night there," Sue said. "Case closed. And he won't starve. His evening meal has already been sent over from the Cook's House. After we finish here, I'll take Simone, and we'll keep him company."

She continued, "Stan Gill was the closest to the explosion and has facial lacerations, burn injuries to his hands and face, most first degree, a few second degree. His hair is singed, and he has multiple bruises from being thrown backward by the explosion. He's also complaining about his hearing. And if that weren't enough, they found a cardiac arrhythmia. The hospitalist told me that it may not be related to this incident. That might be a preexisting condition.

"Gill's a vet with multiple deployments and a lot of combat experience," Sue continued. "I talked with his wife, Charlene, briefly. She says he's blowing the whole thing off. She's not. The woman was distraught. She thinks it's time for him to retire.

"I know you've been getting bits of information all day as you attended to your duties. And I know everyone's tired, but we must put our heads together on this. With Sergeant Larson's help, let's try to get a handle on what happened today." She directed their attention to the large screen.

"As you can see, first there's a call from a landline to dispatch at 5:27 a.m. reporting a fire on Cannery Road. The sector officer, Gill, is sent. He arrives on the scene at 5:56 and reports a vehicle fire. The township fire department is dispatched to the scene. They arrive at the scene at 6:22. At 6:42, they report the fire is under control. This is also the time the sheriff arrives at the scene.

"At 6:57, an explosion is reported at the site. EMTs are dispatched. And from that point on, you were all involved one way or another. Sergeant Larson comes to the State Police from ATF and has expertise in both arson and explosives. She spent much of the day at the site and will share with us her preliminary findings."

Larson, tall and muscular, was wearing a blue jumpsuit and moved around the conference table to the side with the giant video screen. Bits of her salt-and-pepper hair extended beyond a baseball cap that bore the bright yellow letters MSP.

"I've only been back in Michigan for over a month. And I've got to admit, I've been looking forward to getting up north. It's been years, but I didn't expect my first trip would come so quickly. Let me start with arson, then move on to the explosive device.

"These events appear to be part of a carefully orchestrated scenario. A derelict vehicle is torched. Gasoline was poured into the interior, splashed on the exterior, and ignited. A red plastic five-gallon can, deformed by the heat and fire, was discarded near the scene. A plastic cap, I believe, came from this container and was found nearby, probably tossed by the perpetrator after opening the can.

"In most cases, a scene like this would suggest vandalism: A warm summer evening, a couple of twelve-packs, two or three guys with time on their hands. It's the dumpster fire scenario. And there's evidence things like this have happened at this property over the years. Maybe not a fire, but lots of broken windows in the building and abandoned vehicles. There must be a special joy in breaking glass and doing graffiti art. Given the locale, the fire might have gone entirely unnoticed. That said, the scene wasn't quite right. There was none of the telltale litter of recreational vandalism—lots of beer cans and cigarette butts.

"And then there's the 9-11 call. It turns out the call was from a landline. And you, Barbara, checked the phone's location?"

"Yes, a landline in a summer cottage. The building is currently unoccupied, and the rear door had been forced."

"And how far was that from the fire at the cannery?"

"I'd say about ten miles."

"So, too far to see the fire at the cannery?"

"I would guess. Too far, heavy overcast, smoke from Canada," Barbara said.

"And the 9-11 call?"

"I listened to the recording," Barbara continued. "The caller identified himself as Mr. Franz and provided the correct address. It was a deep male voice. When I went to the address, there was a sign on the drive—*Franzes' Retreat*. From our county tax records, I got the owner's phone number in Columbus, Ohio, and talked with Mrs. Jane Franz. She confirmed that she and her husband owned the property. They are elderly, and she was unsure they would come north this summer.

"I asked if anyone had been given permission to use the building. She said absolutely not. I told her about the break-in. It took a while to reassure her that nothing else seemed to have been touched besides the damage to the door."

"So how did you leave it with her?" asked Larson.

"They have a handyman up here. She was going to call him to secure the building. I'm going to follow up with him tomorrow."

"Good. And the purpose of the call to dispatch from this cottage?" Larson directed her question to Sinclair.

"I think to bring an officer to a deserted building to check on a fire," answered Barbara.

"Exactly. So you got two things here," said Larson. "First, the person making the 9-1-1 call had to know about the unoccupied building and the available landline. Second, at least two people are involved—the 9-11 caller and one person at the cannery."

Sinclair's expression became quizzical. "Couldn't one perp have set the IED up and left the scene to make the call?"

"Let me explain," Larson said. She removed two evidence bags from her pack and held one up for her audience. It contained the remains of a walkie-talkie, the inexpensive kind that kids play with.

"As you can see," she said, "all that is left of this walkie-talkie are plastic bits, a small circuit board, and some wires. And this thing has been around for a while. The perp may have bought it and its partner at a yard sale. They used this walkie-talkie to ignite the device— gunpowder packed in a cardboard shipping tube. Essentially, it is a huge firecracker. When Officer Gill kicked the door open, someone watching ignited the device using another walkie-talkie. There were no enhancements in this bomb, meaning items like ball bearings, nuts, bolts—anything to cause damage. That's atypical."

"So one person was making the 9-11 call and a second person with a walkie-talkie was nearby watching the site and triggering the device?" said Brett.

"Yes," answered Larson. "At least that's my theory. The caller might have been able to hustle over here and get in position, but two would have made the operation easier."

Sue said, "Sergeant Larson and I climbed up to the ridgeline above the cannery. There's a sand trail that runs along the top. It looks like a popular place for dirt bikes and ATVs. The area backs up to state forest land and the National Shoreline. It is easy to access the trail system and get to the cannery. And from the ridge above, you have a clear view of the back of the cannery and most of the site."

"Did you find anything up there?" asked Barbara.

"Tire tracks and a well-worn path, nothing more," answered Sue. "We'll go back tomorrow for a more thorough search." She looked toward Brett, who administered patrol staffing. "I'll need all the interns in the morning and maybe a couple of officers on overtime."

"You've got them," he responded. "Sergeant Larson—?" he began.

"Emily," she said.

"Emily, given your experience, what does this device tell us about the bomber? And I'm also wondering about motive."

"Motive is always the central question. But let me talk about the bomb first. Quite frankly, I've never seen one like this. The electronics part, without the bomb, of course, looks like something an eighth-grade boy might have cobbled together for a science fair project. It's a straightforward device."

"In your experience, what's a typical bomb?" Brett pursued.

"There is no typical. That said, specific bombers tend to build the same type of device over and over. It's almost a personal signature, which helps us eventually track them down. Almost without exception, the bomb makers are male. What guy doesn't love a big explosion?"

She made an exploding gesture with her hands.

"And you don't have to be a technology wizard. There are a lot of electronic tools now, including phone apps, that can be easily modified to control explosive devices. You can find how-to instructions and buy the needed electronics online. Getting some of the more exotic explosive materials requires a bit more ingenuity."

"And motives?" asked Sinclair.

"Probably as varied as the devices. Maybe someone wanted to kill, maim, or frighten Officer Gill or Sheriff Elkins. I've mostly worked on bombings connected to organized crime or gang violence. We were also involved in tracking possible foreign and domestic threats."

"Anything else for Emily?" asked Sue. She waited for a moment, then continued, "Okay, get some rest. Tomorrow will be a busy day."

The other two had left the room as Sue waited for Emily Larson to collect her things.

"Sounds like you're doing your best to look after the sheriff," Larson said as she came to Sue's side.

Sue, wondering where the conversation was going and whether or not Larson was aware of her past relationship with Mike Ogden, answered, "Yes."

"I noticed something about your tone when you provided a medical update. And the piece about taking the dog into seeing him tonight."

Sue explained that they first co-parented the dog for several years and finally became a couple.

Changing the subject, Sue said, "You're new to the department."

"Yes, not quite a month yet. I had been watching for postings in Michigan and doing some networking. My dad is going downhill. Nothing new, just getting worse. In recent months, I've been commuting home to the Lansing area for many weekends to help my mom. She's overwhelmed, and her health is starting to go, too. So I decided to return to Michigan for at least a bit."

"Where were you?"

"Philly, ATF. I liked the job there, but I had no real roots. I was in what I thought might be a long-term relationship, but it suddenly went lopsided."

"Whereabouts in Michigan?" Sue asked.

"St. Johns, north of Lansing. I was born and raised there. After high school, I wandered down the road to State and got a BA in criminal justice. Got a job with ATF and headed to D.C. for training. It was a heady time. The first assignment was knocking down doors in Baltimore."

"How was that?" asked Sue.

"Brutal. Barely made it through the first month. I wasn't prepared for it… didn't know that world existed. But we humans, we adjust to all kinds of bad shit. The unimaginable becomes the new normal. For me, things got a lot better when I got to move to Philly—not that we didn't have our share of gangbangers and pyro-psychos. And, like I said, I had a relationship. It wasn't nine-something on the Richter scale but had a certain smoldering charm. I had a balance of sorts."

32

After Larson left, Sue remained, checking her email and messages and attending to a few that required immediate responses. Then she called the medical center and talked with Ray's charge nurse, explaining her situation and asking permission to arrive after regular visiting hours.

The charge nurse, Gary, granted her first request but took a bit longer to agree to her second request to bring their terrier, Simone, along. Finally, he asked, "Is your dog small enough to be easily carried?"

"Yes."

After a long audible exhale, he said, "I guess it's okay. He's in a private room. But please limit your stay to less than an hour."

As she walked through the near-empty hospital corridors a few minutes before 10:00 p.m. with Simone tucked under her arm, Sue attracted little attention. Stopping at the nursing station, she identified herself to the nurse, Gary—tall, rail thin, and clad in plum-colored scrubs. He escorted her to Ray's room, entering first as she waited just beyond the open door, Simone squirming impatiently.

"He was sleeping when I last checked, but now he's awake. Please remember the hour limit."

"How's he doing?"

"Everything looks unremarkable at this point. If that holds, he should be good to go by morning." He studied Simone's earnest, whiskered face impassively. "The doctor's note said the patient would be discharged for home rest. He should not return to work for several days."

Sue nodded, knowing it was unlikely that she could keep Ray from the job.

As soon as Sue entered Ray's room, Simone tensed, ready to spring from her arms onto Ray. Sue restrained the terrier and set her on the bed at Ray's side instead. Simone stepped onto his chest and showered him with kisses.

"She knows," said Sue.

"They always do," Ray agreed. "She sensed your tension." He gently lifted Simone off his chest, allowing her to snuggle in at his side, the dog's head resting on his shoulder.

"How are you feeling?"

"Sore, especially my upper body. And my head still hurts. Maybe it's the stitches. And I've got this ringing in my ears. Stan's wife, Charlene, stopped in earlier. She said that Stan is complaining about the same problem with his hearing. But besides that, some singed hair, and a few cuts and bruises, she says he's okay."

"How well is Charlene coping?" Sue asked.

"She seems fine. She's always struck me as a determined woman. Anything new?"

"It can wait till morning."

"You must have something new."

Sue didn't say anything. She reached out and rested her hand in the crook of his elbow, then slowly ran her hand along his tanned arm until she reached his hand, which she clasped with her own.

"It could've been much worse," she said.

"How about the explosion?"

"The new sergeant, Emily Larson, former ATF, seems very skilled. I will probably learn a lot more tomorrow."

"What the hell was it? A fertilizer bomb?"

Sue sighed. "Larson says the device appeared homemade, essentially a huge firecracker, gunpowder tightly packed in a cardboard tube."

"What? Why? What's the motive?"

"I have no idea. You get to sleep on that."

Sue leaned over Ray, kissed him, and scooped up Simone.

"Can't she stay? I'd sleep better."

"Sure, Elkins. Gary would happily take Simone for her late-night walk."

As Sue exited the elevator on the ground level, a woman asked, "How did you pull that off?"

She turned to see if the speaker was addressing her.

"Charlene?" said Sue tentatively.

"The dog," Charlene Gill explained. Without waiting for an answer, she continued, "How's your… the sheriff?"

As they walked toward the entrance, Sue answered, "Impatient, impossible, just wants out. How is Stan?"

"Just the same. Wants to sleep in his bed, not some damn hospital bed."

"How are you doing?" asked Sue as they paused near some benches in the entrance atrium.

Charlene breathed in deeply, then out again—a heavy sigh. "What do we women always say? I'm okay."

"But you're not," said Sue, settling onto a vinyl cushion, Charlene following her lead.

"No," she responded.

Sue had only met the woman in passing a few times before. Now, she observed her closely for the first time. In her fifties, Charlene was dressed in jeans and a cotton shirt. Her tan ankles were visible between the hem of her jeans and a pair of worn Tretorn sneakers.

"I didn't see this coming, this possibility." She looked away, gazing at the dark windows of the almost empty atrium. "You know, it's not like… I haven't been here before. Army wife for years, lots of deployments along the way." She met Sue's eyes once more. "I mean, there were the kids. I was a single parent during the deployments. And I was teaching—middle school English. If something had happened to Stan, I would have been crushed, of course." Her eyes welled with tears, and her voice thickened. "But I knew the kids and the job would hold me together. You hear what I'm trying to say?"

"Yes," Sue answered, passing Charlene a tissue.

As Charlene regained control, Sue asked, "Your children?"

"Two girls and a boy. Grown. The oldest, Sherry, is married. I'm a new grandmother. Lynne, the middle child, just completed nursing school. And Skyler, our baby, is on a gap year, which has become two gap years. He wanted to be a ski bum before starting college. So we're officially empty-nesters."

"So what brought you to Cedar County?" asked Sue.

"One of Stan's army buddies retired up here. We visited several times and fell in love with the area." Her face relaxed briefly, and then the tension returned. "The job wasn't part of the plan. We were going to retire. Period. But Stan couldn't deal with that. His line to me: 'I can only fish so many days.' And you guys were advertising. And he's loved it. He needs those adrenaline rushes."

"So neither of you has much history in this area?"

"No."

"Do you know of anyone who might want to hurt Stan?"

"Absolutely not. We have our little house in the woods. We found a church that's a good fit. We have a few good friendships. Until this, things have been idyllic."

"Can you think of any incidents connected to his police work that were…?"

"Nothing like that. He likes working the third shift, especially in the northern sector. As he says, his job mostly involves helping people, you know, with medical emergencies and domestic problems. He needs to serve. I don't think I've ever seen him happier."

"Your kids, nearby?"

"I wish—the skier is in Utah, the nurse in Minnesota, and the grandbaby and her parents in Vermont. Lynne is driving from the Twin Cities tomorrow. She's taking a couple of days off. She and Stan are close. Having her in the house will help keep Stan under control. I'm so happy she's coming."

"Any indication of when Stan's going to be discharged?"

"Tomorrow, but I don't know just when, I hope. He's scheduled to see an ENT and someone else. He's chomping at the bit to get out."

Sue passed Charlene a card. "Let me know if there's anything I can do. The department has a support system in place, including counseling. We encourage our people to take advantage of these services, which are also available to family members."

The two women hugged, and Charlene made her way to the inside entrance to the parking structure. Sue followed more slowly, opting for the automatic doors leading outside. Once she cleared the last set of doors, she found a bench and sank onto it, still holding Simone. The heat of the day had dissipated little. She listened to the sounds of the city: the wind in the trees, the traffic on a busy thoroughfare a few blocks away, the rhythmic sound of a basketball hitting pavement, and voices—male, teenage.

Her eyes filled with tears. She wiped them away. Then she tried to push the tears back, inhaling deeply and letting the air escape through pursed lips. She sensed her world spinning out of control. Simone squirmed, making her presence known.

"Okay, we're on our way," Sue said, getting to her feet and heading into the mostly empty parking structure.

Hours later, Sue awoke, her pajamas soaked with sweat. She reached out, only to find cool sheets spanning the space on the other side of the bed. Her head throbbed, and her breathing came fast. The past day's events unfolded again, from the first call from dispatch about the explosion. She had been too tired to shower before bed, and the stench from the vehicle fire and the bomb scene still clung to her hair and skin.

Though a very grueling day, Sue had been in control. She selected and implemented the appropriate crisis plan, assumed leadership responsibilities for the department, and contacted other police agencies for assistance.

Many times during the day, after news of the bombing and injuries spread through county government and across the community, people asked her, "How are you doing?" A certain tone to the question implied, "You can't be all right." And Sue's response was, "I'm okay."

Holding Simone in the darkness sometime after midnight, she finally admitted it aloud: "Not okay." She whispered the words several times as she pulled up the blankets, chills sweeping through her body. She focused on her breathing: slow inhalation, slower exhalation. That did little to quiet the pounding in her chest. Finally, the grief and anxiety began to uncoil. Tears came like a storm, accompanied by head-to-toe spasms and an uneasy slumber that lasted into a gray dawn, one marked by thunder and lightning that ushered in a stormy summer day.

33

As Barbara Sinclair passed through the medical center's corridors, the morning activities were in full swing. Tall aluminum food carts were scattered along the hallways, and the air was redolent with the aroma of stale coffee and institutional food mixed with the usual clinical smells, including hints of Pine-Sol and bleach.

Barbara slowed as she neared her destination, tracking the ascending room numbers. Finally, she stopped at a doorway and peered into the room. Ray's left arm was encased in the cuff of a sphygmomanometer. A nurse stood at his side, watching a digital display.

"How is it?" Ray asked.

"Unremarkable," the young woman—short and lean with narrow shoulders—responded as she keyed the numbers into a form on an iPad. She nodded in Sinclair's direction before continuing. "The hospitalist signed your discharge. You're good to go. And it looks like your driver has arrived."

"Driver or minder?" Ray muttered.

"Has he been a good patient?" Sinclair asked.

"During the first three-quarters of my shift, he was perfect—slept like a baby. Things didn't start to go south until I served him a cup of our almost-gourmet hospital blend. Then he got grumpy."

"This will probably remedy the problem," said Sinclair, holding up a large thermos cup and passing it to Ray.

"This is Misty," Ray said, motioning toward the nurse. "Other than giving me that coffee, she's been wonderful."

"Missy, Sheriff, Missy." Looking at Barbara, the nurse said, "He keeps calling me Misty."

"The bump on the head, could that be the cause?"

"Yeah, possible."

"And then there's that old Erroll Garner piece." Sinclair snapped her fingers four times, slowly, and then softly launched into the first few bars of the song. Her best torch-singer voice filled the room.

"Hey," said Missy, "anytime my presence can engender that kind of vision, they can call me anything they want."

"Anything I should know about how to look after this patient today?" asked Sinclair, swiftly changing gears.

"It's all here," said Missy, waving a sheaf of papers in Sinclair's direction. "The neurologist's instructions and the CDC guidelines for concussion care. When he was here this morning, the neurologist made it clear that the sheriff should not return to work for several days. He is to rest at home and have someone monitoring his condition. Isn't that right, Sheriff Elkins?"

Ray nodded without enthusiasm.

Sinclair set a bag of clothing at the foot of the bed and accepted the documents.

"I'll read this thoroughly while he's dressing. Thank you."

Missy pulled the curtains in place around the bed before departing. A few minutes later, Ray pushed them apart. He stood beside the bed in cargo shorts, a navy T-shirt, and Birkenstocks.

"Why am I dressed in mufti?" he demanded. "What was Sue thinking?"

Sinclair couldn't contain her laughter.

She loaded Ray into her Dodge Pursuit, her hand on his head as she gently guided him into the passenger seat.

"Where to now?" he asked exasperatedly after she was seated next to him. "Back to the ranch?"

"No. Sue knew you wouldn't rest. So I will look after you as I complete some nonhazardous duties."

"Like what?"

"Interview of Delbert Witz, owner of Del's Cottage Service."

Sinclair started the car and maneuvered out of the parking structure. Once on the highway, Ray asked, "Del, what's he done now?"

"Is he known to the department?" she asked. "I checked the database, and his name didn't appear."

"No, it probably wouldn't," said Ray. "He's a real old-timer. He has to be pushing ninety. There aren't many left like him."

"Like him, what's that supposed to mean?" asked Sinclair.

"Where do I begin?" Ray considered what he knew of the man's life. "Del was probably born in the early thirties, I imagine on the family farm at the peninsula's North End. If that's where we're going, he still lives in the same falling-apart farmhouse where he was born. Life was never easy on those farms—poor soil, short growing season. I heard stories from the old-timers as I was growing up about how tough things were during the Depression years."

Ray sorted through a rush of memories. "What I'm going to say comes from things my mother shared, stories from my grandparents' and great-grandparents' lives. I imagine you also have rich family stories?"

Barbara nodded.

"Most of the farmland here was close to worthless. It was subsistence farming, just enough to keep a small family from starvation if you were lucky enough to have a small family. Fishing and hunting were necessary for survival, and little attention was paid to the conservation laws.

"That's the story of Del's family. When people used to talk about 'those people up north,' that's what they were referring to. And now that kind of life is gone.

"For many of these people, the only source of cash was seasonal work for the summer people—odd jobs, handyman chores, housecleaning, laundry, just lots of manual labor. Over the years, people have drifted away to better lives in urban America. Sorry to be so long-winded, but Del is one of the last of his kind, a real contrast to the turnkey concierge services most of our seasonal residents now employ."

"So, do you know this guy, Del, personally? Is he known to law enforcement?"

Ray chuckled. "Sort of. He lives off the land and takes what he needs. Some of it's acceptable. Roadkill disappears quickly near his place. And there were other... incidents."

"But he's old now?" Barbara asked.

"Yes, but it was his modus operandi for decades. Probably his father's, too. Normative behavior for a lot of people for generations. Survival mode. Once, for example, some purloined beehives appeared on his property."

"How did you handle that?"

"I knew the aggrieved beekeeper. We worked it out. There have been other things, too, like his cottage services. For a modest fee, he's supposed to check his customers' property every few weeks during winter. But I'm not sure that happens."

"And sometimes people complain?" said Sinclair.

"Sometimes. I've had him return the money he was paid, or we've worked out an arrangement with the wronged party to provide some services, like chopped and stacked firewood. Del is hard to dislike. People don't usually push it too much. His few remaining customers have been with him for years. They cut him some slack."

Sinclair pointed to the GPS screen. "Where am I going?"

Ray put his index finger close to the screen. "See this township road here? It runs into a two-track that forks and almost circles Little Pike Lake."

"Okay," said Barbara. "I suppose I go straight when I get to the fork?"

"No, not in this case. This time, you go right. There's another two-track that's not showing on the screen. I'll guide you in. And your first turn is coming up on the right in about a mile."

The slamming of the patrol car doors brought Del—barefoot, dressed in coveralls with a flannel shirt on top—out through the screen door. "What's going on, Ray?" he asked.

"Hey, Del, how are you doing?"

"Not dead yet. See you got a driver. Must be moving up in the world."

"This is Barbara Sinclair. She's been with us for a few years."

Del threw a salute in her direction. Then he motioned for them to follow him into his home.

Once inside, he offered them a seat at the kitchen table. He asked, "What brings you?"

"Did you hear from Jane Franz about the damage to her cottage?"

"Yeah, she called me yesterday," he said. He went to the sink, chose three coffee mugs from the counter, and rinsed them out, one by one. "I just screwed a piece of plywood over the whole opening. I'll go back and fix it right in a day or two. They're not coming up soon."

"How long have you been working for the Franzes?" asked Ray.

"Can't remember when I wasn't," said Del. Without drying the mugs, he set them on the table. Then, he pulled a coffee pot from the top of the stove and filled the cups.

Sinclair gazed at the chipped enamel mug and then at Ray, who cautiously sipped the steaming liquid.

"So you made a temporary repair?" said Ray.

"Yeah, temporary, of sorts."

"Has this happened before?" asked Sinclair.

"The Franz place?"

"Yes."

"Might have." Del shrugged his shoulders. "Those out-of-way places. It happens. Those old doors and windows, all it takes is a pry bar. And no one is around. If you break a window or make a little noise, no one's gonna notice."

Del took a big gulp of coffee. "You know what I tell my people, the ones with these old places? I tell them not to have me fix it too good 'cause the next time, the bad guys will need to do more busting up to get in and it will just make everything worse."

"When was the last time you checked this property?" asked Ray.

Del wagged his head from side to side and chewed on his lower lip. "Oh, probably sometime in March when the snow was finally disappearing. Things looked okay then. And the Franzes did everything right."

"What does that mean?" Sinclair asked.

"I tell my people—well, there ain't that many anymore—I tell them don't you leave any booze or guns. Someone finds that once, and they come back every year looking for it again. Same goes with those big TVs."

"The phone in the cottage was still in service," said Ray.

"That's crazy," said Dell. "Guess they got money to burn."

"Did you know about the phone?"

"No. It's all cells now."

"Anyone work for you who might have noticed a landline at the property?"

"No, it's just me and Kid now." He pointed to the dog bed next to the stove, upon which rested a mound of shaggy black fur that hadn't moved since they had been inside the house.

"The places that I used to check on are disappearing," said Del. "The old cottages are teardowns—new people, new buildings, security systems. I just got a few customers left. And that's about all I can do."

"Okay, thank you, Del," said Ray, standing. "If you think of anything that might help, call me." Ray placed a card on the table. "You've got a working phone, right?"

"A landline impersonator," said Del, pointing to a black pushbutton phone partially hidden among the debris on a kitchen counter. "It's hooked to some cell device. Ma Bell gave me that last winter when something went bad with the line. That's what they do now."

"Good to meet you, Mr. Witz," Sinclair said.

Once back in the car, she asked, "How was the coffee?"

"Theater, just theater," Ray answered.

"You didn't taste it?"

Ray shook his head from side to side, signaling his answer.

34

〰

Emily Larson filled a mug of coffee before joining Sue at the conference table.

"You saw my memo?" said Larson.

"No, I haven't gotten to it yet," Sue replied, opening her laptop.

"The lab did identify the material used in the explosive, a compound called flash powder," explained Larson.

"How is that different from gunpowder?" asked Sue.

"It's the kind of explosive found in pyrotechnics, meaning commercial fireworks," Larson said. She observed her younger colleague. The woman looked exhausted and anxious.

"You can buy that online?"

"I think it's getting harder to find. But you can also fabricate it from easily obtainable materials. And if that's too heavy a lift, you can buy a bunch of fireworks and drain the powder out of them. The actual construction of the device used in this case is relatively simple. You can get anything you need with Google. Ain't technology grand?" Larson changed tacks.

"How's the sheriff?" she asked.

"Ray? He had a good night. His CT results are satisfactory, and he was discharged this morning. The neurologist recommended several days of bed rest. I knew that wouldn't happen, so I assigned Barbara Sinclair as his driver and companion. She's intelligent and insightful. She'll get him back to the medical center fast if need be."

"And how are you doing today?"

"Okay," Sue said, her tone mechanical and without affect.

"Did you get any sleep?"

She exhaled sharply. "It was one of those nights. We're

understaffed. There was a multi-vehicle accident sometime after midnight. Ray usually does these middle-of-the-night runs when extra officers are needed for, in this case, a couple in their 80s T-boned by a drunk."

"Did you get any sleep?"

"Three or four hours before the call from dispatch. When I returned home, I tried but was totally wired by then. The couple had to be cut out of their car. It didn't look like they would make it, especially the woman…" Sue's voice faded.

"And you've got a lot more than that on your plate," said Larson, encouraging Sue to vent.

"Yes, this murder investigation. I want to get justice for this kid." Her voice cracked.

"And then the man you love almost got killed." Larson studied Sue's face. Her lower lip trembled almost imperceptibly.

"One of the things I learned during the bad days in Baltimore is that we women don't have to be one of the guys keeping it all in or finding relief in a bottle."

"What do you do?"

"Sometimes I have a good cry. Sometimes, I go to the gym and beat the crap out of a heavy bag. I also have one tough therapist. I don't see her regularly anymore but I can Zoom with her when needed. And then there's yoga, running, or bicycling with friends. Did I mention reading a sizzling romance?" Larson stood. "Let's go outside and have a smoke."

"I've never smoked," said Sue.

"Me, either. That's got nothing to do with it. You go outside, walk around for a few, yell and scream if you need to, say *fuck* or *fuck it* a couple of times and come back in feeling better. And we can talk as we walk but don't have to."

It took a few minutes for their eyes to adjust to the bright summer sun as they walked away from the building. Larson set a brisk pace and sensed the tension in Sue's body easing a bit.

At the top loop of the empty lot—an overflow area parking

area—Sue asked, "What's our chance of finding anything that might…?"

"Well, so far, we've got no fingerprints, DNA, or sticker on the gas can that might lead us to Bob's Hardware and the guy that bought it," Larson said. "Now, if you find where the bomb was constructed—some basement, barn, pole budding—we could connect the material collected at the scene and the things on the guy's workbench. Unfortunately, there's no roadmap from the bits back to the perp. Do you have a team working the trails that might have been used to access the scene?"

"Yes, a couple of our officers, our summer interns, and a conservation officer. They've been at it since early this morning."

"No doorbell or trail cams?"

"I wish," said Sue.

"Too bad. Back in Philly, in the city and burbs, the hood, too, everything is videoed up. One thing you know is that the perp or perps in this case are familiar with the area. They also have access to an M15, which brings the number of suspects down to five or ten million Americans." Larson chuckled. "Now, if you can come up with a motive. How about Gill? How much do you know about him?"

"Not much," answered Sue. "Ex-military, retired, married, excellent recommendations. We were happy to get someone with his background and experience."

"So there's probably nothing there. But we need to know if there's someone out there with a motive to injure or kill Gill. You know, love life complication, or someone he's arrested or sent to prison, or something from a past life. I don't know how much time you should spend on that, but it's gotta be looked at." Larson's pace slowed a bit. "The same thing goes for the sheriff."

Then she picked up her cadence again. "I'm just ticking off the boxes. And I don't pretend to have the world's greatest shit detector, but this is the situation here; it's ringing loud and clear. I mean," Larson stopped and turned to face Sue, "if they wanted to off someone, it would have been an easy lift. But no, we've got a carefully planned and executed stunt. It's a piece of theater. Could this be a game some reasonably bright kids are playing? It's kind of like a video game without a good soundtrack."

"Have you ever seen anything like this before?" asked Sue.

"No, never. That's why it strikes me as theater. There's no blood on the ground—well, not much, anyway. If there's another bombing or suspicious fire, I'll get up here right away. And I'll give you the contact info for my therapist. She does cops and military. Like I said, Zoom. Women, strong women who need someone solid to talk to."

35

The waiter balanced the tray on the corner of the table as Amanda Slosson served the meals.

"For Ray, roasted tofu on a sourdough bun, a side of kimchee slaw, and green iced tea with one slice of lemon and one of lime. For Ms. Sinclair, a salmon croquette on a whole-wheat bun, green salad with gorgonzola dressing on the side, and a Diet Coke."

Slosson grabbed the last plate with a burger and fries and slid into the booth next to Sinclair.

"Anything else?" asked the waiter, a skinny teen, as he set an iced tea and two packages of sweetener in front of Amanda Slosson.

"No. Thank you, Tyler."

As he retreated, she said, "Nice kid. Good worker. He's been with us for three years. He is heading east to college. We'll probably not see him next year." After a bite of her burger, she continued, "Finding workers, good ones especially, it's just getting harder."

"The sheriff's tofu sandwich, part of your regular menu?" asked Sinclair.

"It is now. The first time Ray ordered it last summer, I had to steal some from my daughter's private stash of tofu. Olivia's the one who showed our cook how to prepare it. Now, it's become a regular item. Ray was always an early adopter, even in high school. The kimchee coleslaw is an Olivia-influenced addition to the menu, too. She says we have to do more with fermented foods. And to tell you the truth, it's the summer's big hit."

"Amanda," said Ray, looking around the room, "you've added security cameras."

She nodded a bit sheepishly. "Yes. When you talked about it,

I said it was something I'd never do. Then, I made a 180-degree course correction. First, you mention it. I told Olivia about our conversation. She said it must be a generation thing. It was time I got with the program, whatever that means. She pointed out how much more we might have learned about Tammy and that guy if we had video.

"She made a compelling case, telling me they're all over Ann Arbor. And after she converted me, Olivia did everything: found a contractor, got the cameras installed, the whole nine yards."

"So you find them intrusive?" asked Ray.

"Well, the first few days. Then it occurred to me that everyone here has eyes; they're checking things out. And with their phones, they often shoot photos and videos. I got over it."

She dipped a fry in ranch dressing, ate it, and then asked, "Is there anything new you can share with me?"

"The investigation is active," Ray said. "We are hopeful. But at this time, there have been no breakthroughs. Any chance you've heard anything new or remembered something you haven't shared with us yet?"

"Ray, I would have called you immediately if there had been. Just after Tammy's murder, that's all the kids could talk about. It was 'What should we have noticed?' and 'We should have protected her!' Then they just ran out of steam. You know, you pursue something hard, trying to fix it, and finally, it just hits you that you can't change the past. That's where they are. Me, too, I guess. For most of these kids, summers are magical, with new friends and, often, romances. Not this summer. Not for any of us."

"Amanda, we're not giving up," said Ray. "We're working with other police agencies. We are hoping for that breakthrough."

Slosson looked at Barbara Sinclair. "This guy," she said, pointing at Ray, "when he says something like that, I know he is not just playing 'Misty' for me. I've known him since eighth grade. He was always a worker and a leader."

Ray pointed toward the main entrance. "Like most area businesses, you still have a 'Help Wanted' sign up."

"Yeah, it's a struggle. I need the kids—bussers, servers, dishwashers. It was difficult before the pandemic. It seems impossible now. Fewer teens are in the pool, and the children of former summer staff are off to hockey camp, football camp, or doing something to improve their SATs, GREs, or MCAPs. Our usual pool of high school and college kids no longer have summers. And then there's poaching."

"Poaching?" said Sinclair.

"Yeah, seasonal businesses, but mostly restaurants, some, not all, trying to lure away employees. I'm paying more than McDonald's. Memorial Day to Labor Day employees get an extra $500 in their last check. I haven't had many kids poached this year, but there have been a few."

"How does that kind of thing work?" asked Ray.

"I don't know for sure. I see the results. Maybe a former employee reaches out to friends, or someone comes in and looks for especially good people. All I do know is that it makes things harder for me. And I know where many of them have ended up."

"Where?"

"The big-money woman at that bespoke joint, Heirloom Foods North. She's lured away some of my best people."

"You're talking about Victoria Wainwright?"

"Yes, that's the one. I don't know if she does it personally or sends someone around. But that's where some of my people have ended up."

"Have you met her?" asked Ray.

"No, just read about her. And in this trade, she's all the talk. But it's not that anyone knows her. At least no one I know."

"She summered here growing up. Her parents had a cottage up on the Cove," said Ray.

"That's what I hear. But no one seems to know her. The summer people, they're here and gone. They dwell on a different planet." Amanda looked around the crowded restaurant, then back toward Ray. "Got to get back to the fray. You will keep me in the loop as much as you can?"

"Yes," he responded as they gently bumped fists.

In the car, Sinclair asked, "What was Amanda Slosson like in high school?"

"Not much different than who she is now," he answered. "She was one of the girls that excelled at everything. Most of us guys couldn't match up. On average, the girls were better students. They did homework, excelled in English, took foreign languages, and usually set the curve in physics and chemistry. I wouldn't have admitted it then, but most girls were much more mature than we were."

"Sounds like you had a crush on her."

"I was intimidated by her. She was my lab partner in chemistry. I was better at the math, but she put in the time. She always earned a higher grade. She always dated older guys; by junior or senior year, she was dating college men."

Sinclair's laughter filled the car.

"What's so funny?" asked Ray.

"When I think about you and high school, it's ancient times, right, like my parents? But dating older guys… Who'd want to date some high school Harry when you can go out with a college man? I guess things haven't changed that much."

After pulling her seatbelt on and starting the engine, Sinclair asked, "Should I drop you home so you can nap?"

"Let's check on the alleged staff poacher, Victoria Wainwright. She emailed me about some new vandalism."

36

~

"Full parking lot," Ray observed. "Looks like the business has quickly caught on."

"Lots of out-of-state plates. The tourists have found this place," observed Sinclair. "Want me to drop you near the entrance?"

"No, continue down to the far end. I need to walk, and I want to look around. When I was last here, I suggested Wainwright install security cameras. I'm curious as to whether or not she's done that."

As they walked from their distant parking spot to the main entrance, Sinclair said, "This place is jammed. I'm impressed. It's at the county's northern tip on a road that comes to a dead end in less than a mile."

"Wainwright's a tech industry veteran," said Ray. "She's probably a master at advertising and social media. If not, she has the knowledge and money to hire people who are." He stopped and turned in her direction. "There is one more thing I've never quite figured out. These tourists have miles of beautiful beaches, dunes, and paths through the forests available to them, and what do they do? They drive hundreds of miles to shop in crowded stores, wineries, breweries, and distilleries. Did I forget to mention fudge shops? But I guess it works out. They keep our economy afloat."

They stopped at a small park across the drive from the barn complex. At the center of the verdant area, a lush flower garden encircled a sculpture: a peace pole—skeletal rather than the usual wood four-by-four post. Instead, five weathered copper beams supported five brass panels. The message *May Peace Prevail on Earth*, in English and four other languages, was laser-cut through the sheets of brass. The sculpture was mounted in a small pool with a terraced waterfall that provided a gurgling sound barely audible above the road noise.

"This wasn't here on my last visit," Ray said. "It sets a tone."

"It's lovely," said Sinclair. "Looks like she also knows how to hire landscape designers and gardeners, in addition to tech people."

They walked across the drive and through the vast, tall barn doors into the brightly lit interior, where artistic merchandise displays provided a panoply of color and texture. The air was redolent with the scent of baked goods emerging from an oven.

"What do you think?" asked Ray as they stood taking in the scene.

"This place is incredible," Barbara responded, adding, "When my mother comes to visit, this will be high on the list. She'd take this over a beach any day."

"Can I help you find something?" asked a young woman in navy shorts and a light blue polo.

Ray peered at the woman's picture ID. "Tess, we're here to see Ms. Wainwright."

"She's expecting you?"

"Yes, I messaged her." Ray showed her his picture ID. "Ms. Wainwright said she'd be available."

Tess guided them through the sales floor and back toward the office area, finally stopping at the end of a long hallway.

She knocked, entered, said a few words, and then opened the door wide, allowing Ray and Sinclair to move into the room.

"Sheriff, nice to see you again," said Victoria Wainwright, standing and moving around her desk, hand extended.

"This is Barbara Sinclair, one of our newer department members and our technology guru."

"Yes," said Wainwright, "and the intended recipient of that basket of goodies you returned to me."

Wainwright held Ray's hand briefly, then clasped Sinclair's with two hands.

Then, pointing, she said, "Please, have a seat. Can I get you anything? Coffee? Something cold?"

"Thank you, no," answered Ray.

"I'm good," said Sinclair.

"You mentioned some new vandalism in your message," said Ray. "What's happened now?"

"The flags. You may have noticed them coming in. Over the main door, I display the US flag, the Michigan flag, and the flags of our neighbors, Canada and Mexico. And in our peace garden, I had a rainbow flag. Last night or early this morning, someone pulled the rainbow flag off the pole and set it on fire in the road."

Ray said, "We came that way. I didn't notice—"

"Good, I had our cleanup crew on it as soon as I heard. I wanted things back in order by opening. So there's that incident, and then there's this." She opened a drawer and set a crumpled piece of paper on the desk, smoothing it with two hands and then passing it in Ray's direction.

Ray held up his hand to stop her. "Is this possible evidence?"

"It came in the morning mail, but there's no stamp. So it's not something the mailman brought. I read it. I passed it around to some of my employees to read. If it's evidence, it's badly corrupted. But here—" She reached into another drawer and tossed a box of rubber gloves onto the desk.

Ray put on gloves and read the letter, while Sinclair also put on a pair. When he had finished, Ray passed the letter to Sinclair.

"I don't mean to make light of this," Ray said, "but you are the devil incarnate to this writer."

"Yes, I've opened the southern border to rapists and drug smugglers. I've stolen jobs from my neighbors and given them to illegals. I've created a business that promotes alternative lifestyles, promiscuity, and grooming of young children. They forgot to mention that some of my employees by night are probably drag queens." She sighed. "Look, it's all laughable, untrue, and yet, it's very frightening to receive something like this."

Ray nodded his agreement. "It's frightening."

"So, how do I get beyond this craziness?" Wainwright asked. "We sell organic vegetables and fruit and bake wonderful ginger-and-molasses cookies. This is all so wild I don't know how to respond. Should I disregard it?"

Ray pondered the question before answering. "No. This is the work of someone who has a distorted view of reality. But you can't dismiss it, because some people following these false beliefs—not many, but some—do go on to commit acts of violence. And it's hard to protect you from random events. However, if we can find out who's responsible…"

"Sheriff, may I call you by your first name?" Wainwright asked. "Everyone in the county seems to call you Ray."

Ray nodded.

"Please call me Victoria. Are you going to offer your security camera solution again?"

"Yes. If we had a video from the front of your building, maybe we could make an arrest and bring this to an end. The vandals know there aren't any security cameras. That's the first thing they scoped out. And they probably know there's only one road patrol officer at this end of the county from eleven to seven. So they know the chances of being caught aren't very high. Security cameras might help eliminate the problem by scaring them away or helping to identify them."

"Cameras, that's not the message I want to send. My customers are up north, away from the intrusions of modern technology." She gripped the edge of her desk. "This has been an orchard for more than a hundred years. The old-time varieties of apples were maintained here. I want to protect them. I've added heirloom vegetables and other produce, all organic. Our bread and cheese are made the old way. I'm trying to preserve things lost in the industrial age—taste, texture, color, and smell. And I'm trying to recapture a way of doing business and treating customers as friends.

"I don't want customers staring at cameras. I don't want my employees to feel like they're being spied on. I want this place to reflect the qualities of an earlier time."

Ray nodded. "I understand that. I respect what you're saying." He held back, not mentioning that most of her customers were carrying smartphones, and many would be staring at a screen, messaging, talking on the phone, or recording video as they wandered through the store.

"Then what's the problem?" she asked.

Ray put his hand out in Sinclair's direction. She passed him the letter.

"Victoria, look at this letter. Consider the other threatening letters you've received. You can't dismiss the content. Yes, it's ridiculous, over-the-top, sheer lunacy. But, unfortunately, there's someone out there writing these things, and they probably believe what they're writing to be true. The anger and hatred in this," he waved the letter in the air, "is palpable."

Ray leaned forward and set the letter on the desk. "This year, we're averaging more than one mass shooting daily in this country. It's wild. There are so many guns out there. Might the writer of this letter pick up a gun and, to their distorted way of thinking, try to make the world better by shooting up this place? What would happen to your customers then? Isn't it in their best interest to protect what you've built here?"

Wainwright went quiet. She stared at the letter. Then she finally looked up at Ray. "I don't know."

"By installing cameras, you'd protect your customers, employees, property, and the trees in your orchard." Ray looked over at Sinclair.

"Security cameras are becoming increasingly small and unobtrusive. With judicious placement, your customers won't notice them," said Sinclair.

"How about the exterior?"

"Then you want the camera noticed. They deter vandals and thieves and provide customers with a sense of security that they and their vehicles are being protected," added Ray.

"You both make a compelling case, but I need time to consider this." She rose from her desk. "I'll be in touch."

As they waited at a stop sign for the highway to clear, Sinclair asked, "Do you think she'll get the security cameras?"

"I don't know," said Ray. "Initially, I wasn't keen on many of these new technologies, either. But I've had to change my thinking. And I don't think it's only about the technology. Maybe it's just those of us of a certain age pushing back at how fast everything changes. We're trying to hold on to a world that's already disappeared."

He remained lost in thought until Sinclair turned onto the highway. Then he said, "Every night before I fall asleep, I wonder what tomorrow will bring. Will it happen here? The possible scenarios flash through my mind: schools, churches, concerts, weddings, a beach crowded with vacationers. And it's the easy availability of guns, especially assault rifles, and so many people with…" Ray got lost in his thoughts for a long moment. "It's so complex; I don't even know how to think about it."

"I hear you," Sinclair said, thinking she could hardly close her eyes without replaying the nightmare scenario—the beach scene and the bodies cold to the touch. The vision still raw and unabating.

37

It was still early morning when Ray rolled slowly into North Bay, a village nestled along Lake Michigan on the east side of Cedar County. The two-block-long business district, with most of the buildings dating from the late nineteenth century, was still quiet. In a few hours, the sidewalks would be jammed with shoppers, primarily tourists, an economic lifeline in the region.

Sue was already at the scene when Ray arrived. Her SOC truck sat curbside at the front of North Bay Pages. The parking lane and sidewalk were closed along the rest of the block. Ray left his car on the opposite side of the road and stood taking in the scene before crossing.

The store was housed in a century-old building. The large windows at each side of the entrance were missing. Shards of antique glass covered the sidewalk and the deeply worn cut-stone steps leading up to the door.

The bookseller, Phillip Noble, dressed in faded jeans, a T-shirt, and sneakers, was holding onto a broom with one hand and running his other hand through a mop of gray hair while talking with a man just outside the tape. Noble looked in Ray's direction.

"Why?" he asked, despair in his voice.

Ray shook his head in sympathy. "I don't know," he answered. But he was thinking that someone's intolerance was overflowing its container. Was it the same perp or perps responsible for the vandalism at Heirloom Foods North? Or was this someone else with cult-like beliefs who acted out their anger with violence?

"I had a display of banned books in the window, a pile of the most innocuous books I could think of—*Romeo and Juliet*, *The*

Scarlet Letter; Anne Frank: The Diary of a Young Girl; Animal Farm; Of Mice and Men; A Separate Peace; Charlotte's Web; Where the Wild Things Are; Twelfth Night; Tarzan of the Apes…"

"*Tarzan?*" asked Ray.

"Half-dressed people swinging from tree to tree. And Tarzan and Jane, are they properly married or living in sin in a jungle hideaway? Will kids grow up wanting to emulate this alternative lifestyle? And Cheetah… Don't even go there." Noble tried to smile but only grimaced. "I was so careful, Ray. And you know this little store better than most. My stock reflects what sells in this community and what the summer people want to read. What triggered this? The display of banned books? And I'm probably closed for a few days at the height of the season."

"So you think the banned book display was the target of the vandalism?" said Ray.

"What else could it be? The table itself and all the books on it have been destroyed. I just put a few books there with a little handwritten sign," Phillip explained, "and as customers wandered around the store, they started suggesting other titles—books that had been banned over many years. It became sort of a game. Lots of laughter and good conversation. It's the kind of interaction that makes a small bookstore fun. People wanted to share stories about how they grew up and how certain books expanded their worldview."

He emptied a dustpan filled with bits of broken glass into a metal wastebasket. "Ray," he said, "it's a minefield these days. And I don't understand what's happening. It's since COVID. And it's not our regulars like you. They are people I've never seen before. They walk in angry. I don't think they're even looking for a book."

Given the unspooling conversation, Ray knew Noble would have more to say. He nodded and listened.

"I can see it when they come through the door." Noble pointed toward the framing on the transom window holding the brass bell. "Even the bell sounds different. I mean, that bell is karma-sensitive. These people are angry when they come through the door. I don't stock much of a political nature; it's a niche market. They'll demand a title I don't stock. I explain that I carry limited inventory. Sometimes they say, 'You are one of those,' and stomp out. The flip side is when they find a title that's made it to one of the woke banned books lists, they become loud and argumentative. The real customers quickly exit."

He motioned Ray toward the door. "The rainbow flag was here, on the outside. Now it's inside. They tossed it in after they smashed the windows."

Ray followed Noble into the store.

"What have we got?" he asked Sue.

"Two cement blocks, two windows. One of the blocks crushed the table, too."

"It was a bit rickety," Noble explained. "Came with the building. But it was good enough to hold a stack of books safely."

"You can see," Sue said to Ray, "old concrete blocks, paint on one side."

Ray pointed to a camera on the ceiling. "Can we look at your surveillance video?"

The bookseller looked surprised by Ray's question. He stammered a bit. "Oh, yes, the cameras."

"The video from the cameras," said Ray. "Is there a problem?"

"Yes, well. They're not working."

Ray gave him a questioning look.

"Well, you know, I was having some shrinkage, and I read in one of the trade journals about cameras, even fake cameras being a low-cost deterrent. And they have been. They've helped, I think. I got a four-pack online for thirty bucks from Amazon." Phillip looked abashed about admitting to the source.

"So you have no actual working cameras?"

"Well… no. Putting in a proper security system was just too dear. But everyone else up and down the street has cameras everywhere."

"I'll have an officer canvas the area and collect video," said Sue, looking at Ray.

"And the rainbow flag," he said, pointing.

"I'll bag it and check for prints," said Sue. "I'll take the blocks, too. We might be able to find the source."

"The rainbow flag," said Ray, "any negative feedback on that before?"

"No, at least not overtly. This is a village bookstore. I've tried to make it inclusive and welcoming—something for everyone: children's and teen's books, NYT bestsellers, beach reads, some poetry…"

Noble stopped and looked around the interior of the store. "This is what I've been thinking. It's about books. It's about print. It's about the ideas books contain. And these angry people don't know books. Their reality is infused with fantastical echo chamber narratives. They look at books, bookstores, libraries, and even schools as the purveyors of God knows what. All these printed words are a secret code of the deep state propaganda. And the people who read books are a dangerous fifth column."

Ray reflected on Noble's comment before redirecting the conversation. "How about the windows? Do you have a repair plan? Will your insurance cover the cost?"

"Just talked to my neighbor. He's a contractor. His crew will be here sometime this morning with plywood to cover the windows. Then, we'll figure out what to do next. I haven't been able to reach my insurance company yet."

"Phillip, we'll make every effort to find who did this. In the meantime, let me know if you hear anything useful to our investigation. And you know, I'm available if you have questions."

"Thanks, Ray. And thanks for your business over the years. You're one of the many people that keeps this store afloat in the winter."

38

*A*nother Day in Paradise! was scribbled across the whiteboard at the front of the conference room.

"What wag's responsible for that," said Ray, pointing.

Sinclair shrugged. "Maybe one of the interns," she suggested.

"Or your secretary," offered Sue.

"Impossible," Ray said. "Her handwriting is better than that. Old school. Palmer Method." He turned to Sinclair. "Any luck with the video?"

"I got some from the BP station and two doorbell cams—4:26 coming, 4:29 going. The suspect vehicle used in the incident is a black Chevy Silverado pickup, the 1998 to 2006 generation, with an extended cab and standard bed. The cab and bed are just guesses on my part, based on what I found on the web. The truck also appears on the security footage from the camera on the front of the high school, both coming and going. The truck entered and left the village on Ridge Road. The headlights were turned off briefly as the vehicle approached and fled the scene. As the truck headed south on Ridge, the headlights were back on."

"Visible plate?" asked Ray.

"No plate light, as you will see. Probably no plate."

"Any distinguishing features?" asked Brett Carty.

"The front of the truck has those extra pieces of steel tubing, as you'll see in the video. I think they're called bull bars. A macho thing?"

"Yeah," said Carty. "Big pickup, extra steel at the front, intimidating. And loud exhausts, too, I bet."

"Bingo. Yes. I've assembled the video showing the truck arriving and departing. Unfortunately, there is no video of the actual vandalism, but you will be able to hear the breaking glass. The first crash quickly followed the second. Everyone ready?"

Sinclair glanced at her audience and then started the video. A truck moved from left to right as it passed the camera in front of the school. The left brake light flashed, but the right one remained dark as the vehicle turned toward the lake. The rumble from the exhaust pipes increased as the truck accelerated down the hill.

Sinclair stopped the video. "Notice here the headlights are switched off before the truck turns onto Harbor View. After it turns, the video sections are from the doorbell cam at the funeral home, then the gas station, and finally, another doorbell cam." She keyed the video back on, and images flashed across the big screen, in and out of focus: the rattle of the exhaust rising and falling, an empty road, an explosive thud, then a second, then the roar of the engine, squealing tires, and images of the fleeing truck.

Sinclair waited until the truck's rumble had receded. The sound of crickets once more filled the audio track.

"Anything you want to see again?"

"Where was the sector officer at that time?" Ray asked.

"Medical emergency," answered Carty.

"Where?"

"At the south end, just inside the county line. It took the first available officer twenty minutes to get to the bookstore."

"Who called it in?" asked Ray.

"Some people living in an upstairs apartment across the road from the bookstore," answered Sinclair. "The sound of breaking glass and squealing tires awakened them. They thought it was a traffic accident."

"You talked with them?" asked Ray.

"Yes, a young couple. They told me it was over when they got to a window, but the damage was obvious."

Ray stretched, his hands over his head, fingers briefly locked together. "The hills are alive with dead and dying Silverados and Sierras from that era."

"Probably not an everyday driver," added Sue. "Just something kept stashed in the barn for special occasions. And who knows where. It could have disappeared over the county line quickly."

"The cement blocks and the flagpole," said Ray, looking toward Sue.

"The only prints I could find on the flagpole were Phillip Noble's. And no prints, soil, or anything remarkable about the blocks other than mold and mildew. They've been around a while, probably from a demolished building. I'm sending them to the State Police Lab. Maybe they can work a miracle."

"The video was skillful, Barbara. I've never seen that done so well," said Ray. "So, what do we have?"

"Well," said Brett, "based on the video, a ratty-assed black Chevy pickup with one working brake light, the left one, rolls into town and stops in front of the bookstore. The driver and a passenger leap from the truck and grab cement blocks from the truck's bed. Using two-handed overhead tosses, they hurl the blocks through the store windows. Back in the truck, they retrace their route out of town. We're looking for two guys with a lot of upper body strength."

"So we have vehicle type, the bull bars, and one nonfunctioning brake light. Anything else?" asked Ray. "Bumper stickers, noticeable damage to the truck body?"

"Nothing I could see," Sinclair said. "The lighting along the route is widely spaced and fairly limited. And the quality of much of the video is poor. I've created a folder with the videos in the incident file. I tried to capture the truck from different angles. Other eyes need to look through those. I might have missed something."

"Where should we go with this?" asked Ray, looking toward Sue.

"I'll get a listing of all the vehicles registered that fit this description, starting with this county. Working through that will take time. With Barbara's help, we'll put photos on our Community Crime Stoppers website and social media. But we all know there are lots of trucks out there fitting that description. Maybe we'll get lucky."

"Anything new on the Ogden case?" Ray asked.

"Messaged with my friend at the Bureau," Sue said. "He thinks our John Doe may be linked to an Eastern European gang operating out of Antwerp. This is based on some old CCTV footage."

"Does that help us?"

"Not yet. They're testing with some new AI technology to help track the operations of crime syndicates across Europe and North America. Maybe they can tell us what our John Doe was doing here."

"Moving on," said Ray. "Looking over the activity log for the last twenty-four hours, we've been stretched almost to our limits. Brett?"

"Yeah, the road patrol is maxed. For the immediate future, we've lost Stan Gill. When he will return is up in the air. We have one officer down with COVID-19—so much for it being over. We usually need a lot of overtime during the summer to cover all the shifts and handle the additional workload. It's much worse this summer, and we don't have the people."

"I hear you," Ray responded.

"Heirloom Foods North, Victoria Wainwright, any calls or reports last night?" asked Ray.

"No," Brett responded. "Do you think the rainbow flag incidents are related?"

"I don't know," Ray answered. "For the most part, up to now, we've been spared from hate crimes. It would only take one or two actors to change that."

Ray stood and looked at Carty, Sinclair, and Sue in turn. "Try to get some rest. Tomorrow will probably be another challenging day."

39

Before starting her drive home, Barbara Sinclair stood outside her patrol car stretching, using the inside edge of the open door for support—first, torso rotations, then neck rolls.

Brett Carty came out of the building and approached her car. "How about a cruise on the big lake?" he asked.

"Um," Barbara said, feeling slightly off balance at the invitation. "I thought I'd just go home and make dinner—a big salad and some good bread. Then I thought I'd take a leisurely bath, followed by a quiet evening lost in a good book. I'm reading Viktor Frankl's *Man's Search for Meaning*." It was only then that she saw the adrenaline in Brett's attitude. This wasn't about spending time together after work. "Oh, wait. What's going on?"

"I just got a call about a lost kayaker, a man in his 70s. A Park Service boat and us. The Coast Guard won't have a chopper available for several hours. Maybe not before sunset. I'd like to have a second person on board, another set of eyes."

Barbara wanted to avoid going on the call, even with Brett. She wanted to go home. "Maybe next time," she said. "Give someone else the opportunity. How about one of the interns?"

"No one's available."

"Is it going to be rough?" she asked, pointing toward nearby trees dancing in the gusty winds.

He looked at the trees, then back at her. "I don't deny. It's starting to blow. But there's no one else," he repeated.

She sighed. Rough water frightened her. She felt her body tense, and her resentment was mixed in with it. "Okay," she finally said. "If there's no one else."

"You can ride to the harbor with me," Brett offered.

"I'll follow you," she answered, "so I'll have a car if I choose to bail if it looks too stormy."

Once onboard, Brett passed her an oversized waterproof jacket and a PFD. "It's going to be bumpy. This will protect you from the spray."

As he hurriedly ran through a prelaunch checklist, Barbara stood near the stern, looking at the conditions beyond the harbor. The gusty southwest winds were propelling tall wave sets interspersed by smaller swells. The still water of the marina was in sharp contrast to the pounding surf crashing over the Brobdingnagian seawalls surrounding the harbor. As Brett started to back the patrol boat out of its slip, Barbara mounted the chair at his left, fastened the seatbelt, and pulled on a headset. She checked to see that her motion sickness bands were positioned correctly on her wrists.

"What am I looking for?" she asked.

"A bright yellow sea kayak or someone in the surf or on the beach."

Brett paused near the harbor entrance, exchanging information on the marine radio—messages stripped of the nonessentials of everyday conversation. He pushed throttles forward and crashed into the turbulent waters. Barbara grabbed and tightly gripped the handles at the side of her chair.

Once clear of the harbor, Brett turned south toward the search area. He pushed the throttles forward again, bringing the hull to planing speed. Barbara relaxed as the ride smoothed a bit. She focused on the horizon as she had learned to do when Brett had once taken her out on a training mission. Her queasiness lessened as they headed toward the search area.

Holding onto the wheel with one hand, Brett pointed to an area on the large digital map at the center of the dash. "That's where we're heading," his words crisp in her headphones. He moved his index up along the coastline. "If the kayaker was riding the following waves, he might be in this area. He could have covered a lot of distance. He could be along here if he paddled into the wind and went to shore for protection. If he capsized, it depends on where and when. And if he got separated from his boat…" He didn't need to finish his sentence.

Brett slowed slightly as they approached the search area but maintained planing speed. He piloted the boat parallel to the shoreline, about a hundred yards from shore.

"Focus on both the surf zone and the shore. He'd probably pull his boat high on the beach if he landed in this area. If the kayak ended up in the surf, it'll be hard for you to spot."

Barbara followed Brett's directions—the surf zone, shoreline, beach, and dunes beyond. She could feel Brett adjusting the speed and direction of the boat.

Barbara scanned the area, looking for a flash of color or texture that differed from the unvarying tones of the water and beach, her concentration occasionally interrupted by a sudden bounce as the boat climbed a steep crest or dropped into a deep swell.

First, she noted a bit of color, just a flash in the surf. Then it was gone. A few seconds later, she saw it a second time, not a distinguishable form, just a bit of yellow in the surf. Seeing it a third time, she punched Brett's shoulder and directed his attention to the area.

"I see it," he said, turning toward the object as he pulled back on the throttles. Once abeam, the boat pitched from side to side in the rough water as he slowly approached the object.

"It's a kayak, but just an end." Brett killed the engines and tilted them out of the water, allowing the patrol boat to float toward the shore. A large swell lifted and propelled it forward, and the bow came to rest on the beach.

Then Brett was over the side, dragging the kayak through the surf up beyond the reach of the waves, rolling its cockpit down to drain.

Barbara climbed out of the patrol boat, dropped to the beach, and came to Brett's side.

He pointed to the personal flotation device—PFD—firmly

attached to the boat just behind the cockpit. "This didn't do him much good. I'll take some pictures of this and send them to dispatch."

Brett climbed back on the boat. She could hear bits of his conversation on the marine band radio. Then he was back at her side.

"What's the plan?" asked Barbara.

"We should search the immediate area to see if he made it to shore and sought cover away from the wind. Let's go about ten minutes in each direction."

He put a hand on her shoulder. "North or south?"

"I'll take south so I can have the wind pushing me back this way," Barbara replied.

As she walked south, Barbara pulled the windbreaker off briefly, carrying it over her shoulder with her thumb hooked inside the hood. Climbing to the high water point, she marched south, checking the beach, the water just beyond, and the rolling terrain that extended away from the shore. As she walked, she felt less hopeful about finding the kayaker. Looking out at the rough water, she sensed the overwhelming power of the big lake. She stopped and peered at the rolling surf, then held steady on the beach. Taking time to focus on her breath, she pushed back at the gloom, knowing the outcome of this search. This feeling of hopelessness was amplified by the number of open cases the department was confronting.

Feeling suddenly chilled, Barbara pulled her windbreaker back on and keyed her phone. "Brett, ten minutes out and nothing. Do you want me to start back or give it a few more?"

"Give it another ten. By then, you'll start seeing cottages. Start back as soon as you reach them."

Barbara turned after reaching the small group of dwellings. She slowly trekked north, the boat finally coming into view. And then Brett appeared, a distant shadow becoming a distinguishable figure as the light faded.

"We did what we could," said Brett.

It didn't seem like enough. "What about the kayak?" Barbara asked.

"We'll leave it here. I've already called in the location. The Park Service will pick it up later." Brett moved close and gently pulled her into his arms. "Not what we hoped for. Thank you for coming with me."

They clambered back into the patrol boat. Brett dug around in his pack.

"Want an energy bar?" he asked. "It's chocolate mint."

"What do I have to do for it?" Barbara teased, breaking through her sadness. "Go on another call tonight before I can go home?"

"No, not at all," Brett said, placing the package in her extended hand, which he grasped in the process and held briefly.

"Can I buy you dinner?" he asked as they were mooring the boat.

"It's been a long day. I need a very long hot shower and some clean clothes."

"How about this? You head home and do what you need to do, and I'll sit here and type up the incident. I'm sure Ray wants to know what's happening. Then I'll pick up some pizza and salad and drop by your place."

"Sounds like a plan," agreed Barbara, but she was feeling a bit ambivalent. She was tired, emotionally drained by the unsuccessful search, and uncertain of where her relationship with Brett was heading.

"What kind of pizza?"

"From Tuscany North. They're New York style. Thin crust, sauce, and cheese. Well roasted, if you know what I mean. And their Greek salad, with the dressing on the side. And I'll pay."

"How about we split it?"

"That will work."

40

Barbara was out of the shower, dressed in sweats with a towel wrapped around her still-wet hair, when Brett arrived with pizza, salad, and beer. As he set the box on the table, he announced, "New York Style, just what the woman ordered. Just sauce and cheese, medium to a shade well scorched. No meat, no veggies, and especially, no pineapple. Feeling better?" he asked.

"I needed that shower. I couldn't get warm. How can you get so cold in 80-degree weather?"

"It's always cold on the lake. Even in the summer, the water temp never climbs out of the sixties. So it may be in the high eighties inland, but if you're out on the water or the beaches, you can get chilled, especially when there's a stiff breeze." Brett opened two beers and passed one in her direction.

"Any news since I left you?" Barbara asked.

"The Coast Guard did one pass over the area in near-darkness. The search will resume in the morning. Sue visited the family. The man's wife said he intended to kayak out to the Crib and back. That was his usual paddle. She watched him launch. The lake was flat. She went to Traverse for a doctor's appointment and some shopping. When she came home, the whitecaps were crashing into the shore, and there was no kayak on the beach or visible on the water. After a brief search, she called 9-1-1. Their children are driving up from downstate. Sue said they were preparing for the worst."

Brett's last comment added to her sadness. Trying to move beyond that, she asked, "The Crib?"

"That's the lighthouse in the middle of the passage, about four miles out from the mainland on the western edge of the shipping channel. A shoal extends out from the north island to the lighthouse."

The conversation fell into a lull as they attacked the food. Finally, Barbara said, "I'm sorry we couldn't rescue him, but I'm also glad we didn't find a body."

"Understood," said Brett. After opening another beer and passing it in her direction, he asked, "Do you mind if I ask how the therapy's going?"

Barbara took a bite of salad to avoid having to respond immediately. Finally, she said, "The therapist, I like her. She listens carefully, and it's right on the mark when she occasionally says something."

"Yes, I've only heard good things about her. But is the therapy helping?"

"I think so. I won't ever be able to erase the memory of finding those two bodies. I wasn't prepared. Confronting violence and death were subjects that some of my classes touched on, but the difference between a… theoretical discussion and the reality…"

Brett allowed the silence to hang in the air.

"The therapist is the one who gave me the copy of *Man's Search for Meaning*," Barbara said. "Do you know it?"

"Yeah, it was an assigned read in an Intro to Philosophy class, maybe my sophomore year. All that ontology and epistemology stuff went over my head, but that book made sense."

Barbara nodded. "Yes, for me, too. How do I survive that dreadful memory and use it to be a better person and maybe a better cop?"

She went quiet, and when she spoke again, a slight change in her tone suggested that she was moving to another topic. "The more I learned about Tammy Ogden, the more I understood what some people's lives are like up here. As you know, I have lived a life of privilege in my suburb in the shadow of Detroit. Growing up, I had no idea what life was like in the city. Only now am I starting to understand the effects of poverty."

She looked intently at Brett. "I grieve for Tammy and the life she lived, and for a life she never got to live… I'm babbling now. It's like I'm trying to wrap my arms around all my feelings surrounding her murder. And the John Doe, there was a life there, too. A family, a history. It's too easy to dismiss him because he was a suspected criminal. We know nothing about him."

Then she asked, "What do you know about the kayaker?"

"His name, age, address, and boat color. I didn't have to deal with a body or knock on a door and deliver the bad news—I handed that task off to Sue. Everything about this incident was at a safe emotional distance."

"But they're not always this easy?"

"No," said Brett. "But some of them are more natural. Like when you respond to a medical emergency involving an older adult. You get there about the same time the EMTs arrive. It quickly becomes apparent the person is already gone. You feel the sadness of the moment. Sometimes, you stay with a spouse or partner until family or friends arrive. And yet, that death is part of the natural order of things. It's not like Tammy's death. It's not like a child at the bottom of a pool. It's not the grief you're describing, the grief for lives never lived."

She let his comment hang in the air. Then she said, "My parents are terrified that I might get injured or killed. Have you ever been injured? Have you ever had to use your weapon?"

"No," he answered. "You probably heard the same thing I did in college: The death rate on the job is low, and most police officers never use their weapons, even over a long career. And the injury rate for patrol officers is not alarmingly high. But we both know it's a dangerous job in some jurisdictions, every shift. Up here, not so much, but there's always the possibility…"

Barbara's eyes sought his again. "But since I left college a couple of years ago, the frequency of mass shootings has continued to climb. My parents are always forwarding articles on mass shootings, the kind that include bar charts. And when you look at the chart, the line starts with a gentle slope, then becomes almost vertical."

"Yeah," said Brett. "Maybe I'm just the frog in the soon-to-be boiling pot of water, but I'd rather not think about it. If I did, I couldn't do my job."

"Well, how about Ray? Seriously wounded once. Injured again just days ago."

"Like I said, I don't think about it. A few years ago, we had a young patrol officer. It was not that he was injured but…"

"But what?" asked Barbara.

"He was responding to an alarm at a veterinarian's office. Third shift, no backup close. He pulls into the drive, passenger side toward the building. As he starts to climb out of his car, it gets sprayed with bullets—everywhere—the windows, the doors, the tires. Automatic pistol—it's a war zone. He's afraid to move. He holds his position. Backup finally arrives: two cars and then a state cop. No further gunfire."

"How did it end?"

"They waited for the SWAT team and a crisis negotiator. You know, bullhorn approach first. No response from the shooter. After several attempts, they surrounded the building, eventually making a forced entry from two directions. They found the gunman had overdosed on horse tranquilizers. He was out cold, barely breathing.

"Result, a vehicle was destroyed, but no one was wounded or physically injured in any way, other than the perp. But the patrol officer, a real good man, was done with law enforcement. A day or two after the event, he told me that he was thinking about his wife and kids all the time he was crouching behind his car. He said he didn't want to put his life at risk again. Not for a job, anyway. He resigned a few days later. It was an unusual situation, but I understand his thinking. And if the shooter had been using an M15 like the one used to shoot up the Ogden place or that old cannery, the car probably wouldn't have given him the protection he needed to survive."

"And that's the unspoken fear?" said Barbara.

"What is?"

"A military-grade weapon in a madman's hands," she answered.

"You have one in your trunk," said Brett.

"And by the time I open my trunk…"

"I understand. Yes, that's the fear we all live with, whether consciously or not." He stretched hugely, then changed the direction of the conversation. "Should we finish the beer? We're both off tomorrow." Without waiting for an answer, he opened a bottle and passed it to her.

"Are you trying to get me drunk?" she asked while accepting the bottle from his hand.

"Not my intention," he answered. "I'm just doing what I can to lift you out of your funk. Is it working?"

Barbara laughed. "Maybe it is," she said.

Brett started clearing the dishes from the table, stacking them at the side of the sink as Barbara loaded the dishwasher.

"One last sip and I should be going," he said, lifting the bottle.

"I doubt you're okay to drive. You must be exhausted, and you've had a lot to drink. Stand against that wall and walk a straight line toward me."

Laughing, Brett staggered in her direction, putting his hands on her shoulders and then pulling her close. "Did I pass, Officer?"

The first light was still hours away when Brett's phone started buzzing.

41

As Ray stood at his writing desk—fountain pen in hand, journal open, staggered by exhaustion and doubt—the words refused to flow.

"Are you coming to bed?" Sue asked.

"I'm struggling with addiction," he responded. "My addiction," he added in answer to her questioning look.

"Elkins, what are you talking about?"

"I need to try to make sense of things, but I can't get started. I've got too many competing thoughts running through my brain. I can't get a handle on—"

"What's that got to do with addiction?"

"It's the damn computer. It's become an addiction. I just type when drafting on a computer, knowing I can return and rewrite it. In the end, I'll have something logical that makes sense. I can't do that with an ink pen."

"Why not? Just cross out what you don't like and start again."

"Can you imagine the mess?"

"Well, just tear out the page."

"I've never done that."

"Elkins, just come to bed. I'm starting to think you haven't recovered from that knock on the head."

Ray screwed the cap back on the pen and returned it and the journal to the desk drawer. Dropping into bed, he pulled the comforter up. Simone, cuddled next to Sue, emerged from under the covers, climbed onto his chest, and stood looking down at him.

"See, Simone is worried about you, too."

After Ray moved Simone to his side and switched off the light, Sue asked, "What's going on?"

"Too much."

"You still hurting?"

"Yeah—back, shoulder, neck."

"How about your head?"

"I know you've been told to be extra vigilant," he responded. "How about my head?"

"It seems all right," she said, "but I'm worried."

A few minutes later, she asked, "Did you ever have a conversation with Stan Gill? I didn't see anything in the case file."

"I did have the conversation. And I have notes. But it's one thing I didn't get written up yet."

"Did you learn anything?"

"I asked the usual man-to-man questions. Is there anything in your past that might motivate someone to harm you? Negative. Then the usual guy questions about his love life. Negative, again. While my gender is not known to be enormously honest when answering those questions, I think Gill was telling the truth. And he's been around a couple of years. Have you ever found him to be dishonest?"

"Never. I think he is who he is."

"So if the explosion wasn't directed at him, was I the target? And how would the perpetrator even know I was on the scene?"

"Emily Larson thinks the perp was just beyond the ridge. And Ray, you're known for being at the scene of most of the major incidents in this county. And the whole incident required a lot of time to unfold. First, there was the vehicle fire that had to be extinguished. And if you took the bait on that and showed up, it would be natural for you to inspect the area thoroughly. And now we know that this whole little drama was being stage-managed from above, so to speak."

Turning on the reading light on her side of the bed, Sue continued. "So let's have a slightly modified man-to-man conversation. That's a dated model, anyway. Let's have a person-to-person, no-equivocation conversation. I know my big words come from hanging around with you."

"So what do you want to know?" he grumped.

"My questions are similar to the ones you asked Gill. Is anyone out to get you? Someone from the past you sent to prison or some new antagonist?"

"Not that I can think of. And you're probably able to answer that question as reliably as I can."

"And your love life. Anyone trying to do you harm because you are messing with their wife, girlfriend, or daughter?"

"You know the answer to that one. So what's your point?"

"Someone is targeting you. You could have been killed."

"Look, as Larson explained, there were no enhancements to the bombs, no shrapnel, the kind of stuff that kills. It was just some kind of prank—albeit a dangerous one." Ray had grabbed onto Larson's prank explanation. He kept pushing back on the idea of being targeted.

"Prank. Elkins, that was more than just a prank. Maybe the perp's intent was not to kill, but it could have happened. Gill sustained multiple injuries. There's a good chance he'll retire because of it. And you were concussed and thoroughly banged up."

"Just a bump on the head. Bad luck hitting some cement."

"Elkins, with a subdural or epidural hematoma, people die. It's not uncommon. And it's one of those injuries that's sometimes missed until it's too late."

Sue struggled to keep her emotions in check. With a quivering voice, she continued, "Elkins, now I've almost lost you twice." She collapsed onto her pillow in tears, and Ray repositioned himself so that he could put his arms around her, trying to comfort her but thinking that she was overreacting.

Once she had collected herself, she said, into his shoulder, "We're tired. With just the normal summer workload, we're stressed. And this year, there's all that and so much more. Starting with the double murder, and… and we're getting nowhere." She sniffled and rolled out of his arms and onto her back. "Ray, this is my life up close. I don't have any professional distance. You being hurt, I'm just struggling…"

"We've been here before, Sue. Things seem impossible, and then—"

"This is different. This wasn't inadvertent. You were the target. You *are* the target. Don't tell me otherwise. The question is, why?"

He didn't respond immediately, trying to pick his words carefully. "I don't know why. Maybe we've just become part of the chaos. The world's on fire; we've been sheltered from much of that. Maybe our isolation is coming to an end."

He moved back to his side of the bed. "Get some sleep," he said. "Who knows what tomorrow will bring?"

Hours later, but well before dawn, Ray's ringtone sounded. He knocked the cell phone off the nightstand in his clumsy half-awake search. The device went silent by the time he found it in the darkness. He fell back asleep as he held the phone in his hand.

Then Sue's phone emitted distinctive dinging from the other nightstand.

Ray struggled to pull himself awake. "What now?" he asked.

"You won't believe—"

"Pestilence, war, famine, war?"

"Fire, Ray."

"That's not on the list."

"Wake up, Elkins. We've got to get going. There's a raging forest fire near the southern border of the National Shoreline, starting near the big lake, gale-force winds pushing it inland, a half-mile wide and a mile deep. The chief at the scene reports the fire is out of control. Requests assistance. Dispatch has implemented fanout: DEQ, Forest Service, Park Service, State Police, DNR."

"Why weren't we called?"

"Elkins, wake up. We've been called. Get dressed and take Simone for a walk. I'll get some coffee going and fill the Thermos bottles."

Still groggy, Ray walked the dog around the perimeter of the land at the edge of the forest. The sky was dark and star-filled, without hinting at the approaching dawn. He noticed Simone occasionally lifting her head and sniffing the air, an unusual gesture. Following her lead, he slowly inhaled several times as he gazed skyward. He couldn't tell if he could detect a hint of smoke or if he was just a victim of the power of suggestion.

A horn blast from Sue's truck ended his somnolent speculation. Holding Simone close to his chest with one arm, he pulled himself into the vehicle's passenger side with his other arm.

"Your cappuccino is ready, sir. Four perfect shots," said Sue, pointing. "Energy bars in the tray."

"Simone?" They always took her along when they were unsure how long they would be away.

"Water and food already packed on the floor behind you. It's early, Elkins. She'll be snoozing early on."

"What do we know?" he asked, his words garbled by a long yawn.

"Weren't you watching the messages?"

"We were contemplating the morning," he said, his hand resting on the small dog curled up tightly on his lap. He yawned again.

"A command center is being set up at the Bass Township Fire Station."

"The hottest, driest spring on record," Ray said. "Another new normal. Our involvement?"

"Brett's coordinating that with MSP. They've activated the Wireless Emergency Alerts system. Patrol officers and troopers will go house to house as evacuation areas are designated."

42

The Bass Township Fire Station, an aging monolith of cement blocks with occasional small steel-framed windows, stood at the center of a sandy field near the edge of the state highway. A disintegrating ribbon of asphalt led from the road to the two large overhead doors at the center of the building, which were now open, the resident fire engines having been dispatched to the scene. In their place, men and women clad in the uniforms of various federal, state, and local agencies were moving about or standing in small clusters. Vehicles from those agencies were parked on the gravel apron surrounding the building.

As Ray and Sue walked through one of the portals, a tallish man, balding with a protruding Adam's apple, standing in front of a large video screen near the back wall of the building, was tapping on a microphone, attempting to get the group's attention.

"Good morning, good morning, good morning," he repeated. Voices dropped, and he became the focus of attention. "Thank you for being here. I'm Moray Bott with the Bureau of Land Management. Usually, when we gather, it's at a planning session or working through a scenario. Today, it's the real thing. We will skip the usual introductions. Fortunately, most of us know one another and our roles in this operation.

"This is what we know: A fire at a vacant building inside the National Shoreline was reported just after three a.m. The Gull Point fire crew was dispatched. By the time they reached the area, the structure was fully engaged, and the fire, propelled by gale-force winds, was spreading east into a woodland area."

Bott used a green laser pointer to indicate specific locations on the topographic map displayed on the screen behind him.

He gestured with his right hand toward the audience. "Over a lot of years, we've worked through worst-case scenarios. This morning, we have one on our hands. As you know, this has been a searing spring and early summer. We imposed no-burning restrictions weeks ago and have been lucky until today."

He circled an area on the map with the laser beam. "The initial scene was right here. The wind is from the south-southwest at thirty to forty. Gusts higher. This is where we're projecting the fire will move, mainly in the National Shoreline and the federal and state forests beyond. Homes and farms are located in this area, too.

"As you all know, wind direction changes and fast-moving fires often create their own climate. We anticipate that will probably be the case at the head of the fire, given that much of this area is tinderbox-dry pine.

"The operation center will remain in this building. We will be following the preestablished command structure with which you're familiar. We're setting up communications; periodic updates will be messaged, and specific instructions will come via your normal command chain. Be safe, be careful. Godspeed."

As the crowd moved out of the building toward their vehicles, Brett Carty caught up with Sue and Ray.

"Where are we?" asked Ray.

"Right after dispatch called, I contacted the State Police to help get the roads closed. As more patrol staff arrived, we helped evacuate the immediate area. But this fire is moving fast; we're just keeping ahead of it. I've got everyone coming in, and I'll keep deploying them as they arrive. I'm worried about the cottages around Arrowhead Lake. The fire has already cut off the access road. And for people who might need help, the cell service there is spotty at best."

"Get the Park Service to help. They can come down the beach with one of their UTVs. It's just a few hundred yards across the dunes into the roads around the lake. Other than a bit of dune grass, there are no combustibles along the way."

"I'll get that organized. Thanks. One more thing. I talked with Griffin Kamrath. He made the initial 9-1-1 call."

"Okay," Ray responded, gesturing for more.

"The man is elderly and lives alone in a cottage just beyond the southern border of the National Shoreline, next to the first place that went up in flames. He says the fire was set. He told me he has insomnia. When he can't sleep, he likes to sit on his porch and look at the stars. First, he saw the beams from flashlights moving around the old cottage beside his, a condemned structure inside the National Shoreline. He says there was a whoosh, almost like an explosion. Then, the whole house went up in flames. In the glow from the fire, he thinks he saw someone running. Then he said he heard an engine."

"Boat, ATV, headlights?"

"He's not sure. Thinks maybe a boat."

"Did you alert dispatch to suspected arson?"

"Absolutely."

"The missing kayaker?" asked Ray.

"Last evening, the plan was for a Coast Guard chopper to start a search pattern this morning. We would do a grid search near shore, then move deeper. NPS and some township departments would search the beach area. It will probably just be the Coast Guard chopper until the fire is under control."

Ray nodded, not happy with the development. "Arrange to have an officer meet with the family and explain what's happening."

"How about our new social worker? Meggie Cameron will handle the situation with skill and sensitivity."

"Sure."

43

"So you talked to a witness who says this all started with an arson at an old cottage?" asked MSP arson investigator Emily Larson. She was waiting for Ray and Sue near the source of the fire late in the day.

Ray explained that Brett Carty had spoken to the man, Griffin Kamrath, and gave her the gist of their conversation.

"Let's see if we can get some evidence to support his story while there's still some light," Larson responded.

"Busy day for you, too?" Ray asked as they walked along the beach high above the water line toward the remains of the Victorian cottage where the fire had allegedly been set. The high southwesterly winds that had propelled the fire inland had started to weaken by late afternoon.

"Yeah, I started downriver at a factory site early this morning. Possible insurance fraud, but given the looks of the place, I can't imagine there was much of a loss. Probably bored teenage boys on a hot summer night."

"You've mentioned the gender connection before," said Sue, keeping a tight rein on Simone as she scampered near them.

"Yeah, the male fascination with fire. I think it's a relic of the caveman era, with an emphasis on the man part. Stunted or regressive evolution. There is a lot of that going around."

They stopped at the top of a small mound overlooking the ruins of the old cottage. The scorched and blackened fieldstone foundation remained, delineating the shape and size of the incinerated structure. Beyond that, nothing recognizable remained in the piles of ash.

"How long was the cottage vacant?" Larson asked.

"I can't say for sure. Probably a few years," Ray answered. "It was one of the last pieces of private property left in the National Shoreline. Property owners were able to negotiate long-term leases at the time the National Shoreline was established in 1970. The lease's maximum length was until the last grandchild's death. Once the property is officially vacated, it seems to take a year or so to accomplish the final demolition. It's probably a funding issue. The Park Service does a skillful job of returning the site to a natural state. And in a year or two, nature does its thing and recaptures the area."

"Well, it will take more than a year or two before all of this ash disappears," said Larson. "Fire scenes are the apotheosis of chaos, a freaking vision of hell."

"What's the plan?" asked Sue.

"I'll collect samples to take back to my laboratory. Tomorrow, I'll confirm the presence of an accelerant and identify the specific substance. But first, I'll try to confirm the presence of these nefarious substances on-site using a sizzling new technology—no, not an iPhone app but a standalone handheld device called a PID."

Larson reached into a voluminous pocket in her cargo pants, pulled out an orange plastic device with dials and a small digital screen, and held it up for her audience. "I know, it's kind of weird looking, like a cell phone with a SimCity vibe. But this metal thing at the top is not an antenna; it's a probe. I can switch on Geiger counter mode so you can hear how excited it gets when it detects—" Larson stopped mid-sentence, her eyes alighting on an object in the fading light. She marched toward it, with Ray, Sue, and Simone following.

"So much for high tech," she said, lifting a red plastic gas can in her gloved hand. "Our perp left his calling card." She sniffed at the opening of a gas can missing a cap. "No mystery here," she said. Looking at Sue, she continued, "Just like the one we found at the cannery. This guy is shouting at us."

"No prints on the other one, right?" said Sue.

"Yeah, right. I'll check this one, too. Probably won't be any. Interesting scenario. They're playing us. But what's the game? Let me collect some samples from the building. Then I want to show you something I was working on while waiting for you guys."

Standing around Larson's truck's tailgate, they viewed a map on her laptop. She outlined the topographical features of the land east of the shoreline, starting at the location of the recently torched building.

"This is masterful," she said. "Gale-force winds from the southwest, and here's where we are. The forest fire starts with the old building going up in flames, the perfect fuse. This is the center of a valley that runs to the northeast, a deep cut with ridge lines on both sides that runs four or five miles. It's probably a bit of sculpting by a receding glacier. I've looked up and down the coastline. There's nothing else quite like this. And it's almost all forest land, second growth, maybe a hundred and twenty years after the lumber era. Lots of pine, with a scattering of American ash, now mostly dead, some still standing, but much of it on the forest floor. Just amazing."

"What are you trying to tell us?" asked Sue.

"This was no random torching. The site was carefully chosen for this result. Abnormally dry conditions. Fire danger signs are posted everywhere, with Smokey looking on. Add the gale-force winds. The perp waited until all the boxes were ticked. I've never seen such skillfully planned arson. Brilliant.

"Most arsonists are not big on planning. It's usually a lunkhead with a can of gas, motivated by rage, revenge, or the desire to terrify or intimidate. I'm no FBI profiler, but I can tell you some characteristics of this arsonist. You're probably ahead of me, so I won't state the obvious…"

"Go ahead," urged Sue. "Give us your version."

"Arson is a low-skill profession. Mensa membership is not required. All you need are sufficient physicality to toss a flammable liquid around and the capacity to use a Bic lighter. Being fleet of foot also helps. As for executive function, not so much.

"But this fire," she pointed emphatically at the ruins of the cottage, "required executive function and background knowledge: the optimum conditions, the best topography to create a hot, fast-moving blaze. And then you'd have to know about that old house, the perfect fire starter when all the other conditions were aligned. Your perp is smart. Knows the area. Perhaps they're even local. And with this fire, they've managed to tie up all the fire and police assets in the region. One of the two main highways is closed. This is just brilliant. Any reports of a bank robbery, a jewelry heist, or a major crime caper going down today? Your witness says he saw more than one flashlight before the fire started. Your mastermind might have a disciple."

Larson looked from Ray to Sue and back again. "I sense something going on between you two. Is there a possible suspect lurking out there?"

"No comment," Ray said.

Larson collected her samples from the scene, and then they parted ways for the evening. As Sue guided her truck along the sandy two-track in the dusk, Ray got an update from central dispatch. The wind speed had dropped, the flanks of the fire were mostly contained, and the aerial suppression from the USFS planes seemed to have slowed the head.

"We got lucky," Sue said.

"No loss of life or major injuries," Ray said. "*Lucky*—interesting word."

"Should we talk about the rather skinny canary in the room?"

Ray didn't respond for quite some time. He busied himself, scratching Simone's back as she stood on his legs. Finally, he said, "There's no evidence that suggests Scott Nelson might be involved. Yes, he's a scoundrel… a liar, thief, manipulator, sociopath, narcissistic personality…"

"Yes," said Sue, "but nothing that would keep him from being elected to Congress legally. But Amanda Bidwell, disciple number one who is doing time, finally understands how manipulative he is."

"Tragic story. Be careful what you do for love. Maybe we should run north and see what Scott Nelson is up to now."

"Elkins, after your visit to Heirloom Foods, that would look like police harassment. We need evidence to connect him to the crime. Or crimes. Given all the vandalism there… he has means and opportunity, but what's his motive?" She looked over at him. "Elkins, what would you do for love?"

"Give me a hint?"

"It's late. I need a shower, some hot food, and a bed. Simone, too."

"Okay, Scott Nelson can wait till morning."

44

As they drove toward their home—Sue at the wheel, Ray in the passenger's seat with Simone curled in his lap—Ray struggled to stay awake and keep the conversation going, knowing Sue was as exhausted as he was. But sometimes, his best intentions were impossible to realize. Suddenly, he awoke as Sue brought the vehicle to a halt near the house's front door.

"Ray," she said, alarm in her voice as she brought her hand down on his shoulder with a slapping sound. "Ray," she repeated.

"Yes," he answered, struggling to open his eyes.

"The door. The door. It's standing open."

"I'll find out what's—" He passed Simone to her and pushed his door open.

"No!" she shouted. "Close it!"

Focusing the spotlight on the dark interior, she quickly comprehended the danger, putting the vehicle in reverse and backing away as a tongue of flame shot in their direction. She continued backing as conflation became visible throughout the building, windows providing a glimpse of the horror in the interior. Seconds later, an explosion within the structure propelled the fire through the shattered windows and up toward the roof.

Sue backed to a far corner of the lot, aware of Ray's call for assistance to central dispatch—fire and police backup.

"Do we stay?" she asked, moving the spotlight over the area around the house and the neighboring forest.

"What are they expecting?" asked Ray.

"Here, we're sitting ducks, but on the road, we're vulnerable from any direction."

Ray dumped Simone on the floor behind him. They each had their sidearms at the ready.

"Stay low. Use the car as a battering ram if you have to."

"My plan."

They ducked, eyes just above the dash, watching for any movement, the area now lit by the raging fire. Ray, vigilant yet lost in thought, struggled to understand what was unfolding. Sue, filled with rage, was ready to strike back against the perpetrators as soon as she saw them.

The first patrol vehicle reached the scene in minutes. The driver observed the fire, then reversed and parked near them. Ray saw George Adler slip out of the car and retrieve his AR15 from the trunk. Then, using the vehicles for cover, he moved around the rear of Sue's truck and tapped on Ray's window. At Ray's behest, he brought two more rifles from his back hatch and passed them through the window.

"Nothing to save here," said Ray. "Let's secure the area for the firefighters." One by one, they slipped into the woods, widely separated, moving cautiously, using the trees for cover, Adler moving clockwise, Ray and Sue moving in the counter direction.

"Nothing here," said Adler.

"Ditto," Sue transmitted.

"Same," said Ray.

They carefully emerged from their protected positions and waited along the perimeter until the first engine, followed by a tanker truck, arrived. As the first company deployed, a second company arrived and quickly joined the fray.

Ray watched the fire-weakened walls of his home collapse, the roof folding into the rubble below, and the last explosive shower of sparks before the overwhelming blasts from the hoses started to quell the flames.

He felt Sue tight at his side, holding onto him. Silent. There was nothing to say.

In the midmorning, under gray skies and cool drizzle, Ray circled the remains of his home. Nothing recognizable remained except the grossly distorted shapes of a few appliances. The acrid fumes hanging over the still-warm remains burned his nose with every breath. His eyes watered.

Ray rejoined Sue, standing behind Emily Larson's van. Both women were dressed in HiVis jackets with hoods on.

Larson, mid-sentence, pulled off her glasses and started wiping away the fog. "I was just telling Sue," she paused, "I was just telling her the obvious. Sometimes you gotta do that. Ray, this is the same MO as the cannery and the cottage." She pointed to a bagged plastic gas container in the truck's rear. "Same calling card."

"Fire started remotely?"

"I imagine."

"So someone was watching?"

"Yeah. Or there's a trail cam on one of those trees. Or maybe a drone was lurking above—I should have thought about that possibility at the cannery."

Looking over at Sue, Larson continued, "You've told me about your friend at the Bureau. I imagine you will reach out to them and other resources, and you should—"

Sue cut her off, "But, but what? Does this look like anything you've ever…?"

"No, my consistent 'No.' So, let me ramble a bit. What was the availability of law enforcement and emergency services yesterday and last night in this county? And you don't need to answer because it is obvious. Your dispatchers were probably struggling to find staff to meet normal needs."

"Exactly."

"And the ongoing murder investigation?"

"Nada," said Ray. "We've had no resources to devote to it."

"And your focus after the cannery…?"

Larson waited four or five *largo* beats, then said. "So this has all been sticking in my craw. What's wrong with this picture? It just doesn't compute. In the cannery explosion, it looks like you were targeted, but if they wanted to off you, they could have. And last night, the same MO. You were being watched. The ignition was perfectly timed to give you the full emotional impact without causing you physical injury. This is psychological warfare. Yesterday, they had a huge window where they could have dropped by and torched the house."

Larson let her words soak in, then continued. "Okay, so let me cut to the quick. All the evidence points to you being targeted, but you're not. You have a small department stretched to its limits. Your plate runneth over. And here's the big thing: other stuff's going on that you're missing. You're being kept occupied. You need to back burner this stuff for a while and see what else is going down."

"What do we do now?" asked Ray, exhaustion and grief permeating his body and echoing in his voice.

"First, don't give the perps the pleasure of media attention for this. Control the news. Only you live on this access road. Keep it closed off; keep the curious away. The fire should be reported in the usual way: structure fire, building a total loss, no one was injured, including the family pet, and the cause of the fire under investigation. Just the facts, no extra material for lurid headlines. The real story comes out later.

"And one more thing. You're pretty autonomous up here. Usually, you can take care of things that happen on your patch. And that's not unusual; I've seen it often as an ATF agent. But right now, you need outside help from the feds and us. I'll work with Sue. We'll make this happen."

<h1 style="text-align:center">45</h1>

S ue found Ray—dressed in department coveralls—sitting at his desk, staring at a dim computer screen. Peering over his shoulder, she quipped, "Should I call IT?"

He didn't answer. He just shook his head slowly from side to side.

"Are you okay? Should I take you to the ER?"

"Do I look as catatonic as I feel?"

She carefully measured her response. "Most people would be horizontal. And you probably should be. You've been without sleep for more than twenty-four hours, and then there's the grief on top of exhaustion. We need sleep, some good food, showers, clean clothes—"

"How are you managing?" he interrupted.

"I feel it, too. But there's also the adrenaline and anger. I want to catch these bastards. But I'm entering the crash zone, too."

Sue pulled a chair close to the front of his desk. Looking at her iPad, she began, "I've just talked with Meggie Cameron. She's looking for emergency accommodations for us—a place that's dog friendly."

"Meggie's focus should be on community needs, crime victims, not the department staff," said Ray.

"Elkins, we are the crime victims. We are part of Meggie's job description. We're currently homeless. Other than these jumpsuits, we have no clothes." She tamped down a feeling of exasperation before continuing. "Meggie is here because you convinced the county board that the department needed a social worker. Elkins, my first week on the job, you told me we are more social workers than anything else here in the woods. We find lost children, look after the elderly, and rescue drivers from snow drifts before they freeze to death. At the end of your speech, you said, 'Occasionally you'll need your handcuffs, probably never your gun.'"

"Sounds like I was a horrible bore."

Sue shook her head and moved on to the next item. "And after emergency housing, we need clothes. You hate shopping. I know what you wear. I'll do the shopping and get you some essentials."

Ray nodded his consent, then stood and came around his desk, pulling her into his arms.

She responded, holding him tight. "We're here, uninjured, Simone, too. That's what's important. I'm so lucky to have you in my life."

"Yes," he responded.

"Sorry about your favorite down vest, your kayak, your fountain pen, the years of journal entries. Some things are irreplaceable."

"Irreplaceable," he repeated, "but many don't need to be replaced. The pen was special, but it can be replaced. The journals were important at the moment. Sometimes, I have to slow down my brain. Putting my thoughts into print, the tactile nature of the act—the paper, the ink, forming letters and words. That's the recursive part. At that moment, it helped me work through things. The critical part, the process, is still here. I can get a new pen. More brown ink, too. The important part remains.

"The books, that hurts more. They're the walls of my cave. My understanding of the world has been shaped by reading. Moments in time, the right moments to understand and internalize. By adolescence, I was time-traveling and living in other cultures. All those pages and bits of information were the building blocks of my awareness of the world beyond. And, like my journals, I didn't return to most of them over the years. But having them around me, a security blanket of sorts?"

"We'll build a new cave, Ray. Our cave."

"Yes," he answered, "I'd like that."

Sue pulled back from the embrace. "Emily Larson has liaised

with her former colleagues at ATF and people she knows at the Bureau. And she'll coordinate the MSP involvement. With her leading that investigation, we can focus on the Tammy Ogden case and maybe find out what Scott Nelson is up to."

"That makes sense," he agreed. "We're barely treading water as it is."

"I'm sure we can ask Brett to step up and take additional administrative responsibilities as he did while you were away. We're going to have to adapt to get through this chaos."

Brett stood with the other agency representatives behind Moray Bott as he gave the initial press briefing to reporters from regional news outlets, including camera crews capturing the event.

"So, in summary, the fire is nearly contained. Fire crews will continue to monitor the scene for any possible flare-ups. With a lot of hard work from multiple agencies and some much-needed rain, we're finally in control of the situation. About three thousand acres of mostly forest were burned, the majority within the boundaries of state forests or the National Park Shoreline. Fortunately, no fatalities or injuries have been reported. Getting people out of harm's way and protecting homes and farms was achieved through skillful coordination by all these agencies."

Bott turned and made a sweeping gesture to indicate the people standing behind him. "Representatives from this group have been meeting for the last several years to plan for the possible emergencies brought on by global warming. As you know, these events are becoming increasingly common: wildfires, devastating rains, severe floods, and tornados—the list goes on and on. The severity of this fire is directly the result of extreme heat and severe drought. We will analyze the effectiveness of our response to this fire. We will work to keep growing our resources and capacities for future challenges. Are there questions for me or my colleagues?"

Holly Pride, a summer intern at the local TV station, asked, "What can you tell us about where and how this fire began?"

"I'll give your question to Emily Larson, a State Police arson investigator. Sergeant Larson?"

Larson moved to the microphone. "We have an eyewitness who identified the probable source of the fire, a building scheduled for demolition just within the southern border of the National Shoreline. We have evidence that the fire was started with an accelerant, gasoline."

"So it was an act of arson?"

"Yes, there is evidence that supports that conclusion."

"Any suspects, anyone under arrest?"

"Not at this time. We're in the early stages of the investigation. Given the location of the alleged crime, federal, state, and local agencies will be involved in this case."

Bott pointed to Abi Gear, a youngish man with a mop of dark hair and a short, neatly trimmed beard from the local NPR affiliate.

"Yes."

"Thank you. This is a bit off-topic, but the missing kayaker in Lake Michigan. Does anyone here have an update on the ongoing search and rescue efforts? Has the fire affected those efforts?"

"Lieutenant Carty?" Bott said.

Brett moved to the microphone. "A Coast Guard helicopter continued search and rescue efforts yesterday. Given the passage of time, we are now in a recovery mode. Fortunately, the wave heights are dropping, and we will be able to put together a more robust search effort. In addition to my department's two patrol boats, we have additional assets from the State Police, the Park Service, and the Coast Guard Station. The Northern Michigan Mutual Aid Dive Team will further assist with their side-scan sonar unit."

Brett carefully surveyed his audience, then continued, "The Manitou passage, with its two islands, many shoals, and great depth in places, presents many challenges. For the family of the missing kayaker, we hope to be able to provide closure."

By early evening, the gale-force winds of the previous day had diminished. The big lake was still working through residual energy from the storm as the sun began to drop toward the horizon.

Every available mooring in the large marina was occupied, sailors seeking shelter from the storm joining the usual boats parked there during the peak recreational boating months. Few, if any, had ventured back onto the lake yet. The prevailing mood favored another evening of revelry—the joys of being in a safe harbor as the sun started to drop below the western horizon.

The mood was more somber in a separate area at the harbor's south end, near the seawall's opening to the big lake. A group had gathered on the dock the Park Service and the Cedar County Sheriff's Department shared.

A Coast Guard response boat slowed to a crawl as it entered the harbor, the hull settling, the alert-orange pontoons becoming parallel to the flat water within the harbor. The crew tossed the lines to secure the craft to the pier. Brett led Dr. Dyskin toward the boat, past the officers controlling access to the dock. With the help of two crew members, the less-than-agile medical examiner boarded and stood on the small deck behind the boat's aluminum cabin.

Dyskin dropped to his knees next to the body bag on the port side of the deck. The veteran pathologist pulled at the heavy zipper, moving it far enough to expose the head and neck. He spread the bag open to get a better view. Looking over his shoulder at Brett, he said, "Your kayaker?"

Brett nodded. "Yes, I think so. He looks about the right age."

"Pretty fresh. Hasn't been in the water long. I'll be able to tell you more after the autopsy." Dyskin pulled the zipper closed.

"What's the story on this one?" asked Dyskin, looking at the second body bag.

"I don't know. We had two boats out there. Two search areas. Each came back with two bodies."

Dyskin moved to the second body bag and steeled himself before pulling the zipper. He inspected the head and upper body. "Looks like less than forty-eight hours on this one, too."

Dyskin pulled the bag open further, using a small flashlight to inspect the face and skull. He moved to the side to give Brett a better view.

Brett swallowed hard, then said, "That person is known to the department. We'll need an autopsy as soon as possible."

46

A few minutes after seven a.m., Dr. Dyskin—dressed in scrubs and with a face mask hanging around his neck—met Ray in a small conference room in the pathology department.

Dyskin gave Ray a once-over and gestured with an open hand. "New department uniform?"

"My clothing choices are limited at the moment."

"So I heard. I talked with Brett last evening. How are you doing?"

Ray didn't respond immediately. As most of his friends had noticed over the years, he wasn't one to give a pat answer to a serious question. And even though he'd slept quite well, Ray didn't feel moored in the world—his mooring was just... gone. Finally, he said, "I don't know. I am still trying to understand what's happened. To suddenly lose my long-term nest... I'm mostly disoriented."

"How about Sue?"

"She's mostly on task. She's never really cared about things very much. She reminded me that we have each other, and we have our dog. And she's right. The other things are just stuff. Mostly replaceable things."

"Yes. So true. Decades of doing PMs. We come in with nothing. We leave with nothing." Dyskin regarded Ray kindly, thoughtfully. "Her intelligence, thoughtfulness, and professionalism have always impressed me. Over the years, I could see she was very fond of you. I wondered if you'd ever get the message. Fortunately, you finally did."

Ray nodded his agreement. "What do you have for me?"

"Should we start with the kayaker, Bruce Kushner? That will only take a few minutes."

"Okay."

"Seventy-three-year-old male. I got most of this man's background from Brett, who had talked with his wife. In this case, it's easy to generate a plausible scenario. Like you, Kushner was a passionate kayaker. As his wife left for town, he started to do an out and back to the Crib on flat water. When she returned later in the day, his boat was missing. I'm sure you read Brett's notes. That evening, his kayak was recovered with the man's PFD securely fastened on the boat's back deck. Do you want to finish the story?"

"Sure, a predictable plot. He got caught in rapidly changing conditions. He capsized, was separated from his boat, and exhaustion and hyperthermia took over."

"Yes, that's how it looks. His lungs were filled with water—accidental drowning."

"How about Scott Nelson?"

"A more complicated case. With little more than a cursory exam, it was clear that you'd want the body to go downstate for a forensic autopsy."

"What can you tell me at this point?"

"The death was caused by drowning. The lungs were full of water, lake water. But it's not a case of accidental drowning. First, there's a large laceration on the left side of the scalp. I suspect that blow was of sufficient force to cause a concussion."

"So he got hit over the head and dropped into the water at a deep part of the channel?"

"Yes, but I can't tell you how closely those two events were connected. And I don't know his level of consciousness at the time of his immersion."

"Well, with lungs filled with water, the body would have gone to the bottom," said Ray. "And it's deep and cold in that part of the Manitou Passage. Without side-scan sonar, there's little likelihood the body would have ever been found. His assailants would have thought they were home free."

"There is also bruising on his hands and arms," continued Dyskin. "These are consistent with defensive injuries. He was involved in a fight. There is significant bruising at the wrists and ankles. Ligature marks. At some point, he had been tied up."

"So what do you think?" Ray asked.

"This wasn't just some dustup between Nelson and another person. This man was fit and could probably put up a damn good fight. Pure speculation here, but I think you are dealing with a planned execution. My guess is he was overwhelmed by several assailants, maybe knocked unconscious, tied up, and dumped in the deepest part of the passage."

"But there were no ropes on his hands or feet?"

"No, like I said, just the bruises. I don't know why he was untied. You're the detective," Dyskin added in a jesting tone.

"Toxicology?"

"Once I decided that a forensic was needed, I went no further. They'll have to do that for you downstate."

"How about the time of death?"

"Hard to approximate, the body being in cold water. But eleven p.m. to four a.m., plus or minus who knows what."

"Understood. Will you send the preliminary findings to Sue? We'll get the paperwork on the forensic autopsy going. And thank you for coming in so early to get this done. We now know what we're dealing with."

Ray stopped on his way to the door, turned, and asked, "How's your summer going?"

"Grandsons this week, Cloe's boys. Rug rats. Dune climb yesterday, beach time at the cannery, and a float trip on the river. Then a hot dog roast and lots of ice cream. My goal every day is to exhaust them. Otherwise, I don't stand a chance."

47

A few minutes after eight that morning, Ray drove along the narrow village roads surrounding the bay. Once past the intersection of Lake and Main, the north-south roads ran from First to Fifth.

Ray parked in front of a modest home on Fifth, the dwelling's original bones dating from the village's earlier days.

The front door swung open before he reached the porch.

"Sheriff."

Ray grasped the man's extended hand and held it for a long moment. Bob Nelson was dressed in faded jeans and a black T-shirt. His tan sockless feet disappeared into a worn pair of boat shoes.

"I was just having coffee. Please come in."

Ray followed Nelson toward the back of the house, through the kitchen, and into a contemporary addition with large windows and a doorwall opening to the backyard. Nelson gestured toward an empty chair at the table, then asked, "Coffee?"

"Please. Black. Is your wife here?"

"She's working today. She clerks at the clothing store during the tourist season." He poured coffee and set the mug in front of Ray. "You're here to tell me something, and it's probably not good news."

"We seem to have that history. Sorry." Ray set his phone on the table. "I will record this conversation if you don't mind."

Bob nodded his consent, then said, "Scott, again, I imagine. What's happened this time?"

"My news is not good. A body was recovered from Lake Michigan late yesterday. The officer at the scene recognized your son."

Bob, visibly shaken, dropped into a chair on the opposite side of the table. After a long moment, he said, "So he was a drowning victim?" Nelson chewed on a knuckle, his face expressionless. Finally, he said, "How could this have happened? He was a terrific swimmer."

"His lungs were full of water," Ray explained. "The cause of death was drowning. But there were other circumstances surrounding his death. He may have been incapacitated before he went into the water."

"So this wasn't an accident?"

"It doesn't appear so. We're treating it as a suspicious death."

Nelson sat silently, looking off into space. "You know, my wife and I talked about this possibility. We felt things were going from bad to worse for Scott. His life appeared to be spinning out of control." Nelson pulled off his glasses, tossed them on the table, and wiped at his eyes with the back of his hand.

Ray waited.

"Scott was a fantastic kid, our oldest, our brightest maybe. He couldn't have been better—a top student, district swimming champ, Eagle Scout, and the first kid from his high school to go East to college. Full scholarship, everything. We just sent him spending money.

"And then something happened. His life just went off the rails. I don't know. Drugs? Was the competition too stiff at college—all those kids from fancy prep schools? Was he struggling with depression? We started to lose him, and after a few years, he was alienated from us. And it wasn't our doing, not one bit. We continued to reach out. Nothing. He wouldn't talk to his sisters anymore. And they had always adored him.

"We sought help from family counselors and psychologists. But nothing worked. This has been a great sadness in our lives. And now this."

"When you said you had a feeling something bad would happen, what did you mean?" asked Ray.

"The situation involving the Ingersolles. I never thought I would get interviewed by the FBI. Not that I could tell them anything. Then there was that thing with Jennifer Bidwell and Gerhard Talmadge's death. All the talk surrounding her trial and Scott's possible involvement in the crime. And also things I didn't understand. Big money seemed to be involved. And that young man from China who disappeared. Was he murdered? Was Scott somehow involved?"

"Did you ever hear about anyone being angry with him or wanting to do him harm?"

"No, nothing like that. But who knows what happened at the Ingersolle estate? And even before that, we had become completely estranged. And it wasn't our doing. It was Scott's."

"Going back to when you were still part of Scott's life, was there ever a time you worried about his safety? Did he have any enemies, anyone who might want to harm him?"

"I don't think so. Everyone liked Scott—the other kids, the teachers, the people in the village."

"Think back to the high school years. Anything?"

After a long pause, Nelson said, "There was just one time. The girls liked Scott, and some of their mothers did, too. He was very polite and knew how to talk with adults, especially women. During his senior year, he may have gotten too close to Mrs. Dalton, the swim coach's wife and Scott's English teacher. I didn't hear about it until after he left for college. The rumor was that Coach Dalton had threatened to run him over if he ever got the chance."

"Is the coach still around?"

"Dalton, no. They left town shortly after graduation that year, but some of my friends said Scott had something going on with the woman. And what can I say? He was good-looking, 6'2", with the body of a swimmer. She was young, pretty, and not much older than Scott. It might have happened."

"Would it be possible for you or a member of your family to come to the medical center and identify the body? We need to get that done as soon as possible."

"I need to tell my wife. We'll need some time to collect ourselves."

"I can arrange to have an officer drive you."

"Thank you. That would help. We hoped that we would get beyond this, that Scott would come back into the fold."

48

Ray slowed and turned off the highway onto the access road to Gull Point, an unpaved lane that snaked toward the big lake. He was surprised by how much the dune grass and weeds had encroached on the narrow two-track since he had last visited the estate four years before.

Rolling to a stop at an imposing gate, he keyed in the number posted at the side of the road. A camera was positioned at the top of the gate. In a few seconds, the two arms of the barrier opened inward.

Piper Ingersolle, waiting for him at the side of the road, waved him into a parking place near her cottage. A patch of old-growth forest hid her home from the estate's main building, a lakeside villa.

"Sheriff, it's been a while. What brings you?" she asked as he emerged from his vehicle.

"Police business, I'm afraid. Is there someplace we can talk?"

"Sure, how about the table just outside the cottage? I just made some coffee. Can I get you a cup?"

"Yes, thank you, that would be great. Black, please."

Minutes later, Piper joined him, setting two cups and a French press on the table. "Great view from here," said Ray, looking out toward the big lake.

"Yes," said Piper. "During the good weather, I make it a point to have breakfast here. The view of the bay."

"And half the pay?" said Ray, reciting an old cliché.

"And half the pay but getting me in touch with where I want to be."

She filled each cup, noting his phone on the table. "I take it this is a formal interview you'd like to record?"

"Is that okay?"

"No prob. How can I help?"

"Scott Nelson's body was recovered from Lake Michigan yesterday. Foul play is suspected."

"You're saying Scott was murdered?"

"Yes, that appears to be the case."

"Sad news, I guess. Scott was my first real love. Then we grew up. He became someone I no longer knew."

She peered out at the water, then back at Ray. "What does that have to do with me?" she asked.

Ray remembered Piper as an attentive young woman who'd had a loving relationship with her grandparents. He had forgotten about her occasional machine-gun delivery. He also noted an edge, a wariness in her question.

"This investigation is just beginning. My department's initial contact with Nelson was here at Gull Point, first during the investigation of your grandfather's murder. Then there was the question of the art forgeries and the missing young Chinese national."

Ray and Sue had found the man's passport in the room above the garage at Gull Point. Who was he? What had happened to him? Was he being held against his will? Had he been murdered, or had he just disappeared back across the border into Canada? The FBI had taken over that case. A body was never found.

"Yes. As you know, Sheriff," Piper said dryly, "the FBI interviewed me several times."

"Yes," said Ray, "there was never enough evidence to charge Scott Nelson. Any relevant phone records, emails, all had disappeared."

"Scott is—was—incredibly smart," Piper responded, playing with a strand of her long blond hair. "He was a techie and always seemed ahead of the game. He was skilled at not leaving any tracks." She stared off into the trees. "The sweet guy I loved as a teen turned out to be a liar, cheat, thief, a complete sociopath. It took me a while to realize the change…"

Ray waited for Piper to complete the sentence, but she never did. Her mind had shifted gears.

Ray moved forward in his chair and laid his forearms on the table. "I'm here, Piper, because you knew Scott for many years. I'm asking for your help. Can you think of people who might want to do him harm?"

"You can put me at the top of the list, Sheriff. As everything was going down, Mother fired him. He announced that he wasn't going and locked himself in his apartment. Our two security guys broke down the door and physically removed him, marching him off the property. Then they tossed the contents of his apartment in garbage bags and piled them by the highway. The only thing they kept back was his shotgun. I've got that now, next to my bed, loaded."

"And you haven't seen him since?"

"I wish. Unfortunately, there was one more confrontation. It was a few days later. There he was," Piper pointed to the small lane that ran through the heavily wooded site from the estate's entrance to a circular drive at the side of the main building, her mother's villa on the lake.

"He was screaming at the top of his lungs. It was pouring rain. His clothes were soaking wet. And it was all about me. Somewhere in the stream of obscenities, he was blaming me for making him homeless and ruining his life. Then he launched into all the ways he was going to get even. It was lizard-brain barbarism. He was going to beat me senseless, then rape me. His language was so vile…" Piper shuddered. "Even just thinking about it…"

"Take some time," said Ray.

After a few moments, she continued, "At the end, he yelled about how he was going to finally kill me, sitting on me, strangling me slowly. He wanted me powerless. And there's one more thing."

"Yes?"

"He said that after he killed me, he was going to dump me in the deepest part of the lake where my body would never be found. How's that?"

Ray let the ensuing quiet hang, his mind flashing back to scenes of savage cruelty, especially from his early days as a patrol officer— women beaten, kicked, raped, killed.

Piper shattered the silence, "And then the cavalry arrived: Sal and Helio, part of Mother's security team. Do you remember them?"

"Yes." Ray had liked them both and was glad they were there when Piper needed protection.

"They just brought him to the ground, put those plastic restraints on his hands and feet, and loaded him not too gently into the back of a pickup. A few seconds later, they were rolling toward the gate. They released him out by the highway.

"They sensed how shaken I was and came back immediately. But at that moment, I wanted revenge. I wished they had battered the bastard within an inch of his life before they cut him loose—but no such luck. Sal and Helio were professionals. They told me they warned Scott never to return to the property or approach me if he saw me elsewhere."

"I don't remember that this incident was ever reported."

"It wasn't."

"Did you consider requesting a PPO?"

She gave Ray a long look. "And how well do those work?" she asked sarcastically.

Ray nodded. "So, did you ever see him again?"

"No. Sal and Helio provided me with a handgun and taught me how to use it." Her tone changed. "I do have a concealed pistol license. They also oversaw the upgrade of the security system. There are cameras, motion detectors, all that kind of high-tech stuff everywhere.

"His death, it doesn't qualify as revenge served cold, but I'm happy he's not out there anymore. He's no longer a threat."

"Understood. Based on what you know about him, can you think of someone who might want to harm him?"

"Given how he used everyone with whom he came in contact, I would say any of them. Few will grieve his passing."

"Yes, but I'm wondering if…?"

"I'm sorry, I don't have anything specific to offer. I feel Scott hid who he was from me all those years I thought I knew him. I think I only started to get a good sense of who he was at the end of our—relationship?—I don't know what to call it. I'm just brainstorming, but Jennifer Bidwell was a big-time loser at Scott's hands. How about someone in her family, or one of her friends, perhaps a love interest?"

Ray nodded. "Yes, that occurred to me as well."

"Other than that, I didn't notice other unsavory characters around here while Scott ran the place for Mother. I wasn't here that much in those days. And earlier, when Scott and I were together, my brain was locked in a teenage paradigm—sex, drugs, and good times. No attention to rectitude. Thank God I grew up."

49

〜

ngie Monti spotted Ray and moved in his direction as soon as he entered Heirloom Foods North.

"Ray, what brings you in today, shopping or criminal justice?" she asked jauntily. "On second thought, you look like a man on a mission. Are you looking for Victoria and Scott?"

"Ms. Wainwright."

"It's her spa day, sorry. She'll be here tomorrow. And Scott doesn't seem to be in, either." She delivered this final bit of information in a playful, saucy tone.

"I need to speak with Ms. Wainwright. Would you give me her cell number?" he asked.

"I can do that, but I guarantee she won't answer. Her spa days are precious. No interruptions." Ray remembered Angie's playfulness as a young teen. It was still there, but now it was a very adult version.

"Which spa does she use? I'll try to contact her there."

"I couldn't answer. Victoria has stipulated that her private time is sacred. And the spa days are transformative. She's always so much happier the next day. Who knows," she winked. "Maybe it's a spa treatment with benefits."

"Is there some private place we can talk?"

"Sure. Follow me," Angie said, guiding him to the back of the store and into the office wing.

After they were seated in her office, which was not as spacious as Victoria's but bright and cheerful, Angie asked, "What gives, Ray? You're very serious today."

Ray placed his phone on her desk. "I am trying to find out as much as possible about Scott Nelson. Do you mind if I record this interview?"

"No, of course not."

Monti's attention was distracted by a tone from her phone. She pulled the device from a pocket, peered at the screen, and then looked back at Ray.

"Do you need to take that?"

"No, it's nothing. My apologies for the disruption. You were saying something about Scott. What's he done now? Another basket of goodies?"

"I've got some very bad news. Scott Nelson's body was recovered late yesterday from Lake Michigan."

"Scott… drowned? Oh no. An accident?"

Ray watched a shudder run through her body. He thought her reaction was authentic, not a product of her usual drama.

"No, not an accident. Foul play is suspected," he answered.

"So you're saying he was murdered?" She rocked forward, staring at Ray intently across the desk.

"That appears to be the case."

"I don't know what to say." Angie hugged herself despite the heat of the day. "These crimes are in the news daily, but you don't think it will be part of your world. I guess we do that…" she looked toward the ceiling "… to make ourselves feel safe. What more can you tell me?"

"There isn't much to tell. We're just beginning the investigation."

"How can I help?" she asked.

"What can you tell me about Scott? We know little about him."

"I don't know much either," she answered. "Scott wasn't ever on my radar before he started here."

"When was that?"

"February or maybe March. Victoria was ramping up the technical staff. She wanted that operation up to speed well before the opening. She thought Scott had the right mix of skills to head that department."

"And did he?"

"Yes, I think so, but I couldn't judge. My focus was elsewhere."

"What are you trying to tell me, Angie?"

I don't want to speak ill of the dead, but…"

"But, what?"

"Well, there are some things a woman knows intuitively about a man."

"What are you trying to tell me?"

"Well, when you're introduced to a guy, and the first thing he does is slowly look you up and down, head to toe, and then he does it a second time, you know he's interested. By Scott's second day here, he had started flirting with me. And the next day, he asked me out for a drink. I mean, really, Ray. I'm almost old enough to be his mother, and I'm old enough to know better. He seemed to think I was a done deal. His flirting was obnoxious.

"But after a week or two on the job, I could tell he had decided Victoria was a better target. Power, position, and relative wealth. He set his sights on the high-value target and seemed to find a willing audience in her."

"So you're telling me he was involved with her."

"Not involved like moving in, but I'm sure they were hooking up occasionally. 'Hooking up,' that's what my daughter calls it— getting together for sex. I shouldn't be telling you this, but during one of my conversations with the boss, after a little too much wine, she told me she prefers boy toys—guys young enough that their bodies haven't run to fat yet. I take it the hookups were on her terms. She needs to be in control of everything. She's not looking for anything long-term. That's not me, Ray. I want something more. I'm still looking for Mr. Forever."

As he held her in his gaze for a long moment, Ray was reminded of her kid version, the little sister who liked to tease and flirt with her older brother's friends.

"Early on, Victoria wanted to know if anything had happened between me and Scott. I told her he had hit on me, I wasn't interested, and I'd let Scott know."

Angie gave Ray a coquettish look. "You have a woman friend, don't you?"

"Yes."

"Long-term?"

"Yes."

"But you're not married, right?"

"True. Getting back to Scott. Has he seemed troubled lately? Has he been in conflict with anyone working here? How about the customers?"

"He was a real people person. Lots of talk, lots of laughter. He went out of his way to be friendly with the staff. Same with the customers." Something seemed to occur to Angie. "But come to think of it, there were a couple of guys in here late last week. Scott got into a heated conversation with them. It started in his office. Then, the three of them took it outside, away from the building. When Scott returned to his office, he was agitated, shaking, and upset. I had never seen him like that before.

"I asked him if everything was all right. He said it was personal, just a misunderstanding between friends."

"The men he was arguing with, can you describe them?"

"They were young, younger than Scott, twenty-something. Both white, but one had more olive skin and looked Mediterranean. And they had those haircuts."

"Haircuts?"

"You know, lots of hair on top. I mean, lots. Short on the sides and in the back; it almost looked shaved. It's not a hairdo you can get away with when you start going bald. And they had those trendy beards."

"Long, short?"

"Well, my daughter calls them—she spends too much time on dating sites, and I keep telling her to turn off the damn computer and go to the beach. I say, 'You've got a good body, kid. You'll attract attention. And you'll know it's not some weird pervert from God knows where.'"

"So, the beards?" pressed Ray.

"Oh, right. Short, maybe ten days or so, but neatly trimmed. My daughter has a way of categorizing features. She calls those one-night-stand beards. She claims to know that guys with that kind of beard are looking for a quick hookup, nothing more."

"How about hair color?"

"Black hair on one, reddish on the other. Not that ginger-red. A darker shade."

"But you don't know what the argument was about?"

"Gambling debt, maybe. I'm just guessing. I've seen Scott at the casino a few times."

"Our local casino?"

"Yes," Angie said. "Someone told me Scott plays high-stakes poker. There was a game at the casino behind closed doors, but they shut it down. I heard the game was moved to Traverse. Weird stuff: It starts at two in the morning in a restaurant closed for the night. I'm trying to remember who told me this. They said Scott was sometimes a big winner, sometimes a big loser. Maybe those guys came about gambling debts."

"As far as you know, there are no security cameras on the premises of Heirloom Foods North, inside or outside?"

"Wainwright is totally against cameras. I think you know that."

Ray nodded. "What exactly was Scott's job here?"

"He was head of technology. He designed the website and handled the logistics and fulfillment—packaging and shipping. His behavior could be annoying, but he was also brilliant in his patch. He was doing a first-class job. The people on his team respected him. His death will be a great loss to us."

"His workday, was it all in this building, or do you have other buildings for administration or fulfillment?"

"It was divided. As I said, Scott headed our tech group, which is all in this wing. The other part of his job was overseeing the shipping and receiving operation. That's all in a new warehouse just down the road. The internet sales and all the shipping have grown much faster than Victoria anticipated."

"We don't have a home address for Scott," said Ray. "When he last renewed his driver's license, he listed this address."

"Well, that was Scott. On the one hand, he was very—maybe too—friendly. But I always felt another Scott was lurking. You know what I'm saying?"

"Do you know where Scott was living?"

"No idea. He was pretty private about things like that."

"How about your other colleagues here? Who was Scott friends with?"

Angie shrugged. "I'm not sure. Maybe he hung out with the tech bros." Ray noted a change in her affect from concern to total disregard. "News of Scott's death, is it public information?"

"A press conference is scheduled for this morning. And a news release will be available after that."

"I'll text Victoria on what's happened. I hope she'll hear me pinging her phone and respond. I'll need her guidance on how the staff will be informed."

"If you're in contact with her, tell her I must speak to her immediately."

"I'll try."

Ray pointed to a notepad on her desk. "Give me Wainwright's contact information, cell, email, and home address."

She complied, writing down the details with a purple gel pen. "Done," she said, sliding the paper across her desk.

"Thank you," Ray said, pushing his card toward her. "If you make contact with Ms. Wainwright, you can call or message me directly or call the department if you're not getting a response."

50

Ray drove to the far end of the main parking lot at Heirloom Foods North, an area on a slight rise that provided an unobstructed view of the employee parking area. He backed into a space between a large SUV and a camper van, his unmarked Dodge patrol car dwarfed by its neighbors. After uploading the audio files of his interviews with Bob Nelson, Piper Ingersolle, and Angie Monti to the case folder, he quickly keyed a message to Sue, requesting a series of search warrants and a quick phone search of local spas for Victoria Warrington. Then he explained why he had Angie Monti under surveillance and that he was requesting backup.

Sue responded a few minutes later by phone. She summarized the morning press conference and reviewed the list of search warrants he had requested. The call ended with her explaining that Barbara Sinclair was already in the process of calling the spas.

After ending the call, Ray slid down in his seat and waited. Angie Monti appeared just outside the store's main entrance a few minutes later. After a few paces, she stopped and slowly scanned the area, left to right. Then she strode warily in the direction of the employee parking lot. Finally, she stopped at the side of a bright red Chevy Blazer, where she again surveyed the area, not just a glance but a thorough sweep. Then she disappeared into the SUV's dark tinted-glass interior.

Starting his engine, Ray lingered until she reached the highway. Then, he drove to the exit and waited for traffic to clear before starting in the same direction. By that time, two cars separated them.

Ray held back, allowing a third car to enter from a side road, providing even more distance. Eventually, one of the cars turned off, then another. With only one car between them, Ray lagged back even further. Then Angie turned off onto Sandy Cove Trail, a narrow asphalt lane with only about a dozen cottages that dead-ended at the border of the National Park Shoreline.

Ray pulled onto the shoulder and made a U-turn, taking a right onto Sandy Cove Trail. He slowly rolled down the road parallel to the shoreline, searching for the Blazer. Reversing at the dead end, he retraced his route, stopping at the only drive on the east side of the road, two tracks of sand separated by a median of weeds—shaggy, determined plants clinging to the barren surroundings. He backed away, parking on the shoulder, and called dispatch, asking for information on the address. The data was messaged back quickly. The property was deeded to Heirloom Foods North.

Ray followed the path through the undulating terrain into a scruffy pine forest. He parked at an angle behind the Blazer, blocking a possible escape. Before exiting his vehicle, Ray ran the plate of the Toyota pickup parked at the side of the road. Then, after turning on his body cam, he advanced toward the old wood structure. If the building had ever worn a coat of paint, it had been worn away over the decades. He positioned himself at the front of the Blazer and waited. Minutes later, Angie, her arms full of clothing, rushed out, the sharp snap of the screen door announcing her departure. Her hurried pace came to a sudden halt.

"Sheriff. Ah, Ray," she started. Then she just stood silently and waited.

Pointing, he asked, "Scott's pickup?"

Angie's answer was slow in coming—finally, just an affirmative nod.

"And this place. Was Scott living here?"

"He crashed here sometimes. He might have stayed with his parents or a sibling occasionally. I don't know."

"What are you carrying, Angie?"

"Things."

Ray repeated the question.

"Some of my things," she answered.

Ray nodded. "Set them on the steps, please."

"Why?" she shot back. "It's my stuff. It's personal."

"Put the items down and step away now," he ordered.

She reluctantly complied, bending and carefully placing objects on the weathered boards.

Ray moved close, dropped to a knee, and looked through the assorted clothing, quickly uncovering a small laptop concealed in the pile of clothing.

He looked up at Angie.

"That's mine, too," she insisted. Then, she reached forward in an attempt to reclaim the computer.

Ray physically blocked her advance. "Leave it," he commanded, tensing, prepared for her possible assault. As she sprang forward, he slowed her momentum with his hands, arms, and finally, a dropped shoulder, a remnant from high school football. They rolled on the ground as she struggled to get the computer. Finally, Ray was able to straddle and then cuff Angie. Then he pulled her off the ground.

"Angie Monti, you're under arrest for assaulting an officer," said Ray, Mirandizing her before he led her to the arriving patrol officer.

"I want a lawyer," she said.

"You have the right to arrange representation before the interview."

"I can explain everything, Ray." She stood sucking air, her fury melting away. Suddenly, she was pleading. "I'm sorry. I didn't mean for that to happen. It's grief. I'm lost. All I wanted was to get my stuff. The things I left." She paused, trying to catch her breath. "I had nothing to do with Scott's death. I didn't want to get pulled into the mess. I'm not involved. Honest, Ray. Not involved."

"Involved in what?" he asked.

"I don't know. Whatever happened." She focused on Ray. "Okay, we were sometime lovers. But I didn't know…" Her words trailed off, and she collapsed into tears. She was guided into the patrol car's back seat and buckled in.

As the patrol car started down the drive, Ray pulled on some rubber gloves and quickly searched the building.

51

It was close to two that afternoon when Barbara Sinclair entered Ray's office.

"Is Monti's lawyer here already?" Ray asked.

She nodded. "Cedar County's only criminal defense specialist must have been sitting by the phone. She arrived twenty minutes ago. They're in the interview room, putting their heads together. Tanner demanded that I prove to her that all audio and video equipment was turned off before I left the room. Is she always so unpleasant?"

Ray nodded. "Karen Tanner, unpleasant to a fault. She specializes in defending the full spectrum of scoundrels. Her professional life has been nothing but rogues for decades. It's given her a negative view of humanity." Ray was about to say more but bit his tongue. "Give me a few minutes. Please do the boilerplate."

By the time Ray entered the interview room, the cameras and audio recorder were running, and Barbara Sinclair had Mirandized Angie Monti.

"Sheriff Elkins has just entered the room," announced Sinclair.

When Ray had settled into a chair, Ms. Tanner—her body encased in a bilious green smock, the color mirroring her disposition, demanded, "Is my client under arrest?"

"Yes, for assaulting a police officer, for starters," he answered.

"Starters? My client has told me she was only trying to protect property, items of a very personal nature that you insisted on fingering. It was an assault on her person. She was only there to collect her possessions. She has bruises on her arms from the way you manhandled her."

Ray looked over at Angie slumped in her chair, clad in an orange jumpsuit, all her fight gone.

"Ms. Tanner, my body cam was running. For the record, I want to review my encounters with Ms. Monti earlier today. Given your scholarly knowledge of the Michigan Penal Code, I'm confident you will understand the basis for the additional charges.

"Ms. Monti was detained at a dwelling we now believe had been occupied by Scott Nelson, who is deceased. Late this morning, at her place of employment, Heirloom Foods North, I informed Ms. Monti of Scott Nelson's death. Let me reference the transcript of my initial conversation with Ms. Monti."

Angie glared at him as he continued, "In our initial conversation, you stated that Scott flirted with you soon after he started working at Heirloom Foods North. When was that?"

"Late winter, February or March. I must look at the HR records to get the exact date."

"That's probably close enough. Thank you. Then you stated that Nelson quickly turned his attention to Victoria Wainwright. Is that still your memory?"

"I would like a copy of that audio file," Tanner interrupted.

"Counselor, you know the procedure. Once you complete the paperwork, we will, as we always have before, immediately provide you with a copy.

"Back to my question, Angie. You suggested that Scott pursued Ms. Wainwright. Is that correct?"

"Well, that's what it looked like to me."

Peering at an iPad, he continued, "At which point I asked, 'So you're telling me he was involved with her,' meaning Ms. Wainwright. Your answer was, 'Not involved like moving in or anything, but I'm sure they were hooking up occasionally.' You went on to explain that *hooking up* is getting together for sex."

"So, what's your point?" asked Tanner.

Ray kept his focus on Angie, not responding to Tanner's question. "You continued, referring to hooking up by saying, 'That's not me, Ray. I want something more.' I interpreted that to mean you were not involved with Scott Nelson."

"Ray," Angie looked over at her lawyer and pointed at the sheriff. "I've known him since childhood," she said. "We're on a first-name basis."

"Yes, childhood," Ray agreed. "Later in the conversation, I asked, referring to Scott Nelson, 'So you have no idea where he might be living?' And you answered, 'No idea. We weren't really friends.' Is that correct?"

"Yes, but…"

"But what?" asked Ray.

"This is all a big misunderstanding. I know how it looks. I know what you're thinking, but that's not the reality." Angie's customary flippant, puckish behavior was gone. The woman sitting across the table from him was frozen in a rigid posture. Her countenance oozed hatred as she glared at Ray.

"Let me ask a few more questions, Angie, and then you can explain what you think I don't understand." Ray referred to his timeline. "After our conversation at Heirloom Foods ended, I went to the parking lot, sat in my car, and got caught up with the office on the phone. I had only been out there a few minutes when I saw you exit the building, walk to your car, and drive off. I followed you. You drove to a remote dwelling just off Sandy Cove Road and parked near the front of the house. A few minutes later, you exited the building with clothing and other items in your arms. Here's an inventory of those items." Ray slid a printed copy of the list across the table. "The clothing and toiletries appear to belong to you: undergarments, sleepwear, cosmetics, deodorant, and feminine hygiene products. You were also carrying a Macintosh laptop computer. *Property of Scott Nelson* is displayed on a label attached to the top of the machine."

"By what authority did you seize these items," asked Tanner.

"When I encountered Ms. Monti leaving the dwelling, I had already established that the residence belonged to Heirloom Foods North. When I ran the plates on the Toyota truck parked near the building, I learned the vehicle belonged to Scott Nelson. By then, I knew the building would be treated as a possible crime scene. So first, Ms. Monti violated 479c, items (a), (b), and (c). Thus, it was unlawful for her to remove anything from the building. Ms. Monti is also in violation of item (d).

"Angie Monti knew that Scott Nelson was dead. She knew where he lived despite insisting that she didn't. She drove to that location soon after our interview at Heirloom Foods North ended. Based on my walk-through of the dwelling after Ms. Monti was arrested, Scott Nelson appeared to live at this address. Nelson's wallet, containing his driver's license and other pieces of identification, was in the building."

Turning to Angie, he asked, "How did you gain entrance?"

"The front door was standing open," she insisted.

"Was the building usually unlocked?"

"I wouldn't know."

"Why were you in such a hurry to remove certain items?"

"Like I said, it was my stuff, everything I was carrying. I wasn't stealing anything. It was all my property."

"How about the computer?"

"It's a company computer. All executive team members have one. I was protecting company property."

"In our conversation earlier today, you told me you were not involved with Scott Nelson. The material you carried away from his house suggests you had an intimate relationship with him." Ray waited, but there was no response.

"As the SOC team works this scene, will they find evidence of a relationship between Nelson and Victoria Wainwright?"

"I have no idea what they will find. Scott liked women."

"So you went there to remove your things because you anticipated we would find evidence connecting you and Nelson. Am I right?"

"I had nothing to do with Scott's death. I didn't want to get involved. That's all. I didn't want to get involved."

"Scott died violently. You know much more about Scott than you're telling me. What was he into, Angie? Why was he murdered?"

"I fell for him. That's all. I don't know anything else." She gave her lawyer a pleading look.

"Are we done, Sheriff?" Tanner asked.

"No, definitely not." He focused on Angie. "You told me that Victoria Wainwright was away from Heirloom Foods today at a spa. We contacted every spa in the area and found the one. We learned she was a regular customer who always arrived for her scheduled appointments. But today, she was a no-show." Ray allowed that information to sink in, watching Angie's face, trying to gauge whether it was news to her. "I believe she's in great danger. Can you help us locate her?"

"Like I told you earlier, Ray. She said she was having a spa day. It was on her calendar. I don't know anything else."

Tanner exhaled loudly, then launched into a verbal assault. "Sheriff, all I'm hearing are a lot of *ifs* and *ands*; you don't seem to have any solid evidence to suggest my client had any involvement in Scott Nelson's death. And given her emotional state after learning of the death of a close friend, the assault that you allege appears to be nothing more than a moment of high emotion with no criminal intent. Perhaps an inadvertent push or shove."

Ray worked at keeping a neutral expression and tone. He focused on his breathing, trying to slow the pace of the interview.

"Angie, you know a lot more than you're telling me. Scott Nelson is dead. Murdered. Victoria Wainwright is missing. She might be dead as well. Or maybe she's been kidnapped. If she is alive, you're the key to her rescue. I need your help."

"Anything my client might say could be misconstrued and eventually used against her in court."

"Angie, we're talking about life and death. Again, I need your help."

She was not forthcoming. To Ray, it appeared she was carefully weighing her options, perhaps wanting to help but unwilling to expose her possible involvement too much.

"It's the fulfillment side, Ray," she finally offered. "There's this contractor Scott hired. He told me they were Canadian. The guy in charge, I think his name is Ben."

"How many people are we talking about?"

"I saw three men."

"Names?"

"Other than Ben, I don't know. I only saw them once. I was looking for Scott one evening late and saw his truck parked at the fulfillment building. He was helping these guys load a van. He said the shipment was going via private jet from Pellston Airport. He said it was something new, the concierge line of Heirloom Farms."

"Anything else about this?"

"I asked why Pellston, what's wrong with TVC? He said the shipper was based at Pellston, which didn't make much sense, but I let it go. Then he said they were considering using a boat instead of a truck to get the shipment to Pellston. That sounded crazy, but I didn't say anything." Angie paused briefly, then added, "Scott always had a small stash of cocaine in the coffee canister at his house. I thought I should get it out of there. Protect the reputation of the dead. Go figure," she said in a tone suggesting the foolishness of her act. "Instead of finding the little stash, there was a big bag of coke. It was a 'holy fuck' moment. It all came together. Scott, who normally showed little emotion, had been terrified for days, and I suddenly knew why. Drugs. It was all about drugs. He'd gotten into something beyond his control."

"Previous to this, you two had used drugs?"

"That's enough," said Tanner.

"Just weed, occasionally, perfectly legal," Monti answered.

"How about cocaine or other drugs?"

Monti paused, then reluctantly answered, "Cocaine, once or twice. Only recently. And small quantities. But that bag. I've never seen anything like that before." She hesitated. "Drugs, a boat. Does any of this help?"

"Yes, it does. Thank you."

"And there's one more thing you should know."

Tanner reached over to clasp Monti's arm. "We're done here."

Angie shook off Tanner's hand. "There's one more thing, Ray. Something's been bothering Victoria. She sensed something was going on. She had security cameras installed in the fulfillment building on the sly."

Tanner was on her feet before Monti finished her sentence. "We're out of here."

"No. Ms. Monti will be staying with us for the next seventy-two hours. We need time to sort this out and talk with the prosecutor. And given what she has just told me, her life is in danger, too. Angie's safe here, and we will provide protection for her daughter, too."

"I'm scared, Ray." The bravado was utterly gone from Angie Monti's demeanor. She stared at him with the fear and trust of a child.

52

〰

When Ray and Barbara entered the conference room, Sue, Brett, and Emily Larson were seated around the conference table.

"Okay, let's start with Victoria Wainwright. Barbara," said Ray, after settling into a chair.

"A few minutes after 10:00 a.m., Emily and I arrived at Victoria Wainwright's home. The garage was empty, the door wide open. We went to check the house—the entry door from the garage to the kitchen was ajar. A spa bag and Wainwright's purse were on a table near the garage door. The purse was open. Her wallet and phone were in the purse, but no key fob. I called dispatch to initiate a BOLO, and Emily requested the MSP SOC unit from Grayling.

"When I caught up with Emily again, she was inspecting the exterior entry door to the garage."

"It had been kicked in," explained Larson. "There were boot marks on the door. The locking hardware was torn from the frame, and the hinges on the other side were almost pulled loose."

Sue asked, "So what are we looking at? A carefully staged disappearance? A kidnapping?"

"I've seen a lot of kicked-in doors. This wasn't staged. I'd put my money on an abduction," said Larson.

"Okay, and about the same time, Ray's tailing Angie Monti to a place in Sandy Cove. He's waiting outside when she emerges from the building carrying some personal items and what turns out to be Scott Nelson's laptop. She sets the items down, and a struggle ensues when Ray picks up the computer. Then he cuffs her and makes an arrest as backup arrives. He does a walk-through of the building. Ray, pick up the narrative?"

"Not much more to add. It appeared that there had been a fight in the kitchen area. There was dried blood smeared on the linoleum. A wallet containing Scott's driver's license and other ID was on a counter. Monti told me about a bag of cocaine she had found hidden in the kitchen. It was sitting on the counter where she said she left it. Was that what his assailants were looking for? How did they miss it? We can only speculate." Ray looked toward Emily Larson.

"As Sue said, I originally asked our SOC team to process Victoria Wainwright's home. I've redirected them to the Nelson place first. Then, the team will move on to Wainwright's. I've also requested an officer with a drug-sniffing dog." She looked at her watch. "They should be in the area soon. We've acquired the door codes for the fulfillment building. It's after work hours, and the building should be locked tight. Hopefully, no one will be around. A three-person team dressed like maintenance workers will arrive in an unmarked van and search the facility. I don't know how they will smuggle the sniffer dog in. We want this piece to be accomplished quickly."

Brett asked how the operation would move forward if drugs were discovered during the search of the fulfillment building.

With Barbara Sinclair's assistance, Sue's laptop screen was mirrored on the large screen at the front of the conference room.

"Here's a decision tree that Emily Larson developed with her MSP colleagues in coordination with other agencies. As you can see, it starts the search for drugs in packages in the Heirloom Farms North shipping building. If drugs are found, tracking devices will be placed in the boxes. From that point forward, we will be tracking the shipments. The crew picking up these boxes may not even know they're handling drugs. We want to capture the people behind this operation and hopefully find Victoria Wainwright. As you can see, we are surveilling the truck's movements. Will the drugs continue by truck to the bridge and beyond, or will they end up at TVC, Pellston, or one of the many small airstrips scattered across the region? And then there is the possibility of using a boat.

"Nelson also told Monti they might use a boat to get the shipments to the Pellston Airport. There is a small problem of fifteen or twenty miles of land between the big lake and the airport. I assume the shipment would be transferred to a truck for the final part of the journey. By the way, Barbara searched the Heirloom Foods website. There's no mention of concierge products. This was Scott Nelson's side hustle.

"Remember that incident recently where a powerboat pulverized a small sailboat? Robert Atwood, the lone occupant of the sailboat, thought the boat intentionally ran over the wreckage of his boat several times. We speculated on whether the people in the boat might have been trying to see what they collided with in very choppy water. The other possibility was malicious intent. No reports of an accident in that area were filed to law enforcement or the Coast Guard. We've never been able to trace the boat. Is this our ghost ship? One used for running drugs. Maybe the one used to dump Nelson into the deep."

"The water scenario. The pieces start to fit," said Brett.

"Our suspected boat type, what do you call those things?" asked Sue.

"A rigid hull, inflatable boat." Brett enunciated each word very carefully. "It would be much like our new patrol boat, but possibly bigger and faster."

"So, if a boat is going to be used, where will it meet up with the truck?" asked Sue.

"Probably not in any of the marinas," Brett answered. "They're jammed right now. And there are security people and lots of surveillance cameras. I think it would be too risky."

"If not a marina, where?" asked Ray.

"Well, Ray, you've been out with me," said Brett. "There are areas along the shoreline with sheer drop-offs near the shore. You can put the bow on the beach and keep the props clear of the bottom. The lake would have to be flat. That said, not many of those places are accessible by road."

Sue flipped the whiteboard to the other side, displaying two diagrams. "Sergeant Larson, would you like to explain this?"

"Here's what the plan might look like. And this is only a sketch. As you can see," Larson gestured toward the board, "on the left is the water scenario, and on the right is the land scenario. MSP will handle the tracking if the suspects haven't been frightened off. We will coordinate with LEAs and the regional response teams. We want this to end in a delivery where we hope to capture everyone.

"If the perps transfer the drugs to a boat, the plan is to close in while they are on or near shore. If that falls apart, the tracking devices are critical. Tonight's weather forecast calls for winds from the southwest at ten to twenty knots and waves to two feet.

"On the right is a tentative plan if the perps stick to land. Again, we don't want to seize just the truck. We want to get the suspects. These perps have favored hours of darkness for their operations. We think that will be the case this time. One more thing, these people must be considered armed and dangerous."

"Emily, can you bring us up to date on Victoria Wainwright?" asked Ray.

"The MSP crime unit has just started processing her home, so I have nothing there yet. And the tags on her car haven't been picked up by the automated plate readers on the main roads running toward Charlevoix and Petoskey to the north or south toward Ludington. The same goes for I-75 in both directions. But there are lots of back roads. Sorry, I have nothing positive to tell you."

Sue broke the silence that followed Barbara's report. "Okay, friends, it will probably be a long night. Catch a nap if you can."

53

After arriving at the marina, Brett and Barbara boarded the department patrol boat moored at the south end of the harbor, away from the closely packed slips filled with pleasure boats. After running through the equipment checklist, Barbara suggested, "Let's walk; it's one way to stay awake."

"Have you gotten your ten thousand steps in yet?" asked Brett.

"Not even close."

They circled the harbor area several times, past the century-old frame buildings, remnants of a once flourishing fishing village, now converted to trendy boutiques catering to the summer people. Then they walked along the east edge of the harbor—a neighborhood of modest homes dating from the mid-nineteenth century. Finally, they dropped down toward the marina, where dozens of boats were crowded together along brightly lit walkways, among them everything from modest cabin cruisers to multimillion-dollar yachts.

On their third lap, Barbara nodded toward a boat and asked, "Is that what you aspire to?"

"That?" asked Brett, pointing to a yacht that towered over its neighbors.

Barbara started to chuckle as she redirected his attention to one of the more modest boats in the marina, one that needed urgent attention. "You can take the boy out of the Thumb, but—"

Brett cut her off and looked at his phone. "The truck is at the fulfillment building. Let's hustle."

They stopped for a moment at Brett's vehicle. He removed two automatic rifles, passing one to Barbara. He started to say something but stopped. She caught the message in his changed demeanor.

Once on board, after the weapons had been secured within easy reach at the front of the cabin, Barbara asked, "What's happening?"

He pointed to a red dot near the top of the screen—the result of the tracking app. "We hurry up and wait. Here's the target vehicle, and it's starting to move. The small harbor at North Bay is the nearest place to rendezvous with a boat. Once they get moving, it's about ten minutes to a possible water transfer site."

They watched silently as the dot moved along the glowing GPS map toward North Bay. The dot stopped suddenly a few hundred yards short of the harbor.

"What's happening?" asked Barbara.

"Don't know," said Brett. Then, a message flashed on the bottom of the screen.

Medical emergency at marina. Police and EMTs on scene.

"Who knows? Heart attack, stroke. But with the ambulance and patrol car at the scene, our perps probably got spooked," said Brett. "The dot is moving again. Coming our way. The truck could be here in ten minutes."

"What's our plan?" she asked.

"We sit tight and let the transfer happen. We pursue the boat when they're out beyond the seawall."

Brett scanned the radar screen. "There's nothing small and fast-moving in the Manitou Passage, just a lake freighter crawling north at twelve knots. We're looking for something moving at forty or fifty knots."

He looked over at Barbara. "Not much chop tonight. But you still might want your wristbands."

Barbara lifted her hands to display the bands in the dim light of the cockpit. "I'm good. If they don't transfer here, where?" she asked.

Brett switched the screen from the tracking app to a map of the area.

"Lots of places. Good Harbor, deserted at this time. It's six miles down the road. Next, Port Oneida, another six miles. Then Glen Arbor, possibly, but Glen Haven would be better, two more miles."

Brett switched back to the tracking app and pointed to the red dot. "It's almost showtime." He dimmed the displays and switched off the cabin light. They waited and watched—the bright headlights of a truck swept across the mostly empty parking area. The vehicle slowed, pausing briefly near the boat launch, then continued away from the harbor and back onto the highway.

"Not here. I wonder why? And still, nothing moving fast in the passage," said Brett. "Could they be having communication problems? Let's move south. We'll stay close to shore."

Brett started the two big outboards and guided the boat from the marina's flat water into a gentle roll on the big lake. Following the coastline south, he gestured toward the screen displaying the tracking program. "We're going to hang out and see what happens."

He positioned the boat facing west a few hundred yards from the shore and idled the engines, switching off the running lights.

The red dot moved down the screen toward their location in the center of the shipping lane. Additional dots started to converge as patrol cars moved into position.

"Bingo, look what we have here," said Brett, pointing to a dot on the screen. "Someone's in a hurry. That boat is flying now, and the truck is heading toward the shore."

"When do we go?" asked Barbara.

"When the boat is near shore and the transfer has started, we go as instructed."

All units in position. The message flashed in a text area at the bottom of the screen.

Brett started the engines, moving into deep water and turning the bow south.

All units go.

As they approached the beach, Brett and Barbara saw the area was ablaze with light from three or more patrol cars.

Officer down. Taking fire.

Brett brought the engines to full power and turned on the spotlights as he approached the other boat backing away from the shore.

"Down!" he yelled at Barbara as bullets riddled the cabin. Brett accelerated, aiming his bow toward the shooter perched at the front of the other boat.

Now lying flat on the deck, Barbara felt the impact as the patrol boat zoomed over the other craft, its powerful engines destroying the other craft as it passed over. The patrol boat ground to a halt in the shallow water near the beach. And then silence.

Barbara pushed through the twisted aluminum sheeting and slid into the water, crawling through the shallows to the beach. She could hear voices filled with urgency. Laser-like beams slashed through the darkness as rescuers searched the wreckage for survivors. Then, the world spun away.

Hours later, her left arm in a cast from hand to elbow, her aching body covered by a hospital gown and robe, Barbara sat at Brett's side in the pre-op area.

The hospitalist, a man who appeared to be about her father's age, explained that Brett Carty was being treated for shock, multiple lacerations, and a ruptured spleen. He would be going to surgery in a few minutes.

"Was he shot?" she asked.

"No, no gunshot wounds, but he's taken a terrific beating."

Barbara collapsed in tears as Brett was wheeled away.

The hospitalist returned to her side and placed a hand on her shoulder. "And you, young lady, will stay with us for observation for a day or two. And you're going to have some company. One of your colleagues said to tell you your parents will be here in a few hours."

54

～

When Ray entered the interview room late the following morning, Angie Monti was seated at the table. Bonnie, the corrections officer, was standing near the door.

Ray Mirandized Monti, then asked, "Why are you not represented by counsel today, Ms. Monti? We can get a public defender if you cannot afford a lawyer."

"I have a lawyer, Ray. I didn't want her here. I want to get this done."

"Okay, let's do this again for the record," he said, glancing up at the camera. "You requested this interview, and counsel does not represent you."

"Yes. I can't stand it anymore. Has Victoria been found? Is she alive?"

"Yes, Victoria Wainwright was found bound and gagged in the trunk of her car in Charlevoix. It appears that she put up a ferocious fight against her would-be captors. She was badly bruised and beaten in the process. In addition to these injuries, she is being treated for extreme dehydration and shock. The physical injuries should heal quickly, but the psychological scars from such a terrifying experience will stay with her forever."

He looked across at Angie Monti. First, she trembled, and then she began to weep. It took several minutes for her to regain control. He slid a box of tissues across the table toward her. Finally, Angie's sobbing lessened as she blotted her tears and blew her nose.

"I never wanted to harm Victoria. She's been so good to me." She struggled to stay in control. "I still don't understand how this all happened."

"Maybe you can start from the beginning," said Ray.

Angie sat silently, her hands clasped on the table, her gaze moving between them. Finally, she said, "It's no one's fault but my own. This all happened because of my… vanity or maybe my neediness."

"What happened, Angie? Help us understand."

"I moved back to the area a few years ago after my divorce. I wanted to be near family, my mother and siblings, and have my daughter spend her teen years here." She blew her nose again. "I didn't even complete my associate's degree, and you know the job market. I was struggling to provide for my daughter. So when I learned about Heirloom Farms North, I got over there and interviewed with Victoria. We clicked, and I got a management job. Finally, all those years in retail paid off."

"So how does Scott Nelson fit into the story?"

"My daughter, Emma, was messing around with online dating, which I disapproved of. I didn't realize that she was looking for a man for me. There was back and forth between them, Scott and Emma. She was impersonating me. Finally, Emma arranged a meeting with Scott and a drink at Art's.

"One night after dinner, she showed me the dating profile she had created. After the dust settled, as we sat on the couch, she showed me the profile of the man I would meet later that evening.

"I protested. The guy was ten years younger than me. But in the end, I went off to Art's. Scott was charming. We stayed till closing. We met for lunch the next day. I was smitten. It was like high school again—more hormones than brains. When I told him where I worked, he said he was job hunting. I carried in his vita and hand-delivered it to Victoria. He had the right job skills. He did well in the interview. Victoria liked him immediately."

"And then he dropped you and turned his attention to Victoria?" asked Ray.

"No. I just said that. It was just a little fib."

"So Scott and Victoria…?"

"No, they were never involved. Victoria's got a man. Someone who flies in from the west coast. I think he's married. He's here about once a month for a few days."

"So why this story, Angie?"

She squirmed in her chair. "The day you came in to return the basket of goodies—something Scott had given to one of your deputies—I knew exactly what had happened. I was being used. And I recognized you, Ray, but you didn't recognize me. I gave you the impression that Scott was Victoria's boy toy. Why did I do that? I don't know. Self-protection? Trying not to get hurt?"

"So where are we going with this, Angie?"

"I should have bailed on Scott, but I got more involved instead. He needed a place to live. I helped make that happen. I knew about the property on Sandy Cove; Victoria had shown it to me. It was one of many places her family had acquired over the decades. I told Victoria that Scott was searching for housing. That cabin was a perfect bachelor pad. She had the place cleaned up and offered to rent it to him. He moved in the next day."

"So, your relationship with Scott?"

Angie looked at her hands, which were clasped on the table. "It's a third-rate melodrama, Ray, but I was all in. And I won't say I was blind, but I became addicted to Scott first and then to the cocaine he supplied when we were together."

"What were you blind to, Angie?"

"Scott was such a manipulator. A narcissist. That said, in terms of his job, he was very skilled. First, he built a fantastic website in a few weeks. He had the online store up and running before we opened. By then, Victoria trusted his ability to make things happen. She put him in charge of getting the fulfillment operation off the ground. And he did. He got the technology piece pulled together and oversaw the hiring and training of the staff. But my shit detector kept telling me something was wrong.

"He created a fantasy and expected me never to challenge anything he said. And then his violent side started to surface, little by little."

"He physically abused you?"

"At first, he would say mean things occasionally—about my age and how I dressed. But then he started slapping me around, and the sex got rough. He wanted complete dominance. I was frightened. I became less emotionally attached to him. I started to see what was happening. You know, connecting the dots. I began snooping around. It was about drugs. He was using the fulfillment operation to move drugs. I think this was his plan from the beginning. I was just a pawn." She bit at a knuckle before continuing. "But during the last few weeks, this changed. He was panicked. I sensed things were falling apart. But I can't give you any specifics. I think everything happened late at night. He bragged about his third-shift workers. I checked HR records. There was only one shift at the fulfillment center, 8:00 to 5:00 Monday through Friday. And no scheduled overtime."

"So when I told you about his death, you immediately went to his place. What was that about?" asked Ray.

"I wanted to get my stuff out of there. I didn't want to be implicated in whatever he was doing. I hoped you bought my story about Scott being involved with Victoria."

"Mixed in with your personal belongings was a bag with a small quantity of what appears to be cocaine."

She shook her head back and forth. "That was just fucking stupid, Ray. As you learned, I knew where he kept his stash, a baggie in a canister mixed in with four or five pounds of espresso beans. I wanted the drugs. I thought he owed me. While fingering through the beans for the stash, I found a big bag of coke, bigger than anything I had seen before. When I saw that bag, it all became clear. It had always been about drugs. And I had been an easy mark—just a lonely woman looking for love."

55

~

The big lake was flat as Ray and Sue crossed to North Manitou Island on the ferry service. After the ship was tightly secured against the dock, the crew, after helping the passengers ashore, piled the luggage and backpacks on the pier.

They lingered off to the side until the crowd thinned, then grabbed their backpacks. Ray lifted Sue's, helped her adjust the shoulder straps, and then pulled on his pack.

"Are you okay with doing this? Are you not too exhausted?" Sue asked as they walked toward the small cluster of frame houses and cottages, some dating back to the earliest European settlement in the 1840s. The Park Service buildings, cocoa brown, rustic, and utilitarian—often referred to by wags as Parkitecture—stood in sharp contrast to the few remaining structures of the nineteenth-century village.

"Yes, I will feel better once we get going," said Ray. "Let's get a trail map and fill our water bottles. Then we can disappear."

They sat on a park bench, packs before them, studying a trail map.

"Camping spot: land view or water view?" Ray asked.

"You're the tour director. What should I consider when making this decision?" Sue asked playfully.

"If we camp on this side, you will be looking across at the mainland, but you'll have an entirely different perspective. You'll suddenly be on the outside looking in. And at night, you'll see headlights and taillights as streaks, like fireflies. You might hear a horn or a siren if there is no wind. Eight miles of open water puts you in a quiet space away from your still-visible world."

"And if we go to the other side of the island?"

"It's a bit farther. The day trippers and most of the campers remain on the east side. The west side feels very remote, even though it's only a few miles. If we hike that way, we'll stay on the main pathway until we find a place with a compelling view. Then we drop off the trail and set up camp in an area where we're not likely to see other hikers. In daylight, we'll see the curvature of the earth. At night, maybe the lights of a few lake freighters. Other than that, it's open water to Wisconsin." He waited, letting his eyes move with pleasure over the curve of her cheek and shoulder. "Well, what will it be?"

"I vote for the west side," Sue said. "As remote as possible. Just the two of us. No mainland noises or light. Or people. Or cell service, hopefully."

After four hours of hiking, they left the designated trail and picked a campsite at the top of a small dune fifty yards from the water. With instructions in hand, Sue guided the assembly of the tent, a framework of fiberglass rods suspending an envelope of synthetic fabric.

"Smells new," he said, looking in, but not entering.

"Ray. It will air out," Sue said, crawling out of the tent and spreading a throw at the top of the slope.

"You get to open this," said Sue, passing Ray a bottle of his favorite sparkling wine, a product of a local vineyard. "I think the chill may have worn off."

"I could toss it in the lake. Ten minutes…"

"You want to walk down there and back up?"

"Chill is overrated," he said, working to release the wire cage and then slowly removing the cork.

Sue passed him two steel coffee mugs, "Up north Waterford."

"I've always liked camping," said Ray. "You're free of all the junk that collects around you. It's just the basics: something over your head at night, a sleeping bag, a stove or fire, a pot, tin plates, and a few books."

Ray half-filled each cup with bubbly, passed one to Sue, and offered a toast: "To beautiful places. Living the life."

Sue lifted her cup. "Cheers," she said. Then she started chuckling. "What's so funny?"

"Oh, Ray," she said, "I'm waiting for a quote from Thoreau. Look around, love." She made a dramatic sweeping gesture toward the packs, tent, hiking shoes, and the few other items in their campsite. "We have simplified. This is all we have."

"It is," he responded. "Think of it: we were able to rid ourselves of the accumulation of decades in a few hours. No sorting, no choosing, no endless trips to Goodwill or the WRC."

Sue's tone flattened. "Seriously, you lost everything. You'd been in that house for years. The books, kitchen stuff, kayaks, and that special paddle. It must be an enormous loss."

"Yeah, the kayak paddle, hand-carved western cedar." He turned his face toward the lake. "Some of the other things, too. But you lost…"

"Not so much. Some clothing, my favorite yoga mat, and my new electric toothbrush. I still have a guy and a dog. Life is good."

Sue passed her empty cup to Ray. "This bubbly on an empty stomach is having a wonderful effect."

Sue scanned the horizon, left to right, then back again. "The earth's curvature, I had never seen it before you pointed it out to me. It was that first summer. You drove me up to the lookout on Sleeping Bear. I think that was part of the orientation you provided. You made an exaggerated arch with your hand and said, 'See, the world is round.'"

"You had a Flat Earth Society sticker on your car," said Ray. "In my rush to hire a woman deputy, I was afraid I had not probed your background thoroughly enough."

"Elkins, that sticker was on the car when I bought it." Sue waited a bit, then asked, "How do we explain this summer? It's like nothing we've ever seen. Have you been writing about it in your new journal?"

"Yes, I've started with Tammy Ogden. That story's closest to home—her struggle to escape poverty. It was also part of my life story, but I had better luck than her. So many people were pulling for her, but the planets didn't align."

"And then there's John Doe," said Sue. "The DEA agent's best guess was he was from the Balkans, but where in the Balkans? Nothing more specific."

"Most of this went down on our patch, but…"

"But what?" asked Sue.

"Only now are we beginning to grasp what happened as bits of information are reported back from the feds. Four people died, two in custody, and this complex web…"

"The gun, the prints, the ballistics. Thanks to the State Police Lab, there would have been enough to charge Scott Nelson with murder. And the evidence found in the shed at the Sandy Cove Trail house—drones, flash powder, new plastic gas cans, electronics— state crimes, federal crimes, for once he wouldn't have walked. I'm surprised he left all this stuff about."

"Yeah, he was getting careless. Maybe the Dunning-Kruger effect. Maybe just hubris," said Ray.

"But that doesn't get justice for Tammy, John Doe, or anyone else Nelson harmed over the years."

"Maybe the feds will get more from the two survivors. In their case, justice might prevail. That's probably the best we can hope for. We'll have an end but no closure," said Ray.

Sue played with a handful of sand, slowly allowing the grains to escape between her fingers. "Do you want to keep doing this?" she asked.

"Camping? I love it, but we might want to find something more permanent by fall."

"Elkins, I'm talking about you. Are you getting burned out?"

Ray watched a seagull swoop toward the beach, catch an updraft, and glide away. "Burned out? No, I don't think so. Why do you ask?"

"You have an election year coming up."

"It's part of the job. In the past, campaigning has helped me stay in contact with the people we serve. I'm willing to do it again."

"The last few years have been so difficult. Maybe it's time to look at other possibilities."

"What else would I do?"

"You could go back to teaching."

He shook his head gently. "Sue, in some small way, I think I make a difference every day. I know this community and its people. I'm lucky to have this life." He reached over, grasped her hand, and waited for her to look his way. "Are you considering running against me?"

"Elkins, did you bring a second bottle?"

Photography by Tony Denim

About the Author

Aaron Stander, over a long life, has been a construction worker, college English professor, ski patroller, radio host, and certified kayak instructor. These adventures have provided the fuel for Stander's literal, and sheriff Ray Elkin's literary, careers. Stander lives deep in the woods of northern Michigan with his wife and his dog. When not writing or thinking about writing, he spends a lot of time exploring the shores of Lake Michigan and Lake Superior.

www.ingramcontent.com/pod-product-compliance
Lightning Source LLC
Chambersburg PA
CBHW020653120726
47906CB00001B/257